I0535576

Majickal

VAMPIRES VRS. ZOMBIES VRS. FAIRIES VRS. WEREWOLVES VRS. GODS VRS. PIRATES VRS. ALIENS VRS. WIZARDS VRS. PRINCESSES VRS. GAY UNICORNS! THE SUPER-MEGA-ARMAGEDDON ULTIMATE SHOWDOWN!

AS PRESENTED IN NEW HIGH RESOLUTION 1-D BOOK FORMAT, WITH DAZZLING BLACK AND WHITE PAGES

BY

C. J. Connelly

Cover and interior art © 2015 – C. J. Connelly

Printed in the United States of America

First Printing, 2016

ISBN 978-0-9978368-0-6

Preface

FEELS IRONIC NOW—but *Majickal* came out of a year that was, in retrospect, one of my darkest times. I think that was half my motivation to write it.

That year, I was struggling with unexpected loss and grief, physical injury and pain and depression all in turns. I spent a lot of time suffering, trying to improve my life but mostly feeling damaged body and soul.

Writing *Majickal* made me laugh on days when I had precious little else to enjoy. I wouldn't say it *healed me* but it certainly *helped* a lot! The laughter and silliness was charming, a much-needed escape from all the emotional and physical pain. It kept my head above water and that alone makes me glad I wrote it. I still find it a funny, engaging read—even if I do say so myself.

So please don't take it too seriously for what it is. I just hope it brings therapeutic laughter and entertains you as much as it did me. We could use more laughter and silliness in this too-often dark and serious world.

Dedication

DEDICATED TO my wonderful family and friends, who stood supportively behind me for the many years I insisted I'd publish something (*nailed it!*).

To *YourHero (& mine) Sarah*, who withstood the many *loooong phone conversations* where we talked out exciting ideas and problem sequences together.

Finally, to *Logan*—for literally everything, but especially for his brilliantly simple advice. He told me not to "stress and overthink" but to "write freely and honestly. Most of all, *to have fun with it!*"

That's just what I did! ☺

Table of Contents

from the nefarious Cap'n Hook. They hire a lesser witch, not Wicked, but Slightly Naughty, to sneak Tinker-Belle out in a miniature flying gingerbread house.

In which our party crosses to Transylvania, Kent Clark (N.R.) whips off his glasses and plays his alter super-ego and is recognized by no one save F.U.-Belle. They encounter a Persian war god, bitching that other ancient pantheons like Greeks, Romans and Egyptians had Hollywood blockbusters named for them but no one has paid any attention to the Persian gods.

In which the real Cap'n Hook is confused by receiving a note from King Clarion requesting the release of Tinker-Belle who he never kidnapped, and discovers she doesn't meet the legal height requirement to be his victim. Smee orders a new pet online (a tiny, hand-eating crocodile) much to Hook's dismay.

In which our party meets Tailored Wear, a friendly and outgoing, as well as handsome werewolf who only wants to play ball, hates vampires and loves the great outdoors! They convince him to speak to the UnderWear Clan of Werewolves and enlist the werewolves to help the fairies in their war.

In which it comes as a *total surprise!*

In which our party attends a not-Family Reunion of all the (No Relations) who aren't related to each other, much to Kent Clark's (also Not Related) delight. This sets him on the right road to uncovering his dormant heroic superpowers.

Introducing F.U.-Belle

S o that's when *the second Zombie Apocalypse* began though technically it only involved one pissed-off zombie and a length of lead pipe.

No wait—you asked where *it all started*, right? Mainly it *started* with the war, of course.

Didn't you hear about that? Well . . . *once upon 3 p.m. a couple Thursdays ago* . . .

The vampire paused halfway through lifting the rock to check his GPS. This was the covert spot where the fairies stashed their magic crackle, or so he thought . . .

. . .right up until the shrubbery arose, developed sharp steely edges and launched like a rocket through the air at him—or at least, toward his knee caps. It was unusual to say the least. That hadn't happened during the last vampire raid, or any of the other raids before that.

"*DIIIIIIIIIIIIIIEEEEEEEE SUUUCKKAHHHHHHHH!!*" the ferociously-armed mystery attacker screeched as it continued its furious assault on the vampire's lower calves to ankle region. *Was it a walking bonsai tree? What the—?*

The vampire blinked, then realized to his relief it wasn't a tree at all. It was a fairy soldier disguised in camouflage war paint and the bonsai tree impression was helped along by the fact that he was very tiny and strapped head to toe with every edged weapon known to exist, giving him a definite "bristly" appearance.

That alone was surprising. Camouflage wasn't included in the spring pastels colour palette, edged weaponry wasn't a trending fashion accessory and overall, fairies were very firm about their designer clothing being correct for the season. Practicality always gave way to 'the look'.

He was followed by another fairy officer, this time in designer-uniforming with a snazzy zebra-striped belt, a large hairdryer and a maxx-hold aerosol hairspray can shoved in his belt loop, in case any flyaway hairs got unruly. Both men were winged and only a quarter of an inch tall, as all fairies were, which was why they were so hard to spot until they stepped (or flew) out into the open.

The vampire smirked. *A hairdryer and an aerosol can.* Yes, that looked much more like what he expected from traditional fairy law enforcement.

"Spread um, corpse-bag! You're under arrest!" the tiny fairy in camouflage ordered. The vampire just blinked at him, puzzled.

"Who are you?"

"I'm Captain –mumble, mumble– and you're under arrest, I said," the fairy captain whipped a pair of handcuffs out too small to fit the vampire's pinkie finger off his belt as he prattled Fairyland's official legal rights.

"You have the right to dress fashionably! Any clothing out of season may be used against you in the Royal Fairyland Court! You have the right to a manicure, and a pedicure may be offered at the Court's own expense! You have the right to consult a stylist; if you cannot afford a stylist, the Court may at its discretion, appoint a stylist for you—"

"I'm sorry?" the vampire interrupted, bewildered by rapidly changing events. "Why am I being arrested? And I didn't quite catch your name, Captain."

The fairy glared at him, "I'm CAPTAIN—*mumble!* And under Fairyland law, I don't need to press charges to arrest you beyond the fact that you are openly wearing a black opera cloak during daylight hours *–you'll be lucky if they don't hang you–* but give me a minute and I'll think up some other charges to add to the docket."

'His name is FOO-Belle," his partner supplied helpfully. The vampire smirked.

"Foo—*BELLE*?"

The fairy captain rolled his eyes. "I've told you before Dum-Belle, it's F.U.-Belle! Not foo! *F! U!*—as in—uh," the fairy captain now identified as F.U. paused and hunted for a suitable illustration but none came to his rescue.

"Actually his name used to be Twinkle-Belle—isn't that charming?" Dum-Belle continued cheerfully, "It's those "twinkly eyes" he has you know—but he had it legally changed. I can't imagine why he changed such a nice name?"

"Yeah, like no one ever bullies a 1/4-inch-tall fairy named *Twink*," Fu muttered under his breath.

In fact, Fu's problems stemmed from being originally born as a human infant. His fairy parents were doting traditionalists and lovingly stole him out of his human baby cradle at birth and replaced him with a brick which naturally is the *proper method* of fairy consummation. They always claimed later it was a very attractive brick.

Still, it took 3 days before Fu-Belle's biological human parents even noticed their baby was missing or the brick in his cradle and called the police so it can be successfully argued that he wasn't too badly off for being stolen away by the fairies.

As traditionalists, Fu-Belle's parents named their new son "Twinkle-Belle" in the proper manner of fairies. The "-Belle" extension was compulsory to tack on every name under Fairyland Law, *male or female*, and Fu-Belle felt he'd dodged a partial bullet because it was only traditional for *fairy girls* to be named after flora. Boys on the other hand, were named either for a pleasant attribute or, in a pinch, the shrubbery. "That-Damn-Leaf-Belle" was a popular name in his neighborhood.

Actually, he came out semi-*okay* with Twinkle-Belle because apparently he also possessed, as an infant, a very small butt which fit inside his Mum's hand and was frequently joked about at dinner parties—so his given name could be *a lot worse!*

But his human side eventually kicked in and objected to the indignity—so, as soon as he was of age, Fu had his name legally-changed from "Twinkle" (but there wasn't much he could do about the "-Belle").

It was supposed to be "F.U." but the congenial 900-hundred-year-old clerk at Pixietown City Hall hadn't the best hearing nor, it appeared, had he understood what Fu was going for (and the old geezer hadn't been helped much by Fu's demonstrative hand-gestures either. He thought Fu had a weird method of pointing his finger).

"Dum-Belle, let me handle the interrogation please," the fairy captain snapped, focusing his attention on their vampire prisoner. "My name isn't the point, sir. Back to the point, *why* is a vampire raiding our fairy magic caches? I don't get it."

"What? I'm not a vampire! What makes you think that?" the vampire asked, crossing his arms against his tuxedoed chest, and defensively tugging his opera cloak around his shoulders. "Actually,

I'm—uh, one of your tall, fairy cousins just visiting from—uh, NORTH FAIRYLAND!"

"Are you fu—" Fu checked himself, "*funning around* with me, sir?" Fairyland had a zero tolerance policy against public vulgarity from its officers while on duty. Also, legwarmers.

"There is no North Fairyland. And it's clear you are *a vampire*, sir. Opera cloak, widow's peak, Transylvanian accent and—what's that other thing?" Fu snapped his fingers. "Oh yeah—the *fangs*. It's rather the *undead giveaway*, pardon my levity."

"Fangs—*me*? Uh—those are just so I can look, a-ha, "sharp" at all times," the vampire replied nervously.

"Oh—how clever," Dum-Belle clapped his hands enthusiastically. "He does look rather sharp at that. I wonder if fangs will make a fashion comeback? I must write to the editor of the Fairyland Times."

Fu-Belle glared, resisting the urge to do something violent with his collapsible club to help this interrogation along. He had a few unresolved (some might call them psychotic) issues with his rage bubbling beneath his itty-bitty surface.

The mandatory addition of "-Belle" led to outbreaks of rebellion and misapplied rage for young fairy males, including bullying of any magical race which didn't have a mandatory "-Belle" tacked on the end of their name.

Fairy men were small in stature with a lot to prove, especially after they'd had a few drinks. Also, the tights—*traditional fairy breeches, dammit!*—and the little glittery wings didn't help. Fairy men were the first to vehemently insist not everything about them was, er, *little.*

After years spent in anger-management therapy *(unsuccessful),* meditation classes *(even less successful),* and finally, advanced martial arts where they had to invent a new level of belt advancement just for him, Fu-Belle joined the Fairy Peace Corp, figuring he could channel his well-trained fists of fury and still-not-quite-managed fits of unbridled murderous rage to use. The denizens of Fairyland didn't whine as much about his sociopathic violent tendencies so long as he was out killing other magical races on their behalf.

Plus, legally he got to carry weapons "on the job" though Fu's weapon selection included more variety and imagination than standard Fairyland issue (although standard Fairyland issue only included an industrial hairdryer and oversized cuticle snippers). Fu favored pretty much everything he could strap to his body without collapsing beneath the weight.

"If I were a vampire, could I be standing here in the middle of the afternoon beneath open sunlight steal—uh, I mean, *doing nothing* much of importance?" the vampire coughed guiltily. "I was just, um, looking around for some fashion magazines. This is all an innocent mix-up, officers."

Both fairy men regarded the vampire critically. True, there was a significant lack of the screaming and bursting into wild, leaping flames that usually characterized vampires being caught in broad daylight. There was a valid reason why vampires inhabited the wild and desolate mountain terrain of Transylvania, official motto: *"The blizzard just ended, now time for some snowfall."*

"You could be wearing very strong sunscreen," Fu pointed out without much conviction, "Look pal, why are you vampires stealing OUR magic anyway? Crackle is fairy magic and we need it on the go for our dealings with humans. Vampires can't wield it, you don't have the right spells or charms."

"Anyway, don't you have some kind of *bat-related magic* of your own? *Batmen* are very popular in the Human World. I've heard rumors."

"Well the *"dark and stormy castle, creatures of the night"* routine isn't working for us anymore," the vampire whined. "Strange but humans don't want to explore spooky old castles or dusty coffins. It's almost as if *they expect* something *bad* to happen."

"Um—"

"But King Armando found out on Majick-Book that sparkling vampires were the new thing! *Humans like that now!* We just rub some of your sparkling fairy crackle on our skin and *viola!* The humans actually come running to us!"

"The sunlight doesn't hurt us and we don't burst into piles of smoking ash! The magic makes our skin sparkle like a diamond, while reflecting the natural sunlight back on itself. It's like—*like*—" the vampire waved expressive "jazz hands" as he sought for the right word, "—*majickal!* Or something! So Armando has been sending us back for more—there's one young vampire in particular it works especially well on. *Howard,* or *Leonard*— something like that. Can't recall."

Ah yes. Well that explained it. Armando Wingsfield Pentagram the 23rd, the King of all Vampires (the other 22 "Armandos" were him too. He wasn't just the last of his line, he was *his own entire linage*) never heard of such a thing in all his 23 generations (nor had any of his forefathers which were, in point of fact, *him* once removed).

Fresh, young food that *came of its own accord* to present itself to his Transylvanian doorstep? It was a never-ending, all-the-blood-you-can-drink buffet! Clearly King Armando was intrigued that fairy crackle made all vampires *utterly irresistible* to humans, a siren call that had the chattel mooing and snorting and throwing large wads of money to the wind just to get closer to Mother Nature's fang-bearing human predator. It was like millions of cows seeking out the nearest barbeque pit, voluntarily smearing steak sauce on themselves, then lining up to be next on the grill.

Besides, it was very chic and sophisticated, sparkling like a jewel in the open sun and that was just the type of thing to appeal to vampires, a vain – *excuse me, "vein"*— and stylized breed of monster. Let alone that they could actually "walk in the open daylight again without consequences" bit.

To exemplify his point, the vampire smeared fairy crackle dust across his bare white expanse of chest, tearing open his black silk shirt to get the full effect. The midday sun refracted against the shimmer, throwing off a million diamond facets like hitting a prism or fractured mirror. It didn't appear to touch the vampire however; he was protected from the sun rays by the magical dust.

Both fairies stared, feeling a loss for words. While fairy men in general were no strangers to body glitter, no one would ever consider using fairy crackle for this purpose due to its many odd and curious side-effects.

Too much crackle exposure without appropriate safety precautions and you began trying to teach British children how to fly using only their happy thoughts and harboring insane jealousy against any humans named Wendy.

"The humans *like that?* Glittery, bare vampire skin *attracts them?"*

The vampire shrugged loosely, "Well humans, you know. Fickle species. Who can account for their tastes? But King Armando is very clever to take advantage of their fascination."

"Not at *our expense* though," Fu objected dryly. "How did you vampires discover our magic? It's not like common knowledge where we keep it."

"Well Captain," Dum-Belle piped up, "naturally you're aware that I posted the secret locations of all our crackle caches to Majick-Book. Treasure maps are always so complicated and hard to follow—I didn't want us to lose track of any of them, you know," he beamed with pride and efficiency of a job well done, sure his fellow officer would be falling all over himself with praise.

Fu just gaped at his partner, "YOU—*WHAT*? You mean ALL OF MAJICK-BOOK knows where our hidden caches of FAIRY CRACKLE are?!"

"No, of course not. That's utterly impossible, Captain," Dum-Belle insisted, "My profile security was set to "Top Secret Mage" and the post itself marked "Do Not Display This Post on Other Majick-Books" so no one else could see it, naturally."

"And Majick-Book has the best security cause all you have to do is click one button and it makes you, like, totally invisible and you can post whatever you want! You should try it, Captain. In fact, I go on there and post my credit card information as soon as the new cards come in. It's such a handy place to keep it, especially since I have to change card numbers often—they keep getting stolen somehow."

Fu-Belle darted a look at their vampire captive who looked suspiciously guilty, then whipped out his iFairy device and pulled up Dum-Belle's profile on Majick-Book. Sure enough, there were all the secret locations posted on his timeline, with handy-dandy hyperlinks stating: *"Lost? Map this location in Fairyland now"* next to them.

No wonder the vampires seemed to have this sixth sense about where those "secret caches" were and their raids were so remarkably consistent. Mysterious, wasn't it? Equally mysterious how 5,328,566 vampires "Liked" Dum-Belle's post.

Well, fine. Fu-Belle could choose to make a big deal about this but he'd just as soon avoid an international incident that could put Fairyland at risk. Simply put, the vampires were immortal and very dangerous if crossed, and the two mystic races had successfully remained at peace for centuries. The last thing Fu wanted was to cause friction between the two.

"Okay look, we could take you in and hold you for traveling across Fairyland borders with intent to commit a crime on our soil—but we won't arrest you if you will return to Transylvania and inform King Armando that no more thefts by vampires will be tolerated. I'm sorry, but he's just going to have to figure something else out."

"His Majesty will never stand for this insolence from you fairies," the vampire fumed, "he was just voted *the Sexiest Vampire on Majick-Book,* you know."

"Didn't he vote for himself?"

"Yeah—*and*—?"

"No point. I was just curious." Fu concentrated very hard on keeping his face as straight as a board but unfortunately it didn't quite work. The vampire could sense he was laughing internally.

"This is an act of *treason!* You can't press charges against me! I have full *diplomatic immunity* under King Armando's directive."

"Not when you've crossed Fairyland borders under false pretenses and stolen our magic, sir. I'm afraid we cannot allow that."

"You'll see," the vampire huffed. "Just wait until I blog about this! I have a huge following on Majick-Book! It will go viral and then you'll be sorry! You'll see! Transylvania declares war on Fairyland!"

"Right, sure." Fu didn't believe him and released the vampire to return to his homeland—but as it turned out, he should have listened. For only two weeks later, King Armando officially declared a state of war with Fairyland!

Bad Year for a World War

F u-Belle found himself at the "First Annual Fairyland Council of War" which began at exactly half-past two in the Palatial Gardens on a beautiful mid-spring afternoon.

It was expected to be the highlight of the Spring Season and naturally, all the A-list fairy celebrities were in attendance, strolling up the rose-petal carpet in their spring finery amidst the "ooh's and ahh's" of the starstruck guests.

A light aperitif was served on the lawn, and the War Council was even expected to stretch into supper which would be served promptly at half-past six. A thirteen-course menu was prepared, with main entrée of poached salmon glazed with lemon-honey and dill, served with capers and paired with one's choice of over twenty-two types of handbrewed ale.

With clear skies and such an excellent meal in store, it was assumed by all that the War Council was going well.

"I'm afraid it's impossible," King Clarion of the Fairies declared, delicately waving a pale, thin hand.

"I don't care if Armando announced it already. He's very presumptive in that respect and I'm afraid a war with the vampires can't even *be considered* for the upcoming social season. There's just no time to work it into the schedule this late." The way he pronounced "schedule" made it sound like there were about 3 extra syllables.

"Between our Midsummer's Eve Annual Dance-a-Thon and the Evening Out with the Silk Worms and let's not forget, Queen Bee's Ostentatious Honey Bee Ball—well clearly, the vampires should have *registered early* if they wanted a timeslot for a war with us."

"But DAAAHHHHling," interjected his wife, Queen Ding-Aling. The fairy king and queen had gotten around the mandatory "-Belle" name extension law by naming themselves after musical sounds instead. No one else really wanted to argue the point.

"I think the thing is, my Virile Stallion, that we're officially at war with Transylvania whether it was prior scheduled or no. Anyway, one might expect *vampires* to be too boorish to plan in advance. I've heard a ghastly rumor that they can't even use a mirror properly."

"No, my Honey Blossom, it can't be done." King Clarion insisted, flipping back his glorious shiny blond locks, because "he's worth it", and again waving a dramatic hand, more to show off his exquisite manicure ("the shade is called *Moondrop*, oh do you like it?") than any genuine display of emotion.

"Ding-Aling, you know how I love a good war! I've always said it's perfect for exfoliation, all that fresh air and screaming—it really opens up the pores but alas, no! We simply *can't* host, we haven't the space in Fairyland and besides the catering alone would take weeks to plan! And you know how difficult it is to feed vampires! They make such a fuss when we arrange a vegan, nut-free, gluten-free menu," Clarion frowned, though he was careful not to crease his face and make wrinkles.

"I don't know when we'll have an opening. Perhaps we can squeeze them in post-autumn once the Golden Leaf Feast and Festival ends. There's a bit of downtime in there before Winter Solstice Shopping Season begins."

"How true, my Brave Samurai," Queen Ding-Aling praised, "But alas, the vampires may not wait so long. I'm afraid this war may end up—" she shuddered delicately "—becoming an "impromptu" affair."

As one, the Fairy Court took a collective gasp and several women fainted. *Impromptu! Say it isn't so!*

There hadn't been an impromptu gathering of the fairies since the field mouse arranged that quickie marriage between little Thumbelina and her neighbor, the rich but very ugly Mole—and even then, the field mouse still managed engraved invitations. They were on cheap cardstock mind you, but it being impromptu and all, no one had the heart to criticize.

The wedding was later called off and Thumbelina was married to the Flower Prince instead, presumably not because of the inferior invitations to her first wedding although that couldn't have helped matters.

"Ding-Aling," Clarion said in a tone of reproach. "I hadn't thought you even knew such a disreputable word! I'm *sure we're not barbarians!* It horrifies me that my own wife would—" he broke off in dismay.

"Next, you'll be saying for this war, we should skip the party favor bags!"

Another collective gasp rose and Ding-Aling meekly lowered her head.

"Of course not, my Robust Quadruped," she blushed and delicately tapped her mouth. "Do pardon my Elvish—darling, all I meant was this war with the vampires may not be avoidable."

"But we could hire a war planner, I suppose, to sort out the catering, invitations, favor bags and make sure all the militia uniforms are in style with this season's colors. Obviously we have a reputation to protect. It's the details that count."

"I s-u-p-p-o-s-e so," Clarion drawled out the word in a tone that clearly indicated no war planner could conceivably hold up to his standards,

"But where will we host, Ding-Aling? Not in Transylvania—there's no suitable venues there. And we can't have it here either. Vampires do leave such large messes behind when they ravage and pillage."

"Well—" Ding-Aling thought hard "—why don't we host the war in the Human Realm? Don't those human beings have lots of—*I don't know*—free space they aren't taking up with their grotesque, mortal, aging and dying bodies?"

"You'd think so, wouldn't you? Their world is so very large and all. I've tried to get on the books over there for months but there isn't any space available."

Clarion huffed. "That stupid *Zombie Apocalypse* affair is already on the books, and the Immutable Forces of Fate and Destiny claim that every event venue in the Human Realm is pre-booked by the zombies, paid out in advance through their year-3000 while they're eating and decimating the humans. They've been advertising that stupid *Apocalypse* of theirs for years, you know—they must have a tremendous budget!"

"There's no way we'll get the zombies to trade dates with us now. We'll never get a space booking this late, Ding-Aling. We'll just have to wait until next millennia and see if something opens up. Maybe someone will cancel?"

He looked a bit smug as he finished, "See? This is what comes of *impromptu* planning!"

He waved at the Chief Scribe of the Fairies to dictate a letter. "Send a polite but firm RSVP response to King Armando of the Vampires that we respectfully decline their war invitation. Do invite us again if they should find another time more suitable and we look forward to warring with them some time next century. Cordially yours, etc, etc."

"Marvelous, my Sexy Monkey, that was so brilliantly done," Ding-Aling beamed. "I knew you'd find the right solution. And, what IS that nail color you're wearing, darling? It's simply FABULOUS!"

Clarion beamed. "Isn't it just? I think I'll have it for my next pedicure, what do you think?"

With that, the conversation transitioned naturally into a discussion of nail shades with all the important Fairyland dignitaries weighing in. Supper was served and it was delicious, all agreed.

With the excellent catering and wine selection and the party bags handed out by their Majesties being top-label Fairy Designer, everyone unanimously felt it was the finest War Council they'd ever attended and it should be made into an annual affair going forward—but with less unpleasant, appetite-ruining conversation about strategy and warfare at the next one. It simply ruined the ambiance of a War Council to discuss war.

Although he was Captain of the Fairy Peace Corps and therefore entirely relevant to any discussion concerning the outbreak of war, Fu-Belle hadn't been asked for his opinion. He and the rest of his disgracefully-attired regiment were ushered to the back of the lawn where they received cold scraps leftover from the kitchen and no wine list at all. Fu was just barely able to hear what the king and queen said from their oak feasting table upfront.

Had he been asked for his opinion which he hadn't, since he was surprisingly pragmatic for a fairy (but perhaps his human origins had something to do with it) he'd have said that Queen Ding-Aling was correct! War with the vampires was unavoidable now! The vampires would raid Fairyland soon.

It was time for the fairies to set aside their party plans, take up arms, be prepared and nix the catering idea. The ugly truth was that the situation would escalate to far worse before it got better.

Bearers of bad news weren't looked on fondly by the fairies. Naturally they wouldn't listen, not without a wardrobe upgrade on Fu-Belle's part and it was a shame really. As was the case with most pragmatic people, Fu-Belle also was correct.

We're Team Vampyr!

wo weeks earlier, Armando Wingsfield Pentegram the 23rd, King of the Vampires, was feeling very pleased with himself. Not just because his name was voted "Sexiest Vampire Name" on Majick-Book which, hold for applause, *he totally WON by a landslide!* Armando voted for himself the maximum allowable times then made it mandatory under Transylvanian law under penalty of wooden stake for all his vampire subjects to vote for him on his current Majick-Book status.

But he didn't see this as cheating because "Armando" was, in fact, the sexiest name of any vampire ever—"*eat your heart and liver and kidneys and pulmonary arteries out, Alucard!*"

But what also pleased Armando was that vampire snacking became easy and carefree. When he felt hungry, he tossed that skinny vampire out— *what was his name? Howard? Leonard?* It was something like that. Armando didn't have a good memory for vampire names—save for *Armando,* but that was the only name *worth* remembering!

Anyway, so they just sprayed him down with fairy—*sparkly magic dust*, whatever that stuff was called, and watched as without fail, a group of teen girls would appear and madly cluster around the sparkly vampire idol, groping and tossing their panties at him amongst high-pitched calls of "omg!" and "squee!"—this part, Armando didn't understand but it appeared to be a strange human mating ritual.

Regardless, the lustful frenzy never took notice when Armando picked out one or two girls that looked juicy and had a light lunch. They just went on giggling and groping and panty-tossing until Armando locked the sparkly vampire up until the next meal. You know, that fellow *Howard*. Or *Leonard*. Whatever that vampire's name was, the one the human girls liked, it was on the tip of Armando's tongue really.

But it was so simple that it was almost like magic! Rubbing some sparkly fairy dust, uh, that crackle stuff, on a gaunt, pale, sunken-eyed vampire sporting so much hair gel his head would snap off in a strong tailwind, and suddenly beautiful young girls were *lining up by droves,* begging to be his entrée!

Although Armando wasn't sure why this siren song was especially strong on virginal, young women or for that matter, why they all wore matching pink baby doll "Team Vampyr" t-shirts instead of flattering lacy nightgowns and sleeping with their windows open as tradition dictated, but it was alright with him. Other humans came along making for a buffet line of sorts and Armando felt he could adapt with the rapidly changing modern times.

Please do come right in! Transylvania is a friendly, family-oriented place just dying, a-ha, pardon me, to entertain you for, a-ha, dinner, yesss! Armando liked plenty of variety in his diet.

Anyway, the whole system was working perfectly therefore it surprised King Armando when he received a notice from the Fairy Court, once he arose from his coffin for the new night.

It was addressed to him in a pink envelope, marked S.W.A.L.K. and covered top-to-bottom with Scratch 'n Sniff stickers —*"Oh, for the Love of Arteries!"*— politely declining the invitation to begin a war that King Armando himself hadn't bothered to issue. Well, that was the underlying message once he decrypted the ornate and embossed calligraphy utilized by the Chief Fairy Scribe and figured out the content of the letter. It began as a lengthy sonnet about *"a clear blue sky and summertime's young lovers"*—47 pages later, *"the fairies were sorry but they couldn't make the war at this time"*.

Actually, it didn't occur to Armando that it was necessary get involved in an interspecies war with the fairies. They were family to a point—although fairies were more the "batty uncle" in the supernatural family tree than a "blood brother" of the vampires.

Sure, Armando had heard the rumors flying around social media about the fairies and vampires being at war. Some vampire apparently vlogged it, then it went viral with "#gotta lose 20 lbs by VampFair War, lol" but Armando himself hadn't paid much attention, expecting the ruckus to die down when nothing came of it.

He was much too busy to worry about urban legends at the time, locked as he was in a VITAL DEATH MATCH for the "Sexiest Name" title on Majick-Book with *Count Alucard!*

HE SO DIDN'T! It was just *stupid,* you know—spelling your name backward didn't make it SEXY! That stupid Count was going down in flames if Armando had anything to do with it. Why did that guy even have a book named after him anyway, Armando could never understand.

As Armando already knew all the locations of the, ahem, *secret fairy crackle caches* and also knew it wouldn't occur to the fairies to *move* said hiding places after they'd been discovered (their planning skills didn't go beyond matching their accessories to their shoes) he saw no need to waste time or resources fighting over it. Swiping what he needed as he needed it was working out fine.

None of his spies were even caught until the last raid. They snuck into Fairyland under such clever guises as looking and dressing *exactly like vampires* and assuring the fairies they were visiting cousins who were unusually tall—*unfortunately* tall even. They were so tall in fact, that they looked almost human but the fairies didn't like to mention this aloud. It might hurt their poor visiting cousin feelings to find out they were so tall and ugly and badly dressed.

A notation even made it into the spring edition of the "Fairyland Chronicle" that their tall, pale, unfortunately ugly cousins had come from abroad to visit and should be warmly welcomed by all, "straight from Transylv—uh, I mean, we travelled here from NORTH Fairyland to visit you! VERY NORTH Fairyland!" The fact that there was no North Fairyland just made this accomplishment all the more impressive.

Anyway, dead fairies were no good to the vampires. They couldn't make that "sparkly dust stuff" if they were dead and it wasn't like they were edible. Fairies were very, very chewy and sticky like saltwater taffy that came in nauseating colors and tasted like pencil erasers. Everyone knew when a newly-turned vampire tried eating a fairy for the first time—you never needed to experience it twice! You had to pick bits of leftover fairy out of your fangs for weeks and there was always some stuck in your hair (impossible to disentangle, you had to cut the stickiness out) or on the bottom of your shoe—sticky fairy bits got *everywhere!*

Plus, where would they host a war? Zombies had the entire Human World booked out and the fairies wouldn't travel to Transylvania! They griped the journey was treacherous and fraught with danger—*well duh! OF COURSE IT WAS!* There were *standards* to uphold!

Armando had the wild packs of hungry, ravaging wolves shipped in special and lets not even discuss how much it'd cost to have those jagged peaks and sharp outcroppings sculpted in the high mountains! Think building "narrow ledges that broke free at just the critical moment when the hero was hanging on for dear life" was *easy,* did you? What was the world coming to? There was no respect for craftsmanship or pride in one's villainous reputation these days!

It took careful planning and prior arrangements with the weather gods to make everything in Transylvania run efficiently. Armando tried for a dark, stormy night each time they had out-of-town guests to frighten but at times he was embarrassed to admit he had to fall back on a bright flashlight, some water being poured through a sieve off the roof and sheet metal pounded at significant intervals when all the appropriately portentous thunderstorms were already taken.

You couldn't have a good, bloody war in Fairyland—it was like trying to set the chainsaw massacre in Who-Ville. The landscape was perpetually bright and cheerful, it looked like the backdrop for a children's animated feature film. Though the initial thought of littering Fairyland with dead fairy corpses was appealing, the overall effect would be spoiled when cuddly, talking animals burst into a lively spontaneous tune promoting touchy-feely virtues. Or when a staff-bearing white wizard appeared to inform everyone that two little people passed this way and were now in the care of a kindly tree herder.

Fairyland was *that sort of place*, yes.

Armando shuddered again. Thinking about all this fairy cheerfulness and gaiety, gross! Now he needed something to wash out his mouth and mind, and make him feel better. Where was *Orlando*—or, *Leonard*? He was needed to draw the human girls out of hiding so Armando could nab a midnight pick-me-up.

"Your Highness? Sorry to disturb you." Breaking the silence, the butler waited until Armando made a gesture to advance. Vampires were sticklers about protocol and they wrote the book on it, literally.

"The leader of the zombies, 'oops-i-forgot-my-name-cause-i-ate-my-own-brain' is here to see you, my lord."

"Repugnant," Armando said brightly in the same tone one might've said "what a delight". "I'm utterly disgusted. Do show him in and fetch some cold brain for our guest would you, Simons?"

After the zombie was shown in, Armando sat as far across the room as he could get and tried not to hold his overly sensitive nose,

"Right. Can I get you some preservatives? Formaldehyde? A chemical peel?"

"No, thank yer lordship," the zombie replied, smiling with green teeth at him. "I'm jist droppin in to—uh—uh—"

"Let me guess," Armando made a bored gesture, "This has something to do with your "apocalypse" . . ." he made sarcastic air quotes. Since the leader of the zombies looked blank, he sighed.

"Came to ask for money did you, or advice on how to duck shotgun shells?"

"Yo—yo drink da blood, right?"

Armando paused. "Um, yes. Human blood, yes. Er, with caveats," he added quickly. "NOT blood with high toxicity levels," he dropped to an undertone, "Like yours. Can't stand the hangovers."

"Well—we eat brains and flesh," the zombie just looked at him like there was connection he hoped Armando would get. "*Human* flesh," he added hopefully.

"Yes—well—yes—I know that," Armando waved a hand. "There's no accounting for some people's tastes, present company accepted."

"Der humans—dey come all put together," the zombie pointed out. "Der bits all attached like so."

Armando just looked at him.

"What I bin tinkin—" the zombie paused and scratched the large hole in his cranial cavity where his brain used to be. "What I bin tinkin is this— humans has lotsa bits. We only eat some bits see, and yo—yo—eat odder bits, see. So—so—I bin tinkin—yo va—bats, and der us z—z—what we is, we—bot eat human bits, see?"

"Wait," Armando paused. "Are you suggesting a mutually beneficial partnership in which we combine our forces and divide the war spoils equally, each taking our own portion of the limited nutritional resource known as humans for the betterment of our respective species?"

The zombie stopped, pausing for a very long moment. "I bin tinkin dat, yah," he said finally.

Armando drummed his fingers on the armrest of his wingback, a-ha, BAT wingback chair, actually.

"And in return, I suppose you want the help of the vampires to win your little apocalypse—party, thing, whatever it is you're doing," he huffed.

The zombie pointed to his chest where, albeit blood-stained, ripped and very bedraggled, he was clearly and proudly wearing a pink baby-doll T-shirt which read: *"Team Vampyr"*.

"I'll admit, I do hate the thought of all that fresh blood going to waste," Armando mused. "I suppose I could just send along a few boys and some mops and Dixon jars for the storehouse but—oh, very well."

He stood and began to pace. "You zombies will need looking after, I can see. An administration committee qualified to oversee the situation with a firm hand and make the difficult decisions you zombies aren't equipped to make. We can't have you wiping out ALL the future generations of our #1 food source naturally—but we can allow perhaps a little pruning the hedges, some light weeding out of the unfavorable or weak human genes. Good for flourishing, making the garden grow back stronger."

"Den yo—yo be "Team Zombie" next," the zombie declared, smiling his gray-greenish-missing-toothed smile again. "We get yo shirts like dis too."

"Oh alright," Armando agreed crossly. "Anything to keep you from slowly disintegrating on my couch, it'll stain. It was left to me by the King of France right after I ate him. I'm very fond of it."

"And we help yo, yo gonna go kill dem—dem—bells—fings, what?"

"The fairies," Armando laughed. "Oh that, no. Just a silly rumor. We're not at war with the fairies."

"Oh. I dun heard wrong den. I heard dey captured yo spy and all dat! Thought yous was mad at dem cuz the fairies dun moved all dem—shiny bits dey haz."

Armando froze in mid-chuckle. "They did— *what?*"

"Yeah. I done heard dem fairies moved it cause yo—yo dun stole dere shiny. So dey dun hid it and now yo dun know where to get some mo."

"How DARE they?" Armando nearly shook with rage. "After thousands of years of complacent idiocy, how dare the fairies actually MOVE something because we took it without permission?"

"The nerve, the utter gall! They EXIST to make that "shiny, um—gunk" so that WE can STEAL IT at our leisure and WE were certainly doing OUR PART of the bargain—how dare they *MOVE IT* without our say so! That is JUST going TOO FAR! I'm just—so ANGRY NOW—"

The vampire king broke off and whipped out a glossy, black iBat phone (yes, it was actually shaped like a bat) from his opera cloak, pulled up the app and started composing himself a Majick-Book rant post until he felt calm again.

The zombie paused, needing time to work this out in his clearly-missing brain. "Uh—yous—kill dis fairies? Or, yous no kill dis fairies?"

"WE KILL DIS FAIRIES," Armando huffed. "Those little winged insects, they're nothing more than glorified bugs—we'll squish them like mosquitoes!

The WAR is SO ON NOW and then I'm gonna stuff their snotty ridiculous sonnet, all 47 pages of it, up Clarion's tiny nose—" he fumbled with his phone again, his attention diverted from the zombie,

"—I'm making the official declaration right now, that Transylvania is at a state of war with Fairyland. But first I have to BaTwingg the news to my vampire bros on BaTwingger! This is SO being tagged, "#ohnotheydidnt!" . . ."

He kept poking his touch screen and getting replies because he kept bursting out with, "I KNOW RIGHT?" and "CAN YOU BELIEVE IT?" apparently not directed at his zombie guest, though he seemed to realize after that only the zombie could hear his vocal outbursts and BaTwingg-ed them instead.

Had he been paying the slightest attention to the zombie emissary, he'd have noticed his guest smiling that gray-green toothed smile again, as if he were unusually pleased by the turn of events. Like the guy holding the smoking gun after a murder had just been committed, that wasn't the least bit suspicious.

Why no, not at all.

Superhero Wanted: Apply Within (No Capes!)

ent Clark (no relation) awoke to find himself floating midair above his bed while he slept. *Oh no! Not again!* He hated when that alien flying power took him unexpectedly while he slept. Last time, he dropped too quickly and broke his bed apart with the force of impact.

"KENT CLARK (no relation)! Get down here, it's time for breakfast!"

Kent Clark (no relation) woke up all over again, this time to the sound of his mother's voice yelling. *Oh. It was the flying dream again, wasn't it?*

Honestly, that dream was becoming annoying though not near as annoying as the one about the frozen cave full of glowing, talking crystals insisting it was his father.

His dreams were getting stranger all the time. It was a wonder he ever got any sleep at all.

By the time Kent Clark (no relation) got down to breakfast in their quaint, shiny yellow farmhouse, his mother and father were both waiting for him. That wasn't a good sign.

"To be honest son, we're worried about you!" Joshua Clark (also no relation) took his pipe out of his mouth to frown.

"I know we found you in a cornfield next to a suspicious smoking crater and rather than take our chances with legal child adoption, we kept you on the spot and knew we'd be asking for some trouble keeping a kid that just fell out of the sky."

"Course, we don't really know you fell from the sky," Marta Clark (not even remotely related) inserted, "But it seemed likely, given the crater."

"Yes, but you're 38 and still in high school," Joshua Clark (still no relation) complained. "That's not *normal*, son! People are starting to talk! You've been attending Tinyville High for the past ten years and even though no one seems to really have noticed that you're the oldest senior on campus, your mother and I want you to get out there and see the world!"

"Or at least be admitted to a psychiatric ward because of a weird genetic mutation caused by the glowing green rocks like the rest of your student body was! They all graduated on time! They all have murderous disorders and rare psychoses for their parents to proudly brag about at dinner parties!"

Kent Clark (no relation) only nodded. When a kid fell mysteriously out of the sky and had flight dreams and a spaceship-shaped cradle, it was widely assumed the future had big plans for him. He rather expected to have big plans for himself.

It was just—well, all the right pieces seemed to be there, right? Yet Kent Clark (no relation) was depressingly ordinary. He had no budding superpowers whatsoever, besides his weird dreams at night but frankly those he blamed on the footie pajamas and red cape he still slept in at 38 years old, because they were lovingly hand-knitted by Marta for him. He was so utterly boring and mild-mannered as a man that he bored himself!

Oh sure, his folks went on and on about how he caught the car when it was about to fall and crush his adopted father—Kent Clark (no relation) hadn't the heart to tell them it because he just happened to be standing next to the hydraulic jack. He wasn't super-powered, just quick thinking.

"No matter what, your mother and I love you," Joshua said supportively. "Son, we just want you to get past high school and go on to lead a successful and productive life. Move to a big city, dress like a hunky nerd, hide your face behind horn-rimmed glasses, be castrated by an emancipated reporter, learn to undress in a phone booth. You'll grow into those superpowers of yours, believe me, son."

"Dad, I'm 38," Kent Clark (no relation) pointed out as gently as he could. Marta beamed.

"And still *super*," she kissed his cheek. "By the way, I'm knitting you a new cape honey. It should be finished by the time you graduate—" there was an embarrassed gap of silence before she rallied positively with, "—and your Dad and I, we're so proud of you, Kent Clark (no relation)!"

"Group hug," Joshua pronounced cheerfully and likewise beaming, he reached to engulf his large son and wife in his arms before adding jovially, "Careful there, my boy! You might just crush me with your super strength."

"Well then, he'll just have to rush you to the hospital with his super speed," Marta happily replied and the two laughed loudly.

"Dad, I don't have super strength—or super speed. I keep telling you, I'm not an alien super hero with special powers," Kent Clark (no relation) wailed. "I'm just an ordinary guy with a personal spaceship. It's really not all that weird."

Fine, it was a little weird. But despite aging, he'd remained consistently not-super. What the hell, world? *Everyone knew* if you were found in a cornfield and apparently an alien, *you were supposed to have superpowers from the alien sun* and a strong allergy to glowing green rocks from your birth planet. Kent Clark (no relation) had neither.

Short of fitting the hand-knitted superhero costume his mother made for him to eye-popping proportions (that's when Mom suggested it, wear the underwear on the OUTSIDE of the tights! Brilliant idea!) he'd shown no signs of manifesting special powers, ever.

Joshua chuckled. "Now son, you lifted a car off me when you were just twelve years old—"

"—oh god—"

"—and you saved your very best friend, billionaire-with-Daddy-issues Les Lytheryn, from driving off that bridge—"

"—I just switched on his parking brake for him, Dad. He's rich so he didn't know how to work it for himself—"

"Now son, you know you don't need any superpowers to be special to your Mom and me," Joshua continued proudly. "You're super special just being Kent Clark (no relation). But we're always here for you to help with your problems be they super—" he nudged his son with a wink, "—or regular sized."

"Thanks, Dad," Kent Clark (no relation) capitulated with a sigh. No matter what he said, no matter what he did, his parents optimistically believed a souped-up hero lived under the skin of their ordinary little alien kid.

Well, there was nothing for it then. He hid out in Tinyville High as long as he could but now he had to face up to facts. If he hadn't grown into his powers by the time he was 38 well . . . they . . . probably didn't exist. He was running out of options.

He'd already tried venturing out in a thunderstorm with a kite and key. Everyone knew a good lightning strike could transfer or imbue supernatural powers.

It hadn't worked. All it managed for Kent Clark (no relation) was turning his hair jet black and curly, including that one persistent, annoying curl that always fell in the exact middle of his forehead no matter how much gel he used to slick back the rest. Sigh.

So all he had left was to head out on some mysterious quest, disguising himself with only his black, horn-rimmed nerd spectacles, in hopes of stumbling across some supernatural artifact with power transference or discovering a mystic portal which would transform him into a hero since genetics didn't have the decency to let him inherit superpowers the easy way, like *that guy* he was no relation to.

Anyway, everyone also knew that's how you met a pretty girl and saved her life and had some encounter with a deranged megalomaniac and it ended up with you and the pretty girl making out.

Plus, special powers often materialized from nowhere just in the nick of time as you needed them to aid you through some perilous, life-threatening situation, bonus. Turns out you had them all along, they were just dormant until the last five seconds of the bomb countdown. Everyone knew that.

So it was settled then. Kent Clark (no relation) needed to go out and leave Tinyville, while possibly graduating from high school first (but *no rush*) and find a noble, heroic quest to join up with.

If the anthem here was, "Somebody Saaaaave Meeee" (for about *ten seasons* but who's counting), then he was that "somebody" doing the saving.

Word.

No Shirt? No Shoes? Caution: You May Be a Werewolf!

t was two weeks before Fu-Belle received a summons back to the Fairyland Royal Court. When he was escorted into the palace throne room, he was surprised to find everyone in the court on high alert. He expected that he'd have to impress upon the rulers of Fairyland the urgency of their situation but it seemed they were ahead of him.

The throne room was transformed with digital, real-time feeds taken from various media and social outlets, displayed on several large crystal balls as fairy clerks dashed to and fro with armfuls of ticker-tape and made careful notations on scrolls with their quill pens. Tacticians, strategists and all of Fairyland's greatest minds were standing in clumps, debating and quantifying the results, working to identify the best method of approach. Other clerks were clustered around crystal balls and making various incantations, keeping up as fast as they could with the news traveling at the speed of technology—and advanced magical-techromancy.

"Oh good. Captain, you're here," Clarion motioned him to approach, once he finished dictating orders into a headpiece hooked on his pointy ear, every tense word clipped and staccato.

"This is a crisis, a *genuine crisis!* The situation is escalating minute by minute, and we need fresh eyes on this, someone we can rely on."

Fu bowed to show respect, then quickly started forward.

"I humbly await your orders Sire, and if it please your Majesties," he nodded to Ding-Aling with that, "I have suggestions on a primary course of action to take under advisement. Now you must have heard that the vampires—"

"Tell me," Clarion interrupted, "am I going crazy, Captain, or is the dress *CLEARLY white and gold*?"

Fu froze, completely lost. "*Dress? Sire?*"

"*Blue and black!* It's preposterous. How could *anyone* possibly see *blue and black*?" Clarion snapped his fingers at a clerk, "what is the vote tally now?"

"Just refreshed the stats. Current 67% in favor of blue/black, Sire. 30% think its white/gold and 3% aren't sure."

"What? Hurry—we need to start a saturation campaign in favor of #White and Gold. We cannot allow this major fashion fallacy to spread any further than it has."

Stunned, Fu took a closer look at the magic feed. On the largest crystal ball, mounted on a huge pedestal in the corner of the room, there was a grainy, poorly lit image of a woman's cocktail dress—so poorly lit in fact that details such as color were fuzzy. The image was expanded to full size, and above it, a caption was posted: *"Can you help me? What Color Is This Dress? My friends and I can't tell and I'm freaking out, lol!"*

Shocked into silence, he tried to recalculate how to approach the situation. Fairies were about to be slaughtered across their lands and they were running a full-scale war room to debate—*the color of a dress?*

"But your Majesties, this isn't the time for *that,*" Fu pleaded. "I beg you to *consider the consequences to our race*. Haven't you heard that they teamed up with zombies to outnumber and crush us to oblivion?"

"Oh yes," Clarion waved that off, "there was something like that—and frankly they're both colorblind! I notice at least 2/3rds of the #Blue and Black votes are vampire votes. What can Armando be thinking of, letting his people post such outrageous lies on a public forum?"

"Sire please, if we could just *focus* here. The vampires are brilliant strategists and just alone they pose a significant force of opposition, particularly when you take under consideration that they're already undead, leaving beheading and staking as the only viable options of dispatching them. But now, backed by the brute strength of another undead opponent, they are nigh undefeatable."

"Captain, you know the vampires only favor evening wear and I try not to judge," Clarion ignored him, pacing the floor, "I mean, at least black is *slimming* and I'm sure we all love a classic look. So "live and let live" I always say."

'That's the point Sire—we won't *live!* Yes, we're *immortal too*—but that isn't the same thing as *not able to kill.* We can be crushed or dewinged, and when I simply think of the massive amount of zombies and vampires stomping around, shouting, *"I don't believe in—in the F-word"* Sire, you know *the one*— we can't withstand a raid like that!"

"Priorities, Captain. I'm sure Armando will be reasonable; after all, we've had a peace treaty with Transylvania for centuries. But really, for a species that only favors evening wear, *one would think* they'd be *experts* on it! Blue and black cocktail dress indeed! Humph."

"All due respect, Sire—I don't agree. Why would the vampires back down now, when they know and we know that they will win this war?"

Fu-Belle sighed. Clarion and his fellow fairies weren't listening to his cautionary tale. They didn't recognize the danger to themselves. They wouldn't until it was far too late. Fairies were practical jokers and tricksters to be sure—a mischievous and careless lot, but at the heart of it, not *evil* per se.

They were innocent, *naïve*—they didn't understand the kind of dark, malicious destructive force that was even now shadowing their footsteps. Between the vampires and the zombies, the entire fairy race would be wiped out. There would be none left alive, once it was all said and done. Even if there were a few survivors, in the merciless hands of the vampires, they soon would wish they were dead like the others.

"Fine," Clarion sighs, "since I can see you're going to make *more wrinkles* on your face about this Captain, what would you suggest?"

Fu tried to think. Well, they could all flee for sanctuary in Never-Never-Land (it was a fairy-safe living environment) but it was always difficult to locate. They STILL hadn't updated the maps since *"second star to the right"*—that was what came of having a shoeless 10-year-old as your Prime Minister. There was a scandalous rumor circulating Fairyland that he didn't even *bathe!* This was disgraceful to fairies as throwing an 'impromptu' without a party planner or favor bags!

Besides fairies, the whole of the land was overrun by wild Indians, pirates, mermaids and a few random inhabitants like The Crocodile. There was no extradition but the paperwork took forever to process (Tootles was renowned for using it as toilet paper), so the place was notoriously overpopulated and during the tourist season, downright claustrophobic.

Reason it was known as "Never-Never-Land" was, even if you managed to get in, you'd never get your Green Card application approved! Word was Tinker-belle had only established permanent residency for herself by arranging a desperate marriage to a firefly (and they were still waiting on the paperwork).

"Well, I don't think fleeing Fairyland is the answer. I think we should stand our ground—and that we need to consider a strategic alliance with another race, Sire. Give us some leverage to make the vampires back down."

"An alliance?" Clarion looked vaguely interested. "With whom, Captain?"

Fu had to find a way to even up the odds and he knew he had to do it single-handed. He was lucky that the zombies and vampires both were currently distracted by their human prey. Once the humans were thinned out however, they'd turn their attention on Fairyland. It bought Fu time to work out a plan, but not much.

"We should to talk to the werewolves, Your Majesty. Natural enemy of the vampire, right?"

Clarion burst out laughing, "Oh Captain, that's a good one! What a delightful wit you are in these troubled times."

Yes, it was strange how it was so commonly known among humans that vampires and werewolves are natural enemies because that "tidbit of gossip" came as a total surprise to both vampires and werewolves!

Neither race is sure how the rumor got started or spread so quickly. Vampires don't suck on werewolves, their animal blood isn't nutritious and frankly, they tasted like doggie kibble. And all werewolves deny a moon cycle reducing them to hunting cold bat, or a "swarm of bats" as the case may be.

But if vamps and weres weren't enemies by default, they weren't allies either. Vampires were arrogant; they looked down on the race of werewolves, seeing them as lowest on the food chain, being half-human and half-animal. It tended to piss werewolves off being treated as an inferior species, enough so that a werewolf might catch and dissemble a vampire bat with his jaws if he felt particularly vindictive about it. Mostly it was simple avoidance. Werewolves and vampires acknowledged one another as mutual predators but coldly and stayed the hell out of each other's way.

Vampires and werewolves, as with most supernatural races, were much too busy picking on the bottom of the food chain (*for clarification: humans*) to bother with each other. Perhaps it's just a comfort to the human mind to believe interspecies warfare was distracting all the deadly predators involved, while the "bottom of the food chain" went and hid under the covers with a stockpile of wooden stakes and silver bullets.

"Natural enemy of the vampire"—yeah right! The werewolves would all laugh until they were lifting their legs and urinating on the nearest tree if Fu put it to them like that. But if Fu could make a convincing case that, with the zombies backing them, the vampires were likely to turn activist, he stood a good chance of drawing the werewolf forces out.

Honestly neither race much liked having to share Transylvania with the other—oh sure, they both pretended to be okay at social functions but it wouldn't be hard to rouse the werewolves suspicions that the vampires would turn on them for a nickel. If the werewolves backed the fairies now, the fairies would naturally return the favor.

"The enemy of MY enemy is helpful to me, even if he's poorly dressed with no manicure." Fu was never sure why but he felt like that old fairy adage rang true. Admittedly it went very wrong somewhere in the middle but there was something to it.

"Sire, at least I could travel to Transylvania and try to sway the werewolves to our side. It seems like the best chance we have to convince the vampires to back down. We simply don't have the manpower or arms to face them alone."

Clarion clapped him on the shoulder. "What a splendid idea, Captain. With the werewolf votes tallied in, I imagine #White and Gold will easily tip the scales to victory."

"In fact, I'm going to give you some sample fabric swatches to take with you," he snapped at a page who hurried off at once, "and Captain, you must make sure you get them to Armando personally and show him which colours are which. I presume wearing so much black has gone to his head—perhaps he forgot what colours actually look like. But we can most certainly help him out there— the vampires are almost like cousins to us, you know."

Fu-Belle closed his eyes a minute, silently counting to ten and ignoring the urge to tack on a subtle dig about *North Fairyland*. "Yes, Sire. You're very gracious. I'll get started immediately."

Great. So this meant Fu had to take a journey all by himself to the treacherous and deadly mountain country of wild Transylvania.

He'd experience new places, get plenty of healthy exercise and fresh air, make new friends and probably have a meaningful experience culminating in some valuable life lesson and bonding with all his newfound companions which brought them closer in a harmonious and treasured experience full of wonderful memories.

Hmm. Not too late then to just stay home and watch TV 'til it all hit the fan. But then, he'd also get to beat the ass of a bunch of vamps and zombies and no one could bring him up on charges for using "excessive force" since he was officially out of Fairyland border jurisdiction. So there was *that* to look forward to.

Plus, the trip to Transylvania itself was fraught with unknown dangers. It was long, dangerous trip by foot. He'd have to pass through the Human World to get there unless he took the S.S.S. (*Supernatural Subterranean Subway*) to Transylvania.

But trusting the S.S.S. to travel across realms was a risk even for those who enjoyed living on the edge. The local news said that supernatural and interdimensional transportation was *"Down For Repairs"* again. It was always *"Down For Repairs"* or *"Under Maintenance; We Do Apologize For Any Inconvenience To Your Travel Plans"* whenever more travelers mysteriously vaporized than arrived at their intended destination.

The latest issue Fu had heard about, the subway made unscheduled stops in alternate dimensions, causing cataclysmic-chain-reactions when the riding passengers ran into their alternate selves or when they fell into temporal black holes or simply popped out of existence due to the tragic circumstance that, in the *other universe*, apparently they were never even born. This rather got on people's nerves.

Not to mention that the problem of farmhouses falling out of the sky to crush random subway riders every time they came to a "Witch Crossing" sign still hadn't been fixed. The S.S.S. Maintenance Team had classified this as, "*A Minor System Glitch Which We'll Soon Have Straightened Out. Thank You For Your Continued Patience In Our Efforts To Make Supernatural Subterranean Your Preferred Method Of Travel! Have A Great Day!*"

So—risky as it was, that left crossing the Human World then. What was he waiting for?

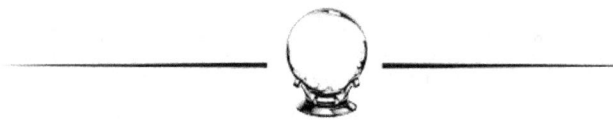

On the other side of the world, Mr. Oubliette awoke. He tried to remember who he was today—and gave up.

He was firmly amidst an identity crisis and wasn't sure *what* he was, let alone *who*. He barely remembered anything past his name. It was doubtless perfectly normal. All the other, you know, Him's (whatever he actually was) probably also had identity crisis's and amnesia at this time in their— lives or whatever, you know, sort of existences they (the other Him's) had.

He'd be over it eventually and back to his old self but for now, he had to pick out "someone new to be" every morning, a decision *almost as weighty* as picking out the day's accompanying wardrobes and shade of eye shadow. He could be a vampire, mind you, or an emperor. Or perhaps an ancient and very well-dressed god of some unknown pantheon, or possibly he was just an unusually beautiful, high-fashion male model.

Whatever he was, he had an excellent sense of style and clearly that was the important point. He hadn't lost his priorities, whatever else he'd lost.

After his usual 6-hour morning routine had commenced, consisting of surveying his ginormous wardrobe spread out over the many levels of his closet which required an giant escalator to get to, then picking out his first outfit and associated wardrobe changes which would be magically occurring at select intervals throughout the day, rigorously applying his lavish eye make-up and hair spray which involved a frighteningly large aerosol can that had to be operated by pistons, and deciding on which accessories to pair with –*hmm, now was it to be the leather gloves or the mini riding crop, or both*— he finally decided what he would be for the day.

He thought he'd seen a parrot someplace. Actually it was an ugly chicken with skinny legs but a few cans of spray paint would fix that.

That settled it then. With a parrot to accessorize with, today Mr. Oubliette would be a Pirate, of course! No eye patch, how gauche—no for this, he needed yards of quality silk and brocade in blood-red, gold and black naturally, and there would be substantial amount of guy-liner and man-bling involved, also a corset. Wardrobe change then, and fetch someone to lace him up good and tight!

There, that was the identity crisis for the day *sorted*. Now he felt a celebratory song and dance number coming on.

It just might involve tossed babies.

Cheerleader, Stubble, Beer Gut. What's Wrong with this Picture?

Travel across the human realm wasn't that hard for a fairy, especially if one had their wings properly maintained regularly for flight in their atmosphere. It certainly was easier to fly than to walk the distance, but in the human's climate the source of natural magic was very low and the air was so dense it made flying rather like swimming. One tended to give out exhausted after a few hours and sink back to the ground, gravity taking hold.

Anyway, even when you were spotted by humans, they were incredibly good at convincing themselves and their eyes that they'd just seen an odd-looking hummingbird or, at night, a firefly perhaps. Neither the first, nor second, nor even ninety-fifth conclusion drawn was ever "fairy" because "padded room" very quickly followed a thought like that.

Fairies also flew high when they could and out of sight, avoiding metropolitan areas where they were less likely to be spotted from ground level. Now, in the days of HD camera phones and faster-than-the-human-eye shutter speed, it was more dangerous to be spotted as a camera could catch what the human eye couldn't and, unlike the human eye, it had a print function. Humans would have a hell of time convincing the others that what their camera phone caught wasn't photo-manipulated, but it was still a risk.

True, cameras couldn't turn out revealing flying fairy photos when they were suddenly transformed into stone by fairy magic—but strangely that had a way of attracting more attention from humans than the photo itself.

Not many fairies crossed over to the Human World as they used to, hadn't for centuries and when they did, it was mostly travelling straight through and they kept to rural routes, or to arrange special viewings of "Tinker-Belle: The Movie" in 3D. The fashion critique post-film release had been on the front page of the "Fairyland Chronicle" for weeks with pictures, and Tink herself was the subject of much ridicule and letters to the editor.

Therefore it quite surprised Fu when, while cutting through an old junkyard that looked deserted, not only to be spotted but actually *caught* by a human—an nigh impossible feat for a fairy in flight was 3 times faster than a hummingbird.

Fu was embarrassed, he knew he was flying too low but he was trying to make good time and taking something of a shortcut against a ferocious wind current. It was easier to fly low, the wind wasn't as strong closer to the ground and he made better progress.

But now, he stared directly at a thumb as tall as he was and wondered how the hell he'd gotten caught by one of those oversized, slow-witted human noobs.

"LET GO OF ME," he threatened, taking out a pair of nunchucks that, admittedly, were like the size of two tiny peas on a string to the giant hand that held him and whirled them around his head, "Unless you wanna be fingerless, bub!"

Then Fu noticed the fingers that held him were had frighteningly long fingernails, fuchsia pink.

Oh-kay. Well, that changed things a bit. Not really for a fairy, even male fairies proudly wore nail color but Fu had aced his "Human Studies" courses at the Fairy Peace Corps academy and he knew the situation was different for human males. In most cases, make-up and nail tint were out.

"Ma'am," he changed his tune slightly and risked a glance upward. He was no authority on human beauty but he ventured to guess this wasn't one of the human's particularly finest specimens— and it had nothing to do with the fact that her gigantic face eclipsed the sun. There was definitely something off about her, but Fu hadn't put his finger on it yet.

"Hello there!" the—well girl, surely it was a *girl*—trilled back at him, blowing his hat clean off with the force of her breath, which reeked of beer. Also garlic—lots of garlic! She smelled like a pizzeria!

"I'm Biffy Winters! Well, aren't you a cute little man?" She batted her obviously plastic long eyelashes at him in a manner she probably thought of as flirtatious, but at her size it was like watching two enormous window blinds flying up and down. Again, falsies were not unusual to male fairies but hers clashed with her Marilyn platinum blonde wig.

"Ah. I see. You're a vampire slayer, aren't you," Fu said dryly, after a moment's careful study.

"N-o-o-o, of course not!" Biffy looked taken aback. "*Obviously* I'm just a sweet, shallow, bubble-headed cheerleader! Besides I'm female! Everyone knows WOMAN can't be SLAYERS, oh the very idea! I'm *shocked* and *insulted*, sir! We belong in the kitchen, barefoot and pregnant. Only BIG STRONG MEN can slay vampires, DUH! Why would you even SAY something like that?"

"Umm, the garlic necklace, the wooden stake hidden in your pom-poms, the holy water capsule tucked in your skirt waistband," Fu ticked off his fingers. "Plus—you need a *shave*, madam."

By reflex, Biffy's other hand flew to the 5 o'clock shadow on his—erm, HER cheek.

"I meant the hairy gut sticking out of your uniform there," Fu clarified, "Attractive, not so much. Too much beer drinking and pizza; not enough Jazzercise, "girlfriend". It gives you away."

"Oh," Biffy sighed. "Yes that. Well, I try to keep in shape but this uniform is very unforgiving. I've issued complaints with the cheer board, they dress us like hookers practically. And those cheer pyramids are HARD man, you just don't even know! I was banned from the squad after the coach saw up my skirt and got a surprise."

"Right, I get it. You're incognito."

"I'm a *what*?" Biffy's face darkened like a thundercloud, "Listen you itty bitty slayer-hater, no need to go around dissin me. It's just my job, so chillax."

"Anyway, like you can talk so big! You're wearing tights there little bro, if you ain't noticed it."

"BREECHES, not TIGHTS—and they're TRADITIONAL," Fu hissed.

"I will kick your ass, though from what I can see of the massive spread down there, it'll take a day's travel to reach it."

"Shut your mouth," Biffy snapped. 'No respect, and for all I'm saving the world. *Save a cheerleader, save the—*"

"PLEASE don't!" Fu insisted. He squinted at the male slayer thoughtfully, "So tell me, why the cheerleader outfit?"

"Disguise, broheme!" the vampire slayer shrugged his burly shoulders, nearly dislodging a dangly, clip-on hoop earring.

"Girls can't be slayers, it's unthinkable! That's what makes it perfect! I'm all like," he trilled in a high falsetto, "Hey boyz, Ah'm just a cute little cheerleader over here, all nice and filled with warm yummy blood 'n stuff, don't you never mind lit ol' me."

Much to Fu's relief, his voice deepened again. "Then I let one of those shiny SOB's think he's gonna get a little somethin-somethin from a pretty girl, and—BAM! STAKE! GARLIC AND HOLY WATER TIME! The poor bastards don't never even see it comin! S'the beauty of it!"

"I guess now you're gonna tell me you're the Chosen One," Fu grumbled. If slayers were born by divine destiny once in a generation, this generation had somewhere drawn the very short stick.

"No," Biffy sighed. "It used to be like that, divine right and proper lineage, and the "one mortal born with the strength to face off with vampires" but there was always something off in the math you know. The slayer-to-vampire ratio was always somewhat unbalanced, especially since the slayer is the bit that can *die*."

"So we traced the line back and now we suspect the slayer destined for *this generation* actually met an unplanned early demise in an abortion clinic. Lucky break for the vampires, that was. We was real idjits."

"I imagine so, yes."

"Well, someone had to step up to the plate and fill in until the next generation is born, didn't they?" Biffy proudly tapped his styrofoam breasts, "That's me. Humanity's pinch-hitter. Now it's just me and my boys, saving the world from bloodsuckers on a regular basis."

"Your boys?"

"Oh yeah, my poker buddies John and Bobby, Sam and Dean. We all got tired of weekly poker night, and I was going to suggest taking up extreme skydiving myself when John suggested we give vampire slaying a try. Turns out I had a real knack for it. Sam and Dean are better with ghosts actually and Bobby does a lean-mean federal agent impression—"

"So you just go around looking for vampires to kill? Is that strictly legal?"

"Broadly, broadly," Biffy made a fiddly motion with one hand. "Fringe law enforcement, it's sort of gaining ground. Right now we have the benefit of covert black ops status without the convenience of government funding—er, in the strictest sense of the word. But we earn our Medicaid and food stamps, thanks."

"I have a treat for you then," Fu drawled. "I'm headed for Transylvania right now to round up an army of werewolves and kick some serious vampire ass. Wanna come with?"

"Do I? The real Transylvania? *Sounds epic!* Wait 'til the boys hear I went to Transylvania to slay vampires with a fairy, oh they'll be so jealous! I can't wait 'til they see my newest status update on Majick Book, 'Visiting Transylvania, wish you were here! Oops, I just ganked a vampire in my sleep cause there are sooo many here!' Ha! Who wears the slayer princess crown now, bitchez?!"

Fu paused. "That was a—yes?"

"That was a HELL YEAH, dude! Let's go gank some vamps!" A pause—then— "Um, so—are you going to be wearing those tights like—the whole way?"

"I don't know. You gonna keep walking around in the little blue ruffled panties with anime princesses on them?"

"Okay, that's fair."

Find Your Arch-Nemesis on SuperMatch Today!

One might think it was a tricky thing crossing the border from the Human World into Transylvania, but not so much really. Vampires liked to encourage tourism, especially from humans.

So there were several entrances placed conspicuously all over the Human World with big flashing neon signs that read things like, "50% off ALL SHOES AND PURSES CLEARANCE SALE! DESIGNER NAME BRANDS! EVERYTHING MUST GO!" if the area in question had a higher population of women, or "Nudie Bar, no cover charge" if it was catering to a male crowd.

Children were harder to trap. One, because many of them couldn't read yet and two, because they were generally accompanied by a parent or legal guardian everywhere they went, and finally, because they had far too much imagination for the vampires overall comfort.

Kids approached by a vampire screamed at the top of their lungs, shattering more overly sensitive eardrums than an acid rock concert, and then kicked it hardcore right in the nads or WORSE, they BIT down on whatever was within reach with all those tiny, razor-sharp baby teeth. A ravenous shark couldn't do greater damage. Kids didn't waste time studying vampires like the adults did. They knew an out-n-out monster when they saw one and they went straight for the jugular.

A few arcades and pizza parlors were rigged as a testing ground but without much enthusiasm. The vampires abandoned their kidnapping project after the first few trial runs and some irreparable damage, blood loss and screaming—mostly by the *vampires!* It proved far too much trouble for little return. Adults didn't believe in "closet monsters" and as a whole, made better prey because of it.

Interestingly enough, one of these portals to Transylvania was placed right next to Tinyville, home of the not-so-super Kent Clark (no relation).

The billboard for this read: *Are you owed millions of dollars in a legal settlement because your life was ruined by those alien green rocks? Come in for a free consultation, there's no obligation but our team will fight to get you the $$$ you deserve!*

Vampires were all about effective marketing.

K ent Clark (no relation) was still looking for the right hook to discover his alien superpowers that surely had to be hidden deep inside someplace.

He just consulted the online manual, "How to Thoroughly Piss Your Super Nemesis Off and Make Him Target You" (included on the "Super Hero Learn-at-Home Training Course for Dummies"). It was quick and easy considering it was less reading and more a page full of big, helpfully numbered, full color illustrations, as most superheroes could crush an entire car under their fist but weren't known as the world's foremost scholars.

The manual suggested if you couldn't kick things off right by killing the villain's beloved wife, child or pet in a freak accident involving your superpower, thus earning their eternal hatred seeking revenge on you (see also *fig 2.B*, "Developing your Super Powers Through Someone's Tragic Accidental Death" and *fig 2.C*, "Ideas To Piss Off Your Super Nemesis") then try taunting them that you know their "secret plan for world domination" /or/ that you know about "the secret device" (see also *2.D*, "Evil Super Villains ALWAYS Have a Secret Plan for World Domination or a Secret Device" and *2.E*, "Witty Banter With Super Villains Basics for When You're A Muscled Super Hero As Thick As A Tub Of Lard")

Kent felt prepped now to face his super nemesis, thus forcing his own dormant powers to spring forth and now was eagerly reading down the invitational page on SuperMatch.

Are you, like many others, looking for your perfect superpowered nemesis to face off with and unsuccessfully try to kill many times over in epic battles, but are having trouble locating the right arch-nemesis for you? Perhaps other nemesi in the past have inconveniently died before the battle was over or didn't fully 100% oppose the causes you fought for/injustices you perpetuated? Or perhaps you simply aren't sure yet who it is you want to fight with?

Well, the wait is over! Take **our free analysis survey** *that's* **guaranteed** *to match you with your ideal nemesis in* **90 days** *or* **less!** *That's right!* **In 90 days, you'll be kicking someone's ass or getting yours brutally kicked, we guarantee it!**

Then view other member profiles to see which Super Hero or Super Villain is right for you! The lack of chemistry and instant loathing will feel just right this time, we promise! Try SuperMatch today and find the SuperNemesis of your dreams!

Click here to create your FREE profile
-OR- Sign in with Majick-Book

Kent Clark (no relation) frowned and clicked the link.

Hi! Thanks for joining SuperMatch! You're on your way to finding the SuperNemesis that's just right for you! Please fill in the blanks below to tell us more about yourself!

I am a: (SELECT)

- ○ girl
- ○ boy
- ○ other being
- ○ not sure

I am a: (SELECT)

- ○ Super HERO
- ○ Super VILLAIN
- ○ Regular HERO
- ○ Regular VILLAIN
- ○ GOD, Demi-GOD, GODLING, or GODDESS
- ○ SUPERPOWERED GOD, Demi-GOD, GODLING, or GODDESS
- ○ E.T.
- ○ Other Immortal Being (explain)

- ○ A Gay Unicorn

Your Alter Ego/Name*:

(*all alter ego secret identities are protected by our patented **Alter-Ego Secure Encryption™** and will never be shown on your public profile or to your SuperNemesis of choice, unless he buys our highest subscription package and you have failed to upgrade from a free account, as covered in our Terms and Conditions for using the site. SuperMatch is not held responsible if this information is used by your arch-nemesis to locate you and then kill you &/or your entire family)

Your Chosen Super Hero/Villain Name: (if undecided, you can change this later)

Age: (if immortal, please round off to the number nearest to when you were born/hatched/god-breathed/sprang fully-formed from your father's forehead)

Are you seeing anyone who could be used against you in a hostage situation:

Do you love/Did you brutally murder any immediate family members:

What cause(s) you stand for/seek to destroy:

Who you'd most like to kidnap/rescue:

What you're looking for in an arch-nemesis:

Your Likes:

Your Pet Peeve:

The Boy/Girl/Other Entity of your dreams:

Finally, tell us a little about yourself in 180 characters or less:

Kent Clark (no relation) filled in the fields as best he could and clicked 'submit', barely even glancing at the ad pop-up before he x-ed out of it.

SUPER HEROES AND VILLAINS! Save 25% off when you get your Super Outfit designed by e.Mode DAHLING! Designer SuperWear by e.Mode DAHLING! comes in all of the hottest new styles and she'll customize your supersuit to fit your own unique superpower and defense structure! Just use the coupon code: SuperMatch25 to claim your discount at the e.Mode DAHLING! online store.

(*additional superpowers not included with outfit. Design of Super Emblem included for an additional fee. Due to safety reasons, all e.Mode DAHLING! designs, new and existing, do not include capes. In fact, e.Mode DAHLING! discourages all Super Entities from using capes; studies have shown capes to be a working hazard to Super Entities that can, in extreme cases, lead to fatalities. e.Mode DAHLING! would like to remind everyone, "Safety is the New Black Daaaaaaaaahling!")

Kent Clark (no relation) started scrolling through the site profiles as his analysis was processing, preparing to match him up with his new arch-nemesis.

VILLAIN PROFILE: MadScientist666

Likes: Creating monsters with lightning, totally screwing with nature, taking walks with Igor, killing every person who calls me crazy!!!, Jazzercise, singing in the shower and cake decoration—I take classes and I'm really getting good with the rosettes.

Pet Peeve: People who say that I am mad, I'll show THEM I'LL SHOW THEM ILLLLLLLSSSHHHHOOOWW THEEEEMMMM!!! MULLHAHAHAHAHAAHA!!!

VILLAIN PROFILE: AssHat82

Likes: Killing random people on the street. That's all.

Pet Peeve: People who say that I am a psychopath. I'm not crazy, I'm a sociopath. I don't give a shit. That really irks me so—I kill them slower. With power tools.

VILLAIN PROFILE: LesLytheryn01

Likes: World domination, megalomania, power and money, a really good single malt. Also, my best friend in the whole world who is just an ordinary farm boy with nerd glasses, no matter what anyone else saw or thought they glimpsed through a crack on the wall or is pretty sure he might have done or someone who looked like him or whatever! So what if Kent Clark (no relation) IS adopted?! He's a nice, ordinary kid okay, everyone got it?

Also, I'm really rich and bald and one day, I'll be president and rule the entire world!

Pet Peeve: My dad. He's a douche.

Les? My best friend Les? Kent was about to click on that profile when an IM popped on his screen.

Dear user: **KC_SUPERM_(no_rltn)**,

User: **Kidnapped_hot_girl_19** has requested you to save her life.

Status: Being held captive by a Super Villain

Predicament level: Extreme Peril/Life-Threatening.

Message: "PLEASE HELP ME SOMEONE! I am being held at 292 N. Ember Pkwy (across from 5th and Elm, <u>click here for iHero Directions app</u>) and I will die in approximately 56 minutes (<u>click here to time this on the iVillain Countdown-To-Death app</u>). PLEASE HURRY! #about to die, lol!"

KC_SUPERM_(no_rltn), *please choose from the following options on how you would like to handle this request:*

- o *Send Reply Message:* 'On my way, just stopping at the phone booth to change' (or choose your own reply message, <u>click here</u>)
- o *Refer to next available Super Hero and decline* (to send decline message, <u>click here</u>, or <u>click to mark your profile as "AWAY - Unavailable for rescues at this time"</u>)

- o *Add to my "Save This Person Later" list* (you can set up a reminder prompt on your smart phone to 'save this person later'. Click here to do that)
- o *Send a witty, Insta-Taunt to the Super Villain who is holding this person captive and begin building an adversarial relationship now. Click here to bring up the integrated iTauntu app.* (Use of iTauntu may incur an extra fee.)
- o *Block all requests from this user and allow them to die.* (It's okay. You can't save everyone. ☹)

After passing the message along to another crime-fighter-in-arms and marking his profile unavailable for rescuing, K.C. (n.r.) noticed that the "loading" button had now changed and a new message popped up onscreen.

Dear user: **KC_SUPERM_(no_rltn)**,

YOU HAVE BEEN MATCHED! Congratulations! We're sure you two will utterly loathe one another for many years to come!

Your new **SuperNemesis** is **ALUCARD (do not spell this backward)**

ALUCARD (do not spell this backward) is a ERIPMAV who enjoys girls who sleep with their windows open, mesmerizing women with my eyes, Bram Stoker novels and fresh blood. He really dislikes King Armando (he's a ponce!), Abraham Van Helsing (I don't want to talk about it!), mirrors, wooden stakes and running water.

You can instant message **ALUCARD (do not spell this backward)** *now to kick-start your feud* (click here to do that) *or send a lovely "how are you" bomb or nest of scorpions to thank him for being your new SuperNemesis* (click here to send something from our integrated SuperNemesis Gift Catalog) *or pay him a surprise visit at his lovely estate in the Transylvanian mountains* (click here to view the iHero Secret Entrances app and find a secret entrance that leads to the Transylvanian Mountains)

Oh look! There's a secret entrance to Transylvania right here in Tinyville. What an amazing coincidence!

Plus, it's very convenient to me getting my GED! I can defeat my SuperNemesis and still be back in time for school. Mom and Dad will be really pleased about that so they'll probably let me go as long as I'm not out any later than 10 p.m.

Kent Clark (no relation) felt very excited. It was all falling together like a perfect superhero plan should. It was like a sign from above that this was his destiny! What could possibly go wrong?

Alien Invasion, Because We Care!

To be very clear, Biffy Winters wasn't born a *proper* vampire slayer with the right pedigree and barbell fists like Hercules.

So in fact he was never formally educated on the careful use of wishes by a stuffy overbearing Englishman who had an extensive supernatural education and never missed an opportunity to ponderously lecture on some interesting caveat of magic, although usually the practical lesson followed *right after* the monster was released in public through improper use of magic as scripted, leading to much exciting and life-threatening action, drama, danger and a cliffhanger two-part episode for sweeps week.

If only Biffy were a properly-trained and officially-licensed vampire slayer, such a hole would never be left in his supernatural education unless, naturally, it provided the opportunity to be terrorized by some new and challenging demon for the make-up and prosthetics department.

Alas, poor Biffy could only struggle through his vampire slaying on magical ignorance, which was why he had no idea when he innocently voiced "a wish" that fairy magic could take them to Transylvania without having to walk all the way, that using the exact words: "I Wish" in a sentence was risky.

Unfortunately for him, the laws governing magic dictated his wish not be granted as he hoped or expected but to fall under the "Humorous Misdirection" clause of magic, which always applies by default when it yields a better shot of disappointing the wishee's expectations. Real magic is very keen on not giving you what you actually wanted but what makes the best drama.

Fairies could, were in fact even compelled by magic, to grant wishes if caught unawares by a mortal. That was common knowledge. But there are secret laws and caveats to the proper use of magic, and supernatural entities are notorious for knowing more tricks and loopholes at getting around "The Helpful or Generous Use Thereof" than a smarmy lawyer who bribed his way past the bar exam. It comes down to the wording and you have to get it *exactly right* or the results will be disastrous!

Another fact useful to know about magic and wishing is that an "open-ended wish" can actually be granted by ANY supernatural entity so inclined who happens to be in the vicinity or feeling indulgent under the magical law clause of "Humorous Misdirection". The universal laws of magic like a good joke as much as anyone.

So whereas Biffy might have been aiming to use magic to *get out of work* (a properly educated mentor would've strongly advised against any such misuse) instead he conjured *something else* entirely.

Universal logic tried to build a legal case on "goblins" not having been verbally expressed by Biffy in the summoning terminology but "Humorous Misdirection" took legal precedence, overruled logic and had the case thrown out of court because *this was clearly the funniest outcome out of all possible outcomes!* It was later explained away by the universal powers that be as a minor paperwork snafu.

Therefore, no sooner had Biffy innocently vocalized his ill-timed wish and before either he or Fu could react to the situation, a bizarre figure appeared, magically summoned by Biffy's wish!

"IT" materialized from thin air right in front of them and "IT" defied almost all available powers of description but "IT" (Fu and Biffy's brains automatically capitalized by default, "IT" fully merited the use of uppercase letters) was something to behold! "IT" was—male at least, yes, *very much male* judging by bulge in the tights, but both Fu & Biffy were earnestly trying not to look. Besides, there was so much ELSE to draw the eye!

His hair took one by complete surprise, frosted blond and humongous with a highlights-wash and 80's rock star written all over it. It brought a single word to mind and the word was "BIG", with about three exclamation marks for emphasis. It also brought a secondary description to mind, if the mind in question substituted pink hair for blonde and moussed, and that was "troll doll".

Then there was the lavish eye make-up. This hadn't been applied with a sparing hand nor, as terrifying a thought as it was, an *inexperienced* one. There was the wave of cheap glitter tossed like rice at a wedding when it (ahem, "IT") appeared, accompanied by the light tinkling of bells—no wait for it, it gets *better!*

"IT" wore a black, sequin-studded cape, and a velvet corset (transvestites everywhere were already DYING to try it on—damn *supernatural entities* just got all the BEST clothes) and the thigh-high glossy black boots and "IT" had shiny balls, no WAIT FOR IT—the "shiny balls" were in fact, *rock crystal glass orbs* which he kept spinning round and round in his black-gloved fingers.

And then—THEN, was that a Man!Purse? Even Fu-Belle, who'd seen a lot in Fairyland that defied many a boundary of where manhood shouldn't venture, was totally taken aback. "IT" carried a Man!Purse dripping with beads around on "IT"s arm, *really*?! His eyeballs were rebelling already, begging to be poked out with a stick and freed from their misery.

A cultured British voice –of course "IT" was British, somehow that completely worked— met their ears. "What ho, me hearties! Say, you remind me of the babe—"

"What the hell are you?" Biffy interrupted. "IT" paused in confusion.

"No, that's wrong. You're supposed to say, "what babe?" Then I say, "the babe with the power," and you say—"

"Really, *what the hell are you*?" Fu demanded, louder. His best guess would've been a fairy but first, he'd never seen one so large before and second, the make-up was too garish. Even *fairies* drew the line somewhere.

"IT" stared down at Fu and then drew back. "Why you tiny bastard!" IT roared.

Fu studied "IT" curiously. While he often took on creatures several times his own size and admittedly, had left them in debatable states of consciousness, let alone functional, once he was done kicking their ass, he was pretty sure he'd have remembered fighting "IT".

"Sorry? Did I try to kill you somewhere before?"

"YOU FOUL LITTLE BITING BASTARD! I DON'T BELIEVE IN YOU LITTLE FUC—"

"No—THAT particular adjective doesn't do anything to us. Others have tried it too. You'd be surprised."

"IT" fumbled in its Man!Purse. "Fairy infestation, yuck! Now where does Hedgewart keep the fairy sprayer?"

"Anyway, I resent being called a biter," Fu grumbled, fists on his itty bitty hips. "I fight clean and fair! Everyone knows using your teeth is cheating!"

"Did I miss the part where he told us *what* he is?" Biffy interrupted.

"Clearly I'm a pirate," indignantly huffed the velvet-corset-wearing, phoofy-haired, Man!Purse-carrying, crystal-balled . . . (nope. The Powers of Description have failed to rise to the challenge presented yet again).

"As if *that* weren't *perfectly obvious*," "IT" flailed, (sorry, there really was no other word) its gloved hands wildly, nearly dislodging what looked to be a spray-painted chicken glued to its right shoulder.

Inexplicably, the glass crystal orb "IT" held didn't drop from his fingers or shatter despite his utter lack of attention. Instead, it slid up and down his arm and across his shoulders to the other arm in a dazzling, gravity-defying maneuver that not only broke the natural laws of science but also tangoed indecently with them and sent them home at a shameful hour.

"I'm having a bit of an identity crisis right now," "IT" continued.

Fu's brow rose, then saw that raise and called with a second raise, "An identity crisis, huh? No shit."

"My name is Mr. Oubliette," "IT declared loudly, "And today I have decided to be a pirate. That is, until I remember what I used to be—very soon I'll remember what I was before, I'm sure. But in the meantime, I'm pirating you! *You're being pirated*," Mr. Oubliette explained, then clucked his tongue, "Such a pity."

"And what are those," Biffy asked warily, eyeing the small puppet-like and fuzzy creatures currently preoccupied playing a comprehensive game of hide 'n seek with Mr. Oubliette's tall, shiny black boots, which he inexplicably thought pairing with thick panty-hose was a good move.

Actually, there was quite a lot that was *inexplicable* about Mr. Oubliette.

"Oh, those?" Mr. Oubliette stared down at his feet as if he wasn't sure what those puppet-y creatures were. "Um, they're my—sidekicks, my little Pirate-Ettes. All pirates have them."

Fu and Biffy stared wordlessly at the very ugly Pirate-Ettes for a moment. Someone clearly thought tying little red neckerchiefs on their stubbly, misshapen heads and adding gold hoops to their ears (to those that actually possessed ears) would make them look more "pirate-ish". It hadn't worked.

"Right. Um, Mr. Oubliette—"

"You have thirteen hours in which to come up with the pirated booty or—or your, well—" Mr. Oubliette trailed off, clearly trying to formulate the remainder of his threat.

"Mr. Oubliette, please!"

"*Fraggin aardvark!* Yes? Well? What is it?"

"Would you like to come with us?" Biffy offered magnanimously. "My good friend here is at war with the vampires and we're off to beat them up. By the way, in case you couldn't tell, I'm just a cheerleader. Perhaps along the way you'll rediscover what you are?"

Fu stared at Biffy like he was crazy for inviting Mr. Oubliette along. Biffy shrugged a little.

"We may need the element of surprise," he explained.

Fu turned to stare at Mr. Oubliette for a minute, "Just *how much surprise* are you thinking we'll need?"

Mr. Oubliette chose that exact moment to burst into an utterly spontaneous, extensively-rehearsed song-and-dance rock ballad, accompanied off-key by the fugly Pirate-Ettes and somewhat by the painted chicken/parrot glued on his shoulder who was cruelly prevented from decorating the shoulder of Mr. Oubliette's jacket with what would prove to be more superglue jammed up a very strategic spot. (I hope you don't need a diagram.)

The Powers of Description tried desperately to rally and witnessed this, then gave up in embarrassment, called it a day and went home.

Words alone would never cover it. You had to be there.

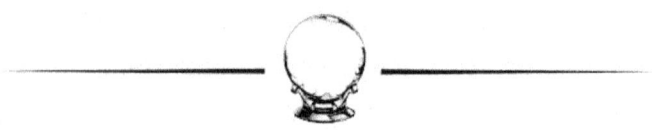

I t was quite the walk to the portal in Tinyville and certainly, after the arrival of Mr. Oubliette, no one was inclined to try wishing instead of walking again.

So they hoofed it and made good progress because, although they came across quite a few generalized attacks of humans versus zombies or humans versus vampires (or both), the party of three, not counting the 'Pirate-Ettes' and the chicken/parrot, were given a very wide berth.

You wouldn't think so as Fu was a fairy and Biffy a human and therefore both were considered to be on the warzone hit-list. Yet the addition of Mr. Oubliette to their threesome threw *everything* out of its natural orbit.

Apparently their "element of surprise" was more accurately termed as an "element of total discombobulation". Neither zombie nor vampire knew quite what to make of Mr. Oubliette—they just gaped and stared—in fact, every living being in the vicinity stared as if the neurons running between the eyes and the brain were being severely cross-examined for accuracy.

And like good soldiers, they awaited further orders from their commanding officer before taking action. It was also possible they were unsure what to do about him short of holding up a mirror so he could see himself, in case he was having an off-day and had somehow missed it.

At any event, Fu and Biffy got a lot of open-mouthed stunned silence and were able to cross human warzones in uncommon peace and safety. You could've heard a crystal ball drop in the dead, 'Xcuse me, "undead", silence. It was better than waving a white flag.

But, as they drew near to the Transylvanian portal located outside Tinyville (everyone knew it was that old billboard outside of town) they were met with an unexpected surprise! The sky above Tinyville darkened like an oncoming thunderstorm and Fu and accompanying party stared up into the swirling black mass above their heads, trying not to get sucked into the vortex.

At first, they were too far to see, but gradually grew nearer, silver orbs slowly rotating in tiny revolutions, making a barely audible humming sound. Billions upon billions stretched across the sky, blotting the light from the sun as they stood poised to attack!

An extra-terrestrial attack, just outside of Tinyville, huh? Whoda thunk? Next stop, Roswell.

A green ray beam split the air and sizzled, rupturing the ground where it hit and filling the air with the smell of scorching atmosphere, burnt grass and upturned earth. There was no female around to scream for them but Mr. Oubliette managed to do an outstanding job regardless, taking one for the team as it were.

A UFO landed with great delicacy for such a gigantic craft and two alien beings disembarked, quibbling as they came down the spaceship ramp in perfect English, technically, even though they were bright green-skinned with large, triangular, bug-eyed alien faces.

"Really Vyxblkzkal?!" the one alien turned to the other, hands, or tentacles rather, on hips, or the general vicinity thereof.

"Weren't supposed to invade Earth for another 20 space-bleems, You, I told! The Planet MARS, it's that, to plug into GPS you were told to, erhm! Zombies already have on Earth everything booked up, and invade until they're done, we CANNOT! Ever *listen*, don't you ERHM???"

He huffed and spun back around to face everyone, despite his apparent lack of knees under his tinfoil spacesuit.

"Hello Earthlings—arrived too early, we have! Sorry about that, I am! It's hard to find good help these days, erhm!" He rolled his giant, iridescent black orbs which, based purely on positioning, had to be the creature's eyes.

"Back to conquer and invade your planet later we will be; You, sorry we are, to interrupt! Carry on with shooting and death and apocalyptic destruction, erhm? May the Forced Captivity of the Zombie Forces Be With You!"

Vyxblkzkal chimed in, "Naturally—fix damage, we did, to your Earth planet, we will, before going! FIRST—PROBE some of you, we MUST! Make some crop circles on our way out, we will also! Visit an alien planet, we cannot, and leave with not dissecting and implanting our spawn children to hatch inside of your bodies and horribly claw their way out! Erhm, To probe first, which of you?! Volunteer, who does?"

He started oiling down a frighteningly large tentacle. Although his face was green and triangular and therefore hard to read as facial expressions went, his said clearly that he rather enjoyed this part.

As one, Fu and Biffy shrank back quickly. Only Mr. Oubliette didn't look bothered, he was too busy checking his make-up in the compact he'd taken from his Man!Purse. The heat from the alien space rays had melted his mascara off. It may have been marked waterproof but the label didn't include ray guns.

"Uh—you should stop by Transylvania," Fu said hurriedly. "Vampires LOVE probing!"

"Erhm?!" Vyxblkzkal's eyes gleamed with a scary green light. It could've been unhealthy interest.

"Oh yes," Biffy hastily agreed, smirking, "why they say you've never really probed right until you've probed some vampires! First thing the Martians did when they came to invade Earth; they went out and probed some vampires then tried our pizza! Everyone knows vampires are total probe-o-holics! They can't get enough of probing! Pass it on to all your alien friends!"

"How come This, I never heard before, erhm?" Vyxblkzkal waved his terribly long, terribly slimy tentacles around and rapped on the side of a spaceship. "Zgvaaadlghf, Ghulooongauhagh! Stop by Transylvania on our way out, we must! Been probing and impregnating the wrong species, we have! ERHM!!!"

"I suppose I could be an alien tomorrow and I do rather fancy the tentacles," Mr. Oubliette mused, regrettably aloud, "we'll just have to see if I'm feeling green enough in the morning."

Fu and Biffy tried their best to ignore him and waved happily as the ships peeled off and headed through the billboard portal to Transylvania. They both stared after the departing alien saucers, far too many to count.

Then Fu said quickly, "You know Biffy, we don't have to cross over to Transylvania TODAY, per se."

"Oh no, NO RUSH, really. We're so close now and all."

"I say we uh, make camp for the night and cross to Transylvania in the morning. We can camp right here, actually. I'm sure Mr. Oubliette has a pop-up tent we can borrow somewhere in those 9 large steamer trunks that he has his Pirate-Ettes carrying."

"Yeah, here's good."

Arrr! A Ransom Note, Me Hearties!

A rmando was feeling annoyed. The war wasn't going as smoothly as promised. Now, thanks to the inconsideration of the fairies, rations among the vampire troops were at an all-time low and they were running out of fairy crackle to tempt human girls out of hiding.

Not to mention vampires kept mysteriously vanishing without a trace all over Transylvania and all that was left in their place was a teeny, tiny crop circle. Some vampires that had reappeared (just as mysteriously) were very disoriented and shaky and had taken to their castles for days and refused to come out. Three vampires had applied for a marriage license with an extra-terrestrial.

But worse than all of that, Armando had just been "un-friended" on Majick-Book by over 27,000 human teen girls. This caused him to take a severe hit on MeIzSoPopular, the newest game available on Majick-Book and his personal favorite. One more level and he'd have been able to wear the title "Mr.

Cool" and his little cartoony-guy (with pointy teeth) that he made to look like himself would have gotten the black "Mr. Cool" shades that came with that special level of the game. It just wasn't *FAIR!*

And there went Alucard bragging on Majick-Book and BaTwingger about how he'd been selected by SuperMatch to be a SuperNemesis to some 38-year-old high-school kid from Kansas. *Pffft, like THAT was so special?*

B!tch, please. Armando created his own profile at SuperMatch and now he had been matched to his own SuperNemesis that was like WAY BETTER! *Beat Prince Phillip the Gay Unicorn, Alucard!*

Oh, fine. Armando had tried getting the human girls attention again by dangling Leonard (or Howard? What was that kid's name?) out in a sequined jacket but the effect wasn't the same. He sparkled but the girls didn't seem much impressed and pronounced it "retro"—whatever that was.

Then Leonard caught on fire without crackle on his skin to protect him, the blazing daylight sun you know—yeah, that hadn't been a good day.

The zombies were no use to Armando there. Nobody wanted to watch a zombie sparkle—now that was just silly!

Fortunately, Armando had a Brilliant Evil Plan™! Of course that WAS why HE, not Alucard, was chosen as King of the Vampires, besides having the Sexiest Vampire Name!

He got to work on his new plan straight-away, after he'd gone up to the roof and eaten the man singing deep bass into the microphone, "You're a Mean One, King Armando! You reeeeaaaally are a heeeeellllllll—"

He pulled out some stationary from his desk, crossed out the bit at the top, "From the Desk of KING ARMANDO" and, while energetically chewing on the tip of his quill pen, began to scribble after a minute or so.

TO: King Clarion and Queen Ding-Aling of the Fairies, Royal Palace, Fairyland

Arrrrrrr! Me hopes these wee tidings finds ye fairy kinfolk well!

Me name is Cap'n James Hook *and I'm holding yer wee lass* Tinker-Belle *for ransom. I'll mercilessly squish her if you don't do as I say and all the other fairies I can find into a fairy pie for dinner 'cuz I'm a ruthless pirate! Did I mention that? Arrrrrr!*

Please send 100 crates of Fairy—Fairy—that shiny fairy stuff ye wee fair folk be responsible fer, to "Cap'n James Hook, Never-Never Land, c/o Transylvanian Post".

Er, send as special rush delivery addressed to "King ARMANDO of the Vampires"—he's, um, just picking up the fairy crumble for me, ye ken? Cuz we're such good mates, we are! He's a hearrrrty, trustworthy vampire he is, with the sexiest vampire name on Majick-Book (I voted for him proudly), and never spells it backward unlike some vampires. Sure sign of a douche, that is, spellin ye name backward for no reason. Arrrrrr!

SIGNED: Cap'n James Hook, pirate.
XOXOXOXOXOXO

PS: Arrrrr, aye we loved your wee sonnet, we did. Read it to me pirate boyos and Smee and t'was the best laugh we had in years!

Armando liked to end his letters on a happy note.

Well, there was that sorted. The fairies would pay the ransom to save poor Tinker-Belle and they'd be all set. Time to resume the war then.

Armando heard rumors that it was all because of one fairy that this war business got started. Apparently there was a Captain of the Peace Corps that was unexpectedly bright for one of those little winged bastards and Armando found out that he was the one responsible for relocating the secret caches and posting guards and just basically being such a pain in the ass that it forced Armando to take further action against the fairies in the first place!

With all due respect to SuperMatch, "Prince Phillip the Gay Unicorn" would have to await his turn on Armando's SuperNemesis roster. First, this little twit of a fairy captain needed to be squished to teach him a lesson about messing the vampires! Not "beware"—'BAT'-ware, a-HA!

Course, he couldn't really *learn a lesson* if he was squished, seeing as that would also technically make him dead also but—but—well, Armando would sort that part out later! THE POINT WAS— actually the point was that he had *annoyed* Armando and now he so would regret it!

Except of course, the fairy couldn't technically *regret anything* after he was squished (e.g. dead) but—BUT—STILL—STILL!

Armando felt it was still a good threat, all things considered. It had *style*; he just needed to work it out a little more. He'd post it as his new status on Majick-Book when he got the wording right.

His current status update: *"tmes R 2 tuff 2 B dscrbed. 2 much war, N no food, V's R stving 2 UN-deth, lol!"* had already received 127 "Likes". He was definitely going to make it to "Mr. Cool" level in MeIzSoPopular, no matter what it took!

He *wanted* those shades!

Transylvania, Here We Come

It was morning and out of the three companions, it was only normal for two of them to awaken and find themselves confronted by a tall, handsome stranger wearing what appeared to be hand-knitted footie pajamas and a cape, wearing his underwear on the outside of his clothing. Although in the case of Mr. Oubliette, he was generally the one in costume every morning.

There was a giant "S" hand-stitched on his chest, then right underneath nested a much smaller (N.R.). One had to wonder what it stood for.

"Brilliant! I love it," declared Mr. Oubliette, the first out of everyone to react. "TODAY, I'll be a Super Hero! WARDROBE CHANGE!"

To all their horrified fascination, he extracted from his Man!Purse, which he was still wearing over his sequined (yes, you read that right, *sequined*) pajamas, and pulled out a pocket-sized fabric square which he then unfolded and kept unfolding until it had a full-sized Chinese screen, which he preceded to dramatically step behind.

A minute or two and a mystery blast of shiny glitter later (witnesses swore they also heard a hair dryer running, despite a complete lack of electrical outlets in the wilderness) out Mr. Oubliette popped in his version of a superhero costume, very neatly folding his Chinese screen back to pocket-size and stowing in his Man!Purse for later.

For your own safety, Mr. Oubliette's superhero outfit shouldn't be described in great detail, just to say there were many, many large rhinestones involved and a giant "Mr. O" emblazoned on his chest plate with muscles built in, of course, in fuchsia pink. There were shoulder pads and pink rubber boots and gloves and a tiny pink mask to cover his eye area and shield his alter ego identity (yeah, as if that helped). Also, yes, the pink Speedos were worn on the OUTSIDE of the outfit (Yes, we told you, you didn't want to know but you insisted. We're not responsible for your therapy bills).

Biffy stared at the humongous "Mr. O" worn proudly at chest level, then face-palmed. "That's just wrong on so many levels."

"Why hello SARAH," Mr. Oubliette leered at Biffy.

"Dude, no! I'm not female, okay? Though whoever this "Sarah" is, she should be warned!"

"Um, who are you people?" Pajama-Footies finally spoke up. He certainly looked right for the part of a superhero, tall and well-built with very bright blue eyes, wearing thick black horn-rimmed glasses and black-haired with one persistent curl right in the middle of his tanned forehead. He also looked much too old to be still wearing footie pajamas and a handmade cape.

"Also," he added to Biffy as if by afterthought, "Why are you dressed like a cheerleader?"

"I wouldn't judge," Biffy replied coldly. "Have you seen what you're wearing?"

"Mr. Oubliette has both of you beat," Fu interrupted, a tiny fairy man wearing a pointy hat and tights though there was definitely an attitude to him that discouraged mentioning this lest your face be chewed off.

"But introductions are in order all around. I'm F.U.-Belle the pixie—yeah say it," he glared, fists balled, "Or laugh! I dare you!"

"Kent Clark (no relation)," the man in footie-pajamas said hurriedly. Superhero or not, he knew better than to taunt a very tiny, very angry fairy who had to carry the name "Belle" around all his life.

"And I'm Biffy Winters. I don't slay vampires at all, I'm just a sweet little cheerleader—unless there are no vampires around, then reverse it."

"And that's Mr. Oubliette," Fu added, jerking a thumb back, "He's currently suffering an identity crisis."

All three men stared in silence at the apparition that was Mr. Oubliette.

"I wouldn't exactly narrow the crisis list down to just his *identity*," Kent Clark (no relation) observed with care.

"Well, hello," a female voice cut in and all the men spun to look—then didn't stop looking. The look stretched on into some minutes and some silence while everyone searched hopelessly for a polite remark that didn't include, "that's some dress," tacked on the back of it.

It was "some dress" indeed. If a southern belle's hoop skirt with phoofy sleeves did a tango with molten pink cotton candy then the whole ensemble was dipped in a vat of glitter and spangles, that would about sum it up. It was amazing she could fit through doorways.

The dress screamed "PRINCESS" in all caps and would beat any fellow claimant to the royal throne into the floor with its hoopskirt.

This impression was only helped along by the blingtastic tiara resting on her golden blonde head—oh, and it should be mentioned, the HAIR! It was huge and braided and fantastically shiny like a shampoo commercial!

Feature film animators were already lining up to sketch its feminine glory and Mr. Oubliette was having the biggest attack of hair envy ever! It was entirely possible her coif was even bigger and phoofier and blonder than HIS!

It was some dress and some tiara and some hair—all at once and clearly the girl knew it. She basked in their stupefied state at her radiance until the spell was broken by Mr. Oubliette fumbling for his Man!Purse and Fu hurriedly preventing it.

"Hell NO! You MAY NOT be a PRINCESS today! The superhero outfit is bad enough," he insisted, yanking the Man!Purse away until Mr. Oubliette could control himself.

"But I could wear the tiara later?" Mr. Oubliette whined. Fu sighed.

"If you behave on the way to Transylvania, then maybe we'll let you wear the tiara for a few hours later on. But that means no fighting with the Pirate-Ettes and potty breaks ONLY when we stop."

"Oh goodie," Mr. Oubliette happily agreed, putting away his Man!Purse.

"I'm Anne Genue," the girl introduced herself proudly, "And I'm training now B/C I'm going to be a princess IRL, I've decided! FWIW!" *

Really, all three male minds noted but no one was stupid enough to say it out loud. They all just smiled and politely nodded, save Mr. Oubliette who was preoccupied with trying to work glass slippers into his good behavior bargain.

"I'm sure you'll make an excellent princess," Biffy said supportively, and was promptly glared at by the other two.

* *Need a translation?*
Check out Anne Genue's chatspk lexicon at the back of the book.

"I was going to say that," Kent Clark (no relation) huffed, "I'm sure she'll make an even more BEAUTIFUL princess, if you hadn't interrupted! Which I am! Sure! Of that! In case you were wondering!"

"I'm taller than I look," Fu cut in, tone hopeful.

Anne was, in the manner of pretty girls often made a fuss over by the male species, not even bothering to listen.

"So, where are you boys headed off to? NP if you don't want to tell me, NMB, but IMHO maybe I could help. I'm working on improving my community skills this week. A princess has to be proactive to her people's needs, RTM."

"Actually, we're headed to Transylvania to kick vampires asses," Biffy bragged, puffing out his chest then, belatedly realizing this didn't look so good in a fake bra, he quickly deflated. "Er, because I SLAY vampires baby, that's just how I roll. Born to be badass, all the way!"

"EXCEPT of course, when you're born a superhero, which actually I wasn't and actually I don't know any superheroes myself," Kent Clark (no relation) pushed the black horn-rims up the bridge of his nose and added, "BUT, if I did know any real superheroes, which I don't, then they'd be the COOL ONES, like Super-Stupendous-Awesome-Man (no relation)."

"Really? *Super-Stupendous-Awesome-Man?* Modest much, is he?" Biffy scoffed.

"He might have had a little trouble settling on a SuperName," Kent Clark (no relation) admitted,

"Also, he might still be working out that quick change in the phone booth. It's not as easy as it looks—if I knew anything about that, which I don't."

"But if he occasionally has to save the world in overalls instead of a cape because it got caught in the phone booth door again—the POINT IS, I think, that he's SAVING THE FREAKIN WORLD not what he's wearing at the time—"

"So why are you wearing his costume then?" Biffy taunted, "At least, I assume that's what the "S" (n.r.) on your chest is about."

"My mom made it," Kent Clark (no relation) huffed. "It would hurt her feelings if I didn't wear it. She likes to dress me up as HIM sometimes—you know, Mom's."

He shrugged his shoulders like, "whatchya gonna do"?

"So your mommy dresses you?" Anne looked at him doubtfully, "SRSLY, you're how old again?"

"NO! Not "dresses me" . . . she, well, likes making—" Kent coughed "—*costumes* for me. She sews. It's a hobby okay?" he huffed, aware he'd lost a step or two in the race to impress the girl and was now actually trailing BEHIND Biffy, a man shamelessly wearing a cheerleader outfit.

"Anyway, MY POINT was, clearly the superhero that I'm not is, you know, very VERY awesome and could pwn *way more* than vampires if he wanted to!"

"Which makes it such a shame *you're not him*," Biffy crowed, well aware he was leading the masculinity polls now and savoring the sweet taste of victory.

"Or related to him or know more about him than his name. You just like to dress up in costume like him," he smirked, "Which is NOT AT ALL nerdy! I bet you have the entire collection of *dolls*—I mean, "action figures", at home don't you?"

Kent Clark (no relation) grumbled, then looked for a way to come back from this.

"But IDK, nerds are really smart," Anne supplied helpfully.

"YEAH, NERDS are REALLY SMART," Kent insisted, glaring down Biffy then, "Also the next time Super-Stupendous-Awesome-Man comes through the phone booth, he's gonna crush your skull in, Biffy!"

"I guarantee you, I've kicked more ass than both of these two put together," Fu inserted as it seemed the scales were starting to tilt towards his favor.

"Plus, I did mention that I'm tall right, as well as handsome? For a fairy, really I am. Tallest in my whole regime, actually."

"OIC! I'm lovin it! VBEG! That's SO G8T, LOL!" Anne giggled, mystifying the males as females have been capable of doing for centuries.

"Well hello SARAH," Mr. Oubliette leered at Anne. Anne drew back a little.

"Um—no, my name is Anne, actually."

Mr. Oubliette fumbled in his Man!Purse for a second and drew out something small and round.

"Peach?" he proffered hopefully, holding it out to her. "It's a present," he added, tone suggestive.

"Oh how kind of you—" Anne started to take it but Fu quickly knocked it out of her hand.

"Miss, I would NOT eat that if I were you! You don't know where it's been!" Fu stared at the peach now in the dirt with great suspicion. "Or even what it IS!"

Anne gave him the same sort of bemused look Snow White might have given the dwarves if they dared suggest the apple given her by the sweet little old lady contained poison.

Fu sighed and tried something else. "Peaches—um, give you cellulite. I read an article in the Fairyland Chronicle about it only last week."

Anne leapt away from the peach like it had just sprouted legs. Fu tried not to smile.

"You know, we're all out here for different reasons and don't know much about each other," Biffy observed. "Shame there isn't someone around who knew all of us to sort of sum things up."

From nowhere, angelic music started to play and golden light streamed down from the heavens, while an equally golden voice intoned, resonating with supernatural acoustics modern sound equipment could only dream of.

"And the facts were these . . . these were the facts: F.U.-Belle the fairy and Biffy Winters, the vampire slayer just happened to be embarking on a dangerous quest, the likes of which was just the sort of dangerous quest that young Kent Clark (no relation, and upon reflection, not entirely young either) was looking to embark upon himself in order to find his own Destiny!

THEREFORE . . . it made sense that they should all embark upon *the same quest* together for perhaps all would thus find what they were seeking along the way. F.U.-Belle to prevent a ghastly war, Biffy some "vampire ass" whereupon to thus "kick", Mr. Oubliette, his real identity and as for Anne Genue, a kingdom to rule o'er that she may become the very princess she envisions herself to be. *Good luck then upon your dangerous quest . . . to you all!"*

The light and voice faded. All was silent.

Then Kent Clark (no relation) ventured a hesitant, "What the hell—"

"It's the Narrator, of course. He's doing a beautiful recap and bringing us all up to speed on the story so far," Anne interrupted with a huff. "SRSLY, don't you know ANYTHING? You SRS?"

"Sounds like the guy who narrated the *"Hubert Pfiffer! Boy Wizard!"* books," Biffy added. While one had to ponder just how Biffy was so familiar, Kent Clark (no relation) again looked blank.

"Oh-kay? Who is *Hubert Pfiffer, Boy Wizard*?"

"RLY? SRSLY? RLY AND SRSLY?" Anne looked hideously offended, "O-EM-GEE, I can't be hearing this! EVERYONE KNOWS *Hubert Pfiffer! Boy Wizard!* You sure you weren't just dropped on your head? Are all caped superheroes this dense?"

"Most of them yeah but I'm not a superhero, just a, um, farm-boy from Kansas in caped pajamas," Kent felt duty-bound to point out. "And I don't know who Hubert Pfiffer is, sorry."

"NYD!! Have you been living under a rock? In a crater? OMGWTFBBQ?"

"Well, actually I was found in a cornfield—"

Anne, like most women, could breathe intravenously while she ranted so she hadn't paused a solo beat to allow him to speak. She just talked right over him, drowning him out.

"HUBERT PFIFFER!! BOY WIZARD!! was *tragically orphaned* at birth and went to Wart-Hogs School for the Blind; an accidental but fortuitous mix-up in paperwork. He was supposed to go to wizard school but cured all the kids of their blindness with his fantastically inherited wizard powers which he prodigiously knew how to use without schooling.

Only *very ordinary* wizards needed schooling, not *Hubert Pfiffer! Boy Wizard!*

Then, he defeated singlehandedly the evil dark lord "He-who-must-not-be-named-except-under-special-circumstances-like-in-a-safe-locked-soundproof-room-but-otherwise-must-not-be-named-except-then-but-only-maybe" in an epic showdown duel to the—oh wait," she paused, "Whoa SRSLY, I shoulda said "spoiler alert" first! SRY!"

"While the name's appropriate for a dark lord, I feel like it could be shorter," Kent Clark (no relation) mused. Anne waved a hand again.

"SRSLY, it's about *ambiance*! Just sends shivers down your spine, doesn't it? For SRS! But I just can't believe you've never heard of *Hubert Pfiffer! Boy Wizard!*"

Anne stared at Kent sadly. "Your very life depresses me, STBYANHPBW!"

Kent hesitated. "I—don't know that one?"

Anne rolled her eyes. "It-sucks-to-be-you-and-not-Hubert-Pfiffer-Boy-Wizard!"

"So, you wanna come along with us to Transylvania?" Biffy invited Anne, tone hopeful, "Great opportunity to recruit some new subjects for your forthcoming kingdom and watch me kick some vampire ass, a lot of it actually."

He tried flexing a little for her benefit, though it lost something in translation when he had on more mascara than she did, "Two or three, or fifteen vampires at a time. I can handle that, no problem."

"What a brilliant idea! Seriously, LYLAS! TEN POINTS AWARDED TO YOU FROM *HUBERT PFIFFERRRR!*" Anne removed her tiara and waved it dramatically at him like a magic wand. Biffy beamed, though his face fell a bit as he mumbled, *"Like a sister* though?"

Kent lifted a skeptical brow. "What the hell would he do with 10 points from a fictional character?"

Anne gasped, outraged. "Watch your language, and don't you dare use such a filthy word around me!"

Kent frowned and did a mental back-check, "Ummm . . . hell?"

"No, *F-I-C-T-I-O-N-A-L!* That's a 9-letter word—eep!" Anne gasped and suddenly pressed both hands to her mouth. "I can't believe I just said that, for shame, Anne Genue, for shame! Such language!"

She reached up, pulled off her tiara again and bopped herself. "That's 10 points deducted from me by *Hubert Pfiffer!*," she said very severely and hung her head. "I'll never win the *Pfiffer! Cup* at this rate."

"BUT HE'S A FICTIONAL CHARACTER!" Kent Clark (no relation) exploded.

Anne sniffed. "You clearly just can't handle the truth. YSDWAL!"

A Rescue Was Being Thought Of!

The "First Annual Rescue Party for Tinker-Belle" was held in the Palatial Gardens although, because of the impromptu nature of the ransom demand and war rations, the catering simply wasn't up to par.

Despite the cheery party hats and colorful balloon animals, large sheet cake, mandatory gift exchange amongst the guests and bright, festive decorations, King Clarion was grumpy.

"I knew something like this would happen, Ding-Aling," he fussed to his wife. "Remember how you said that terrible woodsy-green number she wore so unfashionably out of season was the worst of it but now you see *I was right!* She moved away to this wild, feral land of Never, and bad fashion is just where it all begins!"

"Yes, my Paragon of Virtue. I see you were right. You usually are."

"When Tinker-Belle ran off with that wild boy, I tried to hope for the best," Clarion still fussed. "I told her he was much too young, let alone *too large* for her! I told her it'd only lead to bad things! But she said she LOVED him and off they went, and now— *now look what's happened!* This is a disaster!" He paced back and forth, fretful.

"You know, that disgusting dirty flying boy didn't even wear proper shoes! And I don't believe he's *ever* had a manicure in his whole dreadful life!"

Queen Ding-Aling nodded sympathetically. She'd heard worse rumors about the boy than that he didn't bathe or have regular manicures and pedicures but knew now was not the time to broach the topic. Clarion was already at the point of nervous breakdown.

"Perhaps darling, we should simply pay the ransom Hook demands and bring Tinker-Belle back safely home?" she suggested as gently as she could.

King Clarion frowned and shook his head. "No, it'll set a bad precedent. I've told you Ding-Aling, we DO NOT, under ANY circumstances, *negotiate with fashion victims!*"

He turned sharply on a heel. "However, I've hired someone to help us. I've found us a wicked witch to distract Captain Hook and give our beloved Tinker-Belle a chance to escape his vile pirate clutches."

"I'm not *wicked*," a new, creaky voice complained. All the fairies turned to look. Unnoticed until then, though one must wonder how as she took up nearly the entire courtyard, a shriveled, elderly human woman stood. Being human, she was at least ten times taller than the fairies and that was while seated. It was clear she was the one who'd just spoke.

Two things were likewise immediately noticeable about her. The first was that her skin was a shade of pale yellow, an unusual shade in humans. And despite her seasonal skin color, she wasn't wearing the appropriate spring colors. Instead she wore a drab brown dress and brown pointed hat, meeting with the fairies immediate ridicule. Really, had NONE of their visitors to Fairyland been introduced to pastels?

"That is, I'm not wicked *yet*," the yellow-skinned woman continued, sounding nervous.

"Wickedness is a Level-5 witch see, and I'm only advanced to a Level-2, "Slightly Naughty" . . . but I promise I'm a quick learner! In fact, my coven says I show potential to be a real badass one day," she beamed.

"I thought witches skins were green, not yellow?" Ding-Aling remarked. The Slightly Naughty Witch blushed—or one must assume. More specifically, she turned a pinkish-orangy shade so it was anyone's guess what emotion that indicated.

"Well—green skin is more a Level-4, but I'm getting there! I get to start wearing the black dress and hat at Level-4 too. Why, when King Clarion hired me, I thought to myself: Effeebilbolia, this is your chance to make your path to true wickedness! If you pull this off, you'll be at a Level-3 before you know it, maybe even advancing straight to a Level-4 without final exams!"

"The Slightly-Naughty Witch?" Ding-Aling repeated slowly, raising a perfectly plucked eyebrow. King Clarion cleared his throat a bit.

"The rental rates were cheaper, dear," he murmured in an undertone, "Level-5 Wicked Witches are very costly."

Ding-Aling sighed. "Ah, I see. Well Miss—um, Slightly Naughty, what can you do? Place a curse on Captain Hook for us?"

"Not *curses* as such," the Slightly Naughty Witch sounded nervous again. "That's on the Level-4 certification and it's a bit out of my league but—but I can manage light incantations and every once in a while I almost work a full spell."

"Right now, I'm at the level where I can safely create minor annoyances on Captain Hook for you, like increased spam-mail about manhood enlargement, and crank-calling him, like "does he have Prime Minister Peter Pan in a can?" See, it'll distract him so Tinker-Belle can make her daring escape!"

"Ah, and I assume you have a plan for that?"

"Oh yes," the Slightly Naughty Witch nodded, "I do. One of the experienced witches helped me out with it. In fact, it's my graduation project and if it works successfully, I will advance to a Level-3: 'Fully Naughty and Nearly-Bad-Girl' for next semester."

She set something down in the open-air fairy courtyard and the fairies all gathered around to study it up close. It appeared to be a miniature gingerbread house, frosted with sugar crystals and decorated with brightly colored candies. It was miniature to a full-grown human that is, to the fairies, it was just about playhouse-sized.

Clarion and Ding-Aling exchanged glances. "Um—what is it?"

The Slightly Naughty Witch waved at it proudly. "It's a homing gingerbread house that actually flies! I baked it myself but I had to get some help to make it functional. Flight is a Level-4 skill; I can only manage brief levitation at a maximum of 22 inches above ground level."

"Anyway, I'm sure it will work! I've tested it extensively—all Tinker-Belle has to do is crawl inside the house and it'll fly her safely back to Fairyland."

"And Captain Hook won't suspect anything when he sees a gingerbread house flying through the air?" Ding-Aling inquired doubtfully.

The Slightly Naughty Witch nodded. "Yes, I thought of that. There's a pre-recorded message that's triggered when Captain Hook pokes the gingerbread house with his hook. Like this, see?"

She fished a silver hook out of her pocket and tapped the house with it. A voice, sounding creaky like an old woman's, came out of the house:

"Hello, this is the magic travelling gingerbread house of the Sli—um, I mean the Wicked Witch. Set it down next to your jail cells, don't look inside and don't pay any attention if it flies away. I can't come to the door right now; I'm busy baking up some nice crispy human children for dinner. Carry on with your pirate business and do have a nice day."

"Brilliant!" King Clarion clapped his hands. "Obviously the pirates won't take any notice of a flying gingerbread house with a child-eating wicked witch inside. But will our dear Tinker-Belle know to climb inside the house when she sees it? And how is she to get out of her prison cell?"

"I've recorded another message with escape instructions for her," The Slightly Naughty Witch explained. "It's triggered by Tinker-Belle's unique tinkling bell sounds and it tells her to climb into the gingerbread house and it will carry her to safety. It also carries a doggy bone. Everyone knows there's a dog holding the key ring in its mouth in all pirate jail cells, so she can use the bone to tempt it over to the cell and free herself with the jail keys."

The fairies nodded in agreement. Well yes naturally, the dog with the key-ring and promise of freedom was a common pirate jail cell fixture so that should work out just fine. Plus, fairies had a natural way with all animals.

"Marvelous," King Clarion clapped his hands. "Tinker-Belle is as good as freed! Thank you, dear Slightly Naughty Witch, and I hope you make it to a Level-5 just as quick as you please!"

The Slightly Naughty Witch beamed, "Yes, thank you! At Level-5, they throw in a free vacation over the rainbow . . . I just can't wait! I'm going to take so many pictures and maybe bring back a pair of souvenir all-powerful slippers—have to watch out for falling farmhouses though. They got my sister like that, you know."

"My condolences on your loss," Clarion replied politely, "and we thank you again for your services. Could we get you a glass of water or—"

He was abruptly cut off and all the fairies looked startled as the Slightly Naughty Witch shrieked at an ear-shattering decibel.

"—or a snack before you go—s-sorry?" Clarion finished his thought weakly. He wasn't sure what just happened.

"Not the 'W'-word," the Slightly Naughty Witch shuddered. "That's how they killed my other sister, and she weren't even doin' nothin' but threatening an ugly little girl and a straw man! I ain't fully wicked so—so there might just be some blurring around the edges, but I ain't riskin' nothin all the same! I ain't goin' out as a puddle, not me!"

"I apologize. That was insensitive of me," Clarion murmured, "No, uh, 'W'-word then."

He cleared his throat and rallied, turning to his wife, "Really Ding-Aling, I do think next time we should be more choosy about who we let Tinker-Belle go out with. Shoeless boys, I think not! You can see it leads to a world of trouble: bad fashion, pirates, kidnappings and running away from home— just bad business all around."

"Yes, my Proud Mustang," Ding-Aling sighed. "But darling, she was so young and you know how headstrong fairies are for those first few centuries or so. Tinker-Belle is more spirited than most. You mustn't judge her too harshly for having an adventurous spirit and wanting to go out and see the world."

With that, the Rescue Party officially broke up and, even though everyone got a free set of luggage to take home with them as their party favor, it wasn't ranked among the social season's best.

But they were in the middle of a war and an Apocalypse so admittedly times were tough.

A God By Any Other Name Gets No Love from Hollywood!

I t wasn't difficult crossing the interdimensional portal between the Human World and Transylvania. In fact, it was cleverly devised to make one think they were stepping through a normal doorway into the next room. It wasn't until the vampires lying in wait jumped you that you realized the final destination didn't fit the packaging but by then it was too late.

When the small band of heroes came through the portal, they found themselves in a normal looking office lobby with armchairs and coffee tables strewn with magazines. Tasteful art lined the walls interspersed with signs which promised to land you big $$$ for your bad encounter with glowing green meteor-rocks.

A busy secretary was typing 90 wpm into a computer at the front desk, a ringing extension at her elbow and she glanced up just long enough for a polite, "I'll be with you in just a minute". It all looked very convincing until—

—a door in the back of the office burst open and out jumped the vampires!

They were grinning broadly, fangs already elongated as they well knew they held the advantage. Someone was just seconds from blurting out, "Ah-ha! What have we here?"

They surrounded the small company, hungry and ready to feast on fresh blood although Fu-Belle barely got a cursory glance. All vampires knew fairies were gummy and stuck in your fangs. And Mr. Oubliette, well—he got a much longer and far more inquisitive stare but doubtless he'd be the last to be eaten and then only if the vampire was starving or willing to risk it! Being toxic or poisonous was only the *start of dietary complications* one could envision after eating Mr. Oubliette.

Kent Clark (no relation) took the dire situation at a glance and knew there was no time to waste! While hungry vampires surrounded his friends, he ducked quickly and quietly behind a large potted plant, whipped his horn-rimmed glasses off and slicked his hair back, save that one persistent forehead curl, with the bottle of emergency Heroic Hair Gel he kept on hand for his quick changes.

Then he casually strolled out from behind the plant, his forearm extended high out in front as if he'd flown in moments before but decided he needed be at ground level to threaten the vampires.

"Well-well, what have we here?" he boomed in his patented "Witty Bantering with Villains" voice. "Vampires, hmm? Lucky thing I just happened to be flying by and saw this surprise attack going on through the window. Have no fear, good citizens! For it is I, Super-Stupendous-Awesome-Man (no relation), here to rescue you and save the day!"

"OMG! Super-Stupendous-Awesome-Man (no relation)," Anne squeed loudly, "Thank goodness you're here! We're saved!" She beamed at him and gushed, "You know you're so much handsomer in person—you aren't by any chance related to *Hubert Pfiffer! Boy Wizard!* are you?"

The look on Super-Stupendous-Awesome-Man (no relation) was less than heroic as expressions went but Anne hadn't bothered to notice.

"WAM," she darted a look around, "Where did Kent Clark (no relation) go? IDEK? ROTFLMAO, he'll be sorry that he missed seeing you, you're his favorite superhero! Oh well, STH!"

Super-Stupendous-Awesome-Man (no relation) nodded solemnly. "Yes, I have heard of Kent Clark (no relation). He is a good man."

"Yeah, he even dresses up like you sometimes," Biffy added, "Which is kind of "geeky" not to mention you two don't even look alike! Dude needs major help—he wears glasses and does cosplay, yikes!" He closed his eyes and shook his head "no".

"But we're total bros now, so I'm gonna give K.C. (n.r.) a clue, and help him out with being awesome. It just doesn't come as naturally to everyone as it does to me," Biffy gave a modest little shrug and squared the shoulders of his bright orange cheerleader outfit, a male mind clearly proud he'd never stooped to a level as geeky as cosplay.

Kent C—er, Super-Stupendous-Awesome-Man (no relation) nodded encouragingly, "That's very kind of you, good citizen," he boomed. "Well done!"

Fu-Belle was watching all this while restraining both confusion and shock. Was he the only one who saw that Super-Stupendous-Awesome-Man (no relation) was simply Kent Clark (no relation) with glasses removed and hair slicked back? He was even wearing the same handmade costume that his mom stitched for him but everyone seemed to be utterly convinced this was a different guy.

Even Mr. Oubliette was complimenting him on the craftsmanship of his super outfit and asking where he got it made. Maybe Kent Clark (no relation) did possess an alien power to alter reality because no one else saw it but Fu.

But Fu wasn't planning to rock the boat. He liked Kent Clark (no relation) a lot. He was a nice kid and obviously he just wanted to be the hero for a change. What was the harm in it anyway?

"Oh hey Super-Stupendous-Awesome-Man (no relation)! It's so great to meet you," he said brightly, "I heard nothing but good things! Er, and as for our pal Kent Clark (no relation), I'm pretty sure I heard him say he had to hit the head. He'd been holding it since we got here from the Human World. He'll be sorry he missed you though."

"Why thank you—" Super-Stupendous-Awesome-Man (no relation) boomed again and squinted at Fu, "—er, small citizen. It's my pleasure to serve the cause of justice and assist all of you in your hour of need."

The vampires were very confused. They were used to eating the temporarily super-powered and not-a-little-psycho meteor freaks who usually came through the Tinyville portal but this bunch was just *weird*! Between the fairy and Mr. Oubliette, whatever the hell HE was, plus a cross-dressing cheerleader and now a superhero was involved too?

They backed away slowly. Lunch was lunch but this situation was getting above their pay grade.

"Hello, Cats and Kittens," the voice came from nowhere, a low, sensual growling purr and it was followed by a flash of gold sparklies, pink hearts and red rose petals, as well as the anticipatory "whooshing" sound effect that should follow every good supernatural entity when they first appear on the scene. Kudos to the sound and CGI effects crew!

A man materialized out of thin air—tall, handsome, outrageously fit and built, toned muscles stretching from here-to-everywhere, in a white leather jumpsuit cut so snug it left little to the imagination, dotted with about 40,000,000 metal studs, and left wide open at the chest. His hair was jet black, and hung in shoulder-length ringlets, his skin so glowing flawlessly golden bronze he could model for a bottle of tanning oil. He beamed at them, his teeth blinding white in his tanned face.

"Hey!" he purred, and the solo, velvety word was musical, a song, "I'm Ares, God o' Loooove!"

Mr. Oubliette was instantly jealous. "A LOVE GOD! That's *brilliant!*" he hissed through his teeth. "I should have thought of it FIRST!" He eyed his rival, measuring skin tight leather pants in his mind.

"But—I thought Ares was the Greek god of war? Right," Biffy puzzled. "Wasn't Eros the love god?"

"Looks like someone at the ancient temples didn't translate their pantheon of gods right," Fu mused, eyeing the god. "If that's the "war god" for ancient Greece, no wonder their whole civilization collapsed."

"That sort of gross oversight never would've happened if *Hubert Pffifer! Boy Wizard!* were present," Anne huffed, "He can speak 47 languages, 7 of which are totally extinct now, and including ALL the languages of the animal kingdom. Plus he *invented* sign language. Obviously he never would have deciphered the text wrong!"

She folded her arms to finish smugly, "After all, he invented True Love in the first place! He probably had something to do with the election of the love god to oversee his invention, now didn't he?"

"Excuse me? Did you just claim *Hubert Pffifer, a BOOK CHARACTER,* invented *TRUE LOVE*???" Kent Clark (no relation) gaped in disbelief. Anne nodded.

"Oh Kent, when did you come back? You totally missed seeing Super-Stupendous-Awesome-Man (no relation) while you were peeing. Oh well, BCNU."

"Um, yeah, um—" Kent pushed his glasses up higher. It was true. He'd ducked back behind the large potted plant to change back to his alter ego after the danger had passed.

The vampires threatening them had fled after seeing a god materialize on the scene. The white leather jumpsuit and Elvis sideburns had proved too much for them to handle. Who knew what revenge a love god might take on the vampire who oh-so-foolishly snacked on his friends right in front of him?

"Anyway," Anne continued blithely, "Yes, I did. "True love" was only one of HPBW's amazing inventions for the good of humanity! Of course, that was AFTER *Hubert Pfiffer* invented time travel and the wheel, but BEFORE he invented fluffy puppies with wagging tails and birthday presents."

"Then as you probably know already, he invented the recipe for cheese doodles but when he saw that the world wasn't ready yet for their deliciousness, he had to hide them away until the proper time. There was this penniless, lonely inventor by the name of Geppetto and *Hubert Pffifer! Boy Wizard!* left the recipe on his doorstep so he could provide for his hungry cat and little wooden puppet boy—"

Ares, the love god was clearly tuning them out. He was a busy god and who cared what mere mortals had to talk about? With another burst of rose petals and melodious theme music, he produced a pair of gold spectacles and a scroll and he was preoccupied scanning it until he got to the right spot.

"Ah, I'm looking for—" he broke off and squinted at the scroll suspiciously, "—no, that *must be* a typo! Surely it isn't F.U.-Belle the fairy?"

"Yeah. F.U.—," his voice dropped about 3 decibels, "—belle. That's me."

Ignoring the other men coughing loudly into their fists and looking at the sky, the ground, anywhere but at him, each other or the love god, he continued dryly, "What can I do for you, Ares?"

"Excellent," Ares beamed and rolled up the scroll. "I'm here to make arrangements with you. King Clarion of the fairies hired me to be your war planner and coordinator. He said you'd be my main point of contact for the arrangements."

He consulted his scroll again. "Mmm, shall we start with the menu? Are you feeling full wine list for this war, or just light champagne for everyone? Or maybe we should go over the battle choreography and seating chart first? I've got some great ideas for decorations, wait 'til you see the napkin rosettes and our caterer is the best! His spinach puffs are out of this world—"

"Wait! A *war* planner? Like a *wedding* planner?" Fu-Belle sputtered.

"Clarion *hired a war*—oh God! *Of course* he did! We couldn't have a spontaneous or aggressive WAR, now could we?" The fairy captain face-palmed.

Ares beamed at the "oh God" part. "Yes, that would be me. Best in the business." He smiled his too shiny smile again at them.

"But aren't you a love god?" Fu frowned. "Suddenly, I'm very confused."

Ares, the love god, waved this off. "Expecting a WAR god to be your WAR planner—dude, that's like, SO cliché! What, are you 500?"

He made a little twirly motion with his finger. "Plus, it's kinda racist too, so NOT cool! I'm experienced and professional, and I have excellent references." He shook his curly head.

"Tough times, recession you know. Hey, we all freelance these days to keep things running on

Olympus, those of us gods who are left anyway. I do wedding planning, birthdays, quinceañeras, bar-mitzvahs, wars—pretty much any gig I can land," he shrugged.

"Keeps the bills paid—*mostly*. We had to rent out the bottom half of our mountain to a bed and breakfast and Ye Ancient Herculean Gym," he sighed. "But at least we didn't go to Uncle Hades for yet another loan extension."

'But you're a god," Fu pointed out.

Ares shook his head again. "Immortal ain't synonymous with rich, bro! We got killed in those last few blockbuster movie deals we signed. They made millions at the box office, but want to guess what percentage of the ticket sales we gods saw?"

"My identical twin cousin, Ares the war god incinerated our previous agent with a lightning bolt but it didn't help much at that point. Personally, I voted for chaining him to a rock while a raven picked his liver out. Always a classic."

"*—BUT Hubert Pfiffer! Boy Wizard! had the most glorious singing voice of all the birds and beasts combined! It was tragically stolen from him by a jealous sea witch who kept it hidden in a seashell and that's what inspired him to invent sign language so people in the world without voices could still express themselves!*

Then, after Hubert Pfiffer! Boy Wizard! defeated the sea witch in an epic water battle, he couldn't bear to keep such an amazing gift all to himself, so he gave it away to a beautiful but voiceless mermaid so she could marry the prince of her dreams—"

Fu tried to tune out Anne Genue's shrill background chatter. "Fine, fine. I'm sure you're an excellent war planner and I get that you need the gig, but I still don't think WE need—"

"F!!! U!!!"

"Huh?" Fu glanced around to see who shouted his name—but apparently it wasn't directed towards him but as an insult to Ares, GOL.

Another god had materialized and he too appeared he was from some ancient civilization. His black beard was bushy and matted, clearly never seen a razor. His ill-fitting toga was rough burlap carelessly stitched and draped across his shoulders and belted at the waist. He held a rough-hewn oak staff and glared at them all.

The reason he hadn't been noticed until just then was he appeared without fanfare of any sort, epic fail by his staging and special effects crew, but his *stench* caught one's attention quickly!

It was very male and extremely organic, and most of all, STRONG! Fu's nose hair started to crinkle, and the metal studs on Ares outfit were tarnishing.

"Oh my g—well, ME," Ares gasped. "DUDE, what the Tartarus?! That's the *worst* outfit I've ever seen! What ancient pantheon are you? You should have your costume designer tortured, dismembered and excommunicated, really!"

"Infidel! Defiler! Grecian scum!" the other god shrieked wildly, "I am Verethraghna, GOD OF WAR, and I shall smite thee with a thousand plagues upon thy soul!"

Ares lifted a brow. "Sorry no—can't say I'm familiar. Bro, where have you been for the past millennia-and-a-half? No one does the "smiting thing" anymore, that's so outdated, or says "thee" or "infidel" either. Wake up and smell the 21st century, dude!"

"And, speaking of SMELL, *body wash—invest!*"

"Oh you Greeks think you are so modern and fancy with your contemporary views on bathing," Verethraghna whined.

"Everybody knows your names and titles, everyone wants to makes movies of you and you get all the good godly effects but we Persians were here FIRST before the Greeks! It was our names that were shouted triumphantly in battle, it was the name Verethraghna that was heard as a victory cry!"

"But no one knows the Persian gods anymore, it's all about the Greeks and Romans and the Norse gods now. And Thor doesn't even chew with his mouth closed half the time." He pouted.

"—so after he invented and perfected the recipe for chocolate, Hubert Pfiffer! Boy Wizard! clapped young Willy Wonk on the back and told him, "Now* *that I've taught you all I know about how to make the world's most delicious chocolate bars, you just need to sell them. Ah, I have it! Perhaps if you put a special prize in five of the chocolate bars so people have to buy the bars to find the prize!*

Also, Wonk sounds wrong for a famous chocolatier but if you throw an 'A' in there someplace, I think you'd really have something—"

Again, Fu put some effort into tuning out Anne's background chatter. Ares, god of love, yawned. "Right. Look Viagra—"

"Verethraghna!"

"—sure bro, but you're never going to land a Hollywood blockbuster about the Persians dressed like THAT, seriously! Dude—LEATHER!"

Ares pointed to his own skintight jumpsuit for emphasis. "It's a look for all seasons, always in style—and if you can "punk it up" with metal studs and an enormous belt, even better! Keep the ladies' eyes aimed below the belt. Sex sells –it's my business and I know the market— so pump some iron and go shirtless. *Always go shirtless, bro!* Also, you need a tanning bed, stat!"

"Uhhh—" Viag—um, Verethraghna looked lost. Clearly it hadn't occurred to him that he might need to modernize.

"Second, I'm sure "Viagra" is like, an awesome name for an ancient god, and it made the local yokels shake in their boots with terror way back, ya know, whenever B.C. era it was you ruled the planet—"

"Verethraghna!"

"—uh huh! My point is, you got competition in the godly arena now! It ain't your solo battlefield anymore! So, if you want to make it big, you'll need a stage name! Take "Ares" for example: simple, catchy, easy to remember and everyone can pronounce it! Which is the point I'm getting at, really."

"—but that was the dramatic moment when Hubert Pfiffer! Boy Wizard! spoke up in the meeting of Rebel Alliance, "If you'll permit me, I did notice some vulnerable points to the Death Star—"

"Looking into the future before it happens is blasphemy against—against me!" Verethraghna huffed.

Ares rolled his eyes. "Dude, we're gods. Sneaking a look into the future before mortals is what you might call a perk of the job. You want to know why you don't have followers? It's because you haven't embraced the modern idea of bathing regularly."

"No, it is a punishment," Verethraghna prophesied gloomily. "A judgment placed upon me for failing my duties as the Lord of War. One day you tell yourself you're just taking a century off to rest, maybe two—a little "me" time. Then your civilization collapses and your entire reputation as an all-powerful war god is ruined. No one takes you seriously after that."

"Maaaybe," Ares looked skeptical. "Regardless bro, when you DO sign a big movie deal, take my advice. Secure the merchandising rights too!"

"—and Hubert Pfiffer! Boy Wizard! suggested to the Fellowship, "If only we had someone small enough, I bet they could creep past the giant fiery eye with the ring undetected. I think I know just the fellow for the job—"

"Now Mithras will take the title of god of war and I'll be completely disgraced," Verethraghna continued, going for most pessimistic god of the ancient world. Ares, god of love, clapped his hands energetically.

"Mithras? Aww, you have a little sidekick—awesome!" He beamed. "We'll work him up a nice leather one-piece in safety pins. Tell me, how does he feel about dreadlocks and guy-liner and laughing really annoyingly whenever he does something bad?"

Verethraghna growled, "Mithras is NOT my second-in-command! He is my wretched half-brother who I've been trying to kill for years, but alas, Father's protective order over him forbids me to do so outright. I will destroy him and all who follow him if he tries to take my place! NOTHING WILL STAND IN MY WAY!"

Lightning materialized on his fingertips, forming a powerful, white-hot bolt of energy and it arced in shiny streaks up and down his forearms.

"Nothing?" Mr. Oubliette piped up, "NOTHING? NOTHING, TRA-LA-"

"Shut up!" Fu elbowed him into silence.

"Sure, chill out dude!" Ares raised both hands in surrender. "I'm a lover not a fighter, bro. War gods; soooo anal. You totally need to get laid."

Verethraghna just glared at him. He wasn't sure what that meant but it sounded like an insult.

Suddenly loud bells chimed in the air, surprising everyone, and there were indistinct words, but "wish" and "goblins" could faintly be heard.

Mr. Oubliette gasped.

"Oh, that's for me. Excuse me," he vanished with a sandblast of glitter, his little 'Ettes', all caped and garbed as tiny superheros today, vanished along with him and glittery script hung in the midair where he was previously standing:

BRB: GK at work.

If you'd like to leave a message, please press *72 now.

No one was quite sure what to do when Mr. Oubliette popped up several minutes later with a human baby in his arms.

"Where did you get that? Why did you take the baby?" Fu demanded.

Mr. Oubliette stared at the baby in his arms in utter surprise, like he wasn't sure why he'd taken it. "Um, I'm—not sure—" he squinted at the child.

"I think this calls for a lively song and dance number," he added jovially, "This little chap looks like he'd be fun to throw up in the air, don't you think?"

He began singing and without explanation, strains of an 80's rock hit mysteriously struck up out of nowhere in accompaniment.

"And so my Baby—"

"PUT HIM BACK!" Fu said loudly, interrupting the musical number interruption. "Go put that human baby back right where you found him this INSTANT! Stealing babies, no! NOT ALLOWED!"

"But he's MINE," Mr. Oubliette whined, then looked puzzled. "I think? What's said is said—except I don't know *what was said actually* but whatever it was, it enabled me to take the child and have thirteen hours to . . . to . . . I don't know? Change its diaper into something chic, perhaps?"

"Go—put—the—child—*back*!!" Fu hissed, "Or tomorrow, we'll make you a circus clown, in oversized, striped pants and a red nose."

Mr. Oubliette instantly paled like he was struck across the face. "I should make you Prince of the Land of Stench for this," he huffed but disappeared with the baby and reappeared later empty-handed, much to everyone's relief. He sidled over to Anne who was still regaling anyone who would listen with *Hubert Pfiffer!* stories.

"—Hubert Pfiffer! Boy Wizard! *scratched his chin, "My good friend Robin Hood, aren't those machine guns a bit heavy for your merry men to carry through Sherwood? I think a bow and arrows might travel better, and I could teach you how to shoot. I'm rather good at that you know—"*

"Well hello, Sarah! We meet again," Mr. Oubliette interrupted, leering at Anne. Anne looked him over like he was something stuck to her shoe.

"My name is STILL Anne, not Sarah! RBTL, okay? Is there something WRONG with you, like SRSLY?" she huffed.

"If you love me, fear me and do as I say, then I will be your slave," Mr. Oubliette told Anne, very earnestly.

Anne just stared at him. She didn't appear to know what to do with that.

"Try not to pay him too much attention," Biffy suggested. "We don't."

"Well hello SARAH, and how are you enjoying my—" Mr. Oubliette began, waggling his eyebrows. Biffy shook his head.

"For the last time, I'm a "dude", dude."

"So it's a *piece of cake* is it—?"

Biffy walked away. There was no reasoning with Mr. Oubliette when he was like this.

Fu tried to concentrate. "Well, we need to reach the werewolf forest in Transylvania. We're looking to recruit some of them in our fight against the vampires—"

"A war is brewing?" Verethraghna looked interested. "Excellent! It's just the thing to win back my reputation! Achieving a great victory on the battlefield will surely win me some new worshippers, especially against such incredible odds."

He eyed the motley crew around him and mumbled, "Scratch that. *Unbelievable* odds! Ha, and they still talk about Troy and that stupid horse now!"

Fu sighed. "Yeah, sure. Why not? Come on then—um, V-Velociraptor?!"

"Verethraghna!"

"Sure, him too."

Revenge of the Neverlands

I t was a heavy mail day on the good ship "The Pirate Way". And it usually *was*!

Unlike government due process in the Human World, in Never-Never-Land the postal service was extremely efficient. Mainly because if Prime Minister Pan and his entourage of Lost Boys didn't get their bi-monthly candy delivery to the "Secret Hideout", all Hell broke loose across the island. If you thought the boys were dreadful on a sugar high, you should see what happens without one!

Due to a surplus of natural magic in the atmosphere, Neverland Post was actually *so efficient* that packages were often delivered *before* one pressed the "Order" button, sometimes even if the "Order" button wasn't pressed at all because the person doing the ordering had changed their mind.

A certain ice cream truck driver in Sheboygan could never explain how his candy supply was mysteriously depleted bi-monthly. Changing drivers didn't help, nor did changing trucks. Soon after, a Hawaiian shaved ice company started experiencing the same mysterious stock depletion with their snow-cone flavors, especially blue raspberry.

Still, life was swell for Hook and his pirate mates ever since they mastered online identity fraud and the concept of "0 Liability" credit cards but recently, Mr. Smee had got ahold of an oil sheik's No-Limit Platinum Card and went to town on e-Buy with it.

Under his well-financed and well-maintained e-Buy identity (mister smee will buy it, 5,215,622 positive feedback), he kept ordering tons of used merchandise online to be delivered to the pirate ship. True, their pirate swag coffers were full to the point of bursting but the ship had sunk 3 feet over the past week just from the empty postal boxes.

Captain James Hook surveyed the staggering stack of boxes that had come in the morning post and popped an earbud from his iPirateMp3sPlayer out of his ear to bellow, "MISTER SMEE!"

"Aye-aye Cap'n," Smee popped his head out and looked delighted when he saw the stack of boxes. "Oh goodie! Are any of them for me, Cap'n!"

Hook compressed his lips together. "They ALL seem to be addressed to yer, Mr. Smee!"

"Oh how lovely! I'm so surprised! I really wasn't expecting anything!" Smee clapped his hands and rushed over to survey the lot. Hook glared.

"Mr. Smee, how many times must I tell yer, we're pirates! PIRATES! We STEAL our pirate property; we do not ORDER IT ONLINE and PAY FER IT, all LEGAL-like! QUIT YER PAYIN, I've tole yer!"

"Aye-aye Cap'n," Smee said obediently. "It's just that, if you don't pay, you get a bad feedback score and my score is perfect—"

"Mr. Smee, we dinna care if our feedback score in't perfect. We're PIRATES!"

"Aye-aye Cap'n," Smee saluted then nodded at his music player. "New Shuffle Mix, Cap'n?"

"Aye, Smee," Hook nodded. "I downloaded new music off iPirateTunes fer me mornin' wakeup routine. Ye ken I'm not meself without a cuppa from that wee Cappuccino machine yer ordered last week, some yoga and me mornin' tunes."

"But you downloaded the music legally, Cap'n?"

"Carse I dint!" Hook slapped his forehead, "HOW MANY TIMES must I TELL YER, MISTER SMEE! We're PIRATES! PIRATES! We NIVER PAY fer MUSIC, MOVIES, GAMING or BANDWIDTH!"

"Sorry Cap'n, but the RIAA says—"

"We don't niver care, we're PIRATES, MR. SMEE! WE HOTLINK ALL OUR IMAGES, DON'T WE MR. SMEE?"

"Aye, Cap'n!"

"AND WE NIVER PAY FER OUR WIFI, DO WE MISTER SMEE? WE SAIL AROUND NIVERLAND TO EVERY FREE HOTSPOT AND USE THEIRS, DON'T WE MISTER SMEE?"

"Aye, Cap'n!"

"AND WE ONLY HACK THE NEWEST VIDEO GAMES, DON'T WE MISTER SMEE? WE NIVER PAY FOR THEM ON THE SHELF, DO WE, MR. SMEE?"

"Er, aye Cap'n. Or—nay Cap'n—I can't remember," Smee scratched his head. Hook glared harder.

"What do we niver do, MISTER SMEE?"

"Er, pay, Cap'n?"

"Unless—" Hook prompted. Smee scratched his head again.

"—unless it's with someone else's credit card, Cap'n?"

"Right. Now quit yer payin afore I make yer walk the plank!" Hook huffed. Smee saluted again.

"Aye, Cap'n. But you'd be proud o' me, Cap'n. At the online check-out, when I was payin with the credit card t'werent mine, it said, "Do you want to make a donation to Prime Minister Pan's Reelection Campaign?" and I clicked "no" Cap'n. Just like that. I mean, I could donate any amount it said but I donated NO AMOUNT, Cap'n! That t'was right, wern't it, Cap'n?"

Hook was eyeing Smee like the latter were a cockroach. "Smee?"

"Aye, Cap'n?"

"Yer a real idjit, Smee."

"Aye-aye, Cap'n."

Hook turned back to survey the stack of boxes, grumbling, "ifen yer bought another Julianne Fry

Maker, Smee, I'll make yer walk the plank anyhow! It in't like we have anywhere to plug it in on the ship, I tole yer, Mister Smee—"

"Aye Cap'n," Smee replied diligently and started digging into the boxes. "Oh look, Cap'n, a box came from Fairyland!"

"Tain't like we got nae potatoes on the ship niver," Hook grumbled. "Just hardtack and five boxes of sweets we dun stole from the Lost Boys."

"Aye, Cap'n." Smee began shaking the box. "Whatdyja spose is inside?"

"QUIT SHAKIN THE BOX, SMEE!" Hook bellowed. "Jist open it!"

Smee slit open the packing tape. "Ooooohhhh, a lot of writing," he murmured, studying the large pile of multi-page sonnets hopefully enclosed by the Chief Fairy Scribe, who'd been overjoyed to know his work was so well received by Smee and the other pirates.

"We were runnin' short on toilet paper," Hook nodded his approval. "Them letters look nice and crinkly soft so that's one problem solved. What's the fat one on top there?"

Smee picked up the pink, S.W.A.L.K. envelope. "Dunno Cap'n, but I like the stickers. Smells like," he scratched one and sniffed deeply, "Petunias, Cap'n."

"Give it here!" Hook snatched the envelope away and studied the curly fairy script for several long minutes, his lips moving with each word.

"Sez here that King Clarion is beggin us to release his sweet lass Tinker-Belle and nae to do any harm to her," he frowned.

"Smee? Is we holdin Tinker-Belle fer ransom fer some of the fairies duster "crackle" stuff?"

"Nay, Cap'n."

"Yer sure, are ye? Didjya check in our ransom bin, make sure we havin't tossed her in there with some other victims by mistake."

"Aye, Cap'n. We kin't kidnap Tinker-Belle. She tain't met our ransom victim height requirement."

Hook paused. "What?"

Smee held up a large sign with a fat, red arrow at about waist-height to a man. Above the arrow, the sign was marked: **YOU MUST BE AT LEAST THIS TALL TO BE TERRORIZED, CAPTURED, HELD FOR RANSOM, TORTURED FOR INFORMATION, PILLAGED OR RAVAGED BY CAPTAIN HOOK. (Sorry, no children allowed under the age of Peter Pan.)**

"See, Tinker-Belle is so small she dun meet the minimum height requirement to be a victim, Cap'n. We tain't allowed to savage or torrent her, by law."

Hook scratched his chin. "This is some legal bit, in't it? Now Smee, we're pirates! I dun tole yer we don't obey the law—"

"Aye Cap'n, but the Cruelty to Minors activists got involved and they were threatenin' to send

LAWYERS after us, Cap'n, ifen we don't stop torturing fairies and kids."

"O-h." Hook froze. That was the key word: "Lawyers". It struck sheer terror, even in his cold, black pirate heart.

Never-Never-Land was the last great untamed frontier of the Wild, Wild West; a primal land without need for laws or government oversight. The factions ran the land, and everyone had their piece, from the Lost Boys to the woodland fairies, to the indians and the pirates and everyone in-between.

Like a perfectly balanced eco-system, the various factions kept any one group from dominating the territory. Instead they kept each other in balance and in check.

The one true threat to Neverland was that law and order might come and instill chaos in that perfect world free from civilization. There might be bills, there might be healthcare plans, there might be taxes, there might be 401K—there might even be (oh no!) proper schooling and social services forcing domestic homes on Peter and the Lost Boys!

But the worst of all, the one that struck fear into the hearts of every free citizen of Neverland—there might be a justice system with (gasp!) actual, real lawyers! Who'd been to law school!

No more blasting your enemies with the ships cannons, no sir! Instead, lawsuits would be the future penalty of Neverland!

Pan would be filing a restraining order against Hook for "Unlawful assault against a minor" while the fairies were prosecuting Pan for "Flying without a proper flight permit or being cleared by air traffic control" and "Unlawful use of public Neverland flightways".

Meanwhile Hook would be suing the Indians for "Paddling their canoes along his ship's boundary line" while the Indians were suing the Mermaids for "Using their bathing cove unlawfully" and the Mermaids were suing the Crocodile for "Unlawful harassment by eating them periodically" while the Crocodile was countersuing Hook for "Not letting him finish dinner before taking his favorite main course off the menu".

Yes, lawyers spelled the end of the great wild lawless country that was Never-Never-Land. So even Captain James Hook himself backed down when it came to the dreaded L-word.

"Fine," he grumbled. "We can't kilt tiny fairies nor kids? How am I s'posed to have any fun?" He thought it over. "But I can BLAST THEM OUT OF THE SKY with me ships cannons at long range, eh Smee—"

"Nay, Cap'n. Read the fine print." Smee pointed to the tiny line of print on the sign which read: **PS: You must also be THIS TALL to be shot by Captain Hook's pirate ship cannons and blown to smithereens. Violators will be prosecuted.**

"Damn! Those lawyers think of everything, dun they, Mr. Smee?"

"Aye, Cap'n. And they made us post signs all around the ship: "Fer yer safety, please keep yer hands and arms inside the ship and yer feet on the plank at all times. Thank ye."

"Damn lawyers," Hook grumbled again. "I dun spose Pan meets the height requirement for me tae gut him and slit his throat with me hook?"

"Well, Cap'n, they say Pan's been flying over to the Human World so much he shot up near a quarter o' an inch o'er the summer. So maybe he does now, we'll have to re-measure him the next time you two duel again."

"Ah," Hook scratched his chin, "Well I guess we dun have Tinker-Belle fer ransom. Must be somebody else. Mebbe its them blasted Redskins what has her, eh?"

"Shall we sail to Fairyland and tell King Clarion there's been a mistake, Cap'n?"

"FAIRYLAND!" Hook roared, "NAY, MISTER SMEE! Niver settin' down boot on Fairyland shores again, I tole yer that! Dun ye remember the last time we sailed there jist to do some innocent pillaging and ravaging?"

"Aye, Cap'n."

"The beauty parlor, Smee! They chained me down, Smee! For 6 HOURS, Smee!"

"Aye, Cap'n."

"Cut off all me beautiful dreadlocks, Mr. Smee and covered me beautiful clothes with perfoom! I think they mighta WASHED me beautiful Captain's hat—in perfoomy SOAP, Smee! Niver could get the right smell back into it! It was ruint, my favorite hat! Ruint, I tole yer!"

"Aye, Cap'n!"

"Made me shave, lost me beautiful matted beard, and then they gelled and moussed me hair, Smee! They spiked it! I looked like a member of a BOY BAND, Smee!"

"Aye, Cap'n."

"And—the—MANNYCURE," Hook shut his eyes and shuddered, "I STILL HAVE NIGHTMARES, MISTER SMEEEEEE!"

"Sorry, Cap'n."

"Such cruelty I niver done saw, and I'm a black-hearted scallywag! All fer a few chests of gold coins, and I tole um I'd give those back if they stopped pluckin' on me eyebrows—oh, Mister Smee, you done niver known torture 'til someone done tole yer eyebrows are too bushy and plucked them. That's cruelty with tweezers, that is!"

"Sorry, Cap'n."

"Send word to Clarion that we pirates dun *niver took her*, NIVER!, and check with Pan that she's safe. Else them fairies might come HERE and bring," Hook shuddered deeply at the horrifying notion, "the PEDDYCURE set this time!!"

"Aye-aye, Cap'n. I'll get on it right away!"

"Mr. Smee," Hook changed the subject as he poked through the second box, "Did yer order a wee ginger house online? Cuz there's one here in this box."

"Nay Cap'n," Smee looked innocent. "Just a chest of Aztec gold coins with certification of *GEN-U-WINE ETHNICITY* and real Aztec curse included with purchase, guaranteed to turn you into an immortal ghost pirate "ifen yer remove but one piece of gold" from the chest."

He scrutinized the tiny gingerbread house suspiciously. "Maybe that's the "surprise free gift included with purchase"?"

They both stared at the tiny baked confection and Hook poked it slightly with his silver hook. The prerecorded message began to play:

"Hello, this is the magic travelling gingerbread house of the Sli—um, I mean the Wicked Witch. Set it down next to your jail cells, don't look inside and don't pay any attention if it flies away. I can't come to the door right now; I'm busy baking up some nice crispy human children for dinner. Carry on with your pirate business and do have a nice day."

Hook looked perplexed, "Mr. Smee, did yer order a magic travelling ginger house wit' a wicked witch inside who bakes and eats children online?"

"Don't think I did, Cap'n. But there were a lot of special offer pop-ups that I needed take advantage of 'cuz they said: Last Chance To Buy!!"

Hook frowned. "I dint rightly know witches could travel around in their wee ginger houses, or that they was so small. Caurse I guess they have to be verra small for the children to fit inside, hmm?"

"Pr'ly so, Cap'n."

"Right then," Hook eyed the tiny house, "The only children round these parts are them Lost Boys. Guess she could be cooking and eating one as we speak, hmm?

"Or eating Pan himself, Cap'n."

Hook beamed. "Well then, everything seems to be in order! Carry on, Mr. Smee and set this wee ginger house down in our jail cells until that loverly witch is done eating all the dreadful children she wants to." He started poking through the other boxes.

"What's this crate with the hole in it, Smee? It's empty but there's teeth marks all over it."

"Oh goodie, my small, smuggled pet crocodile came!"

"SMEE—"

"I thought we could train him and—"

"MISTER SMEEEE!"

The pirates watching television on their little mini set on deck groaned as the news cut in:

We interrupt this program to bring you a special news bulletin. Transylvanian officials have warned all residents to be on high alert:

A dangerous, hand-eating crocodile was stolen earlier today from captivity and smuggled out of the country. Local officials lost track of the perpetrators after they crossed the last star to the right and headed straight on 'til morning.

Be advised: the crocodile is green, small, about 5 feet in diameter, notorious for escaping custody and likes to eat hands.

If you or your loved ones encounter this dangerous crocodile, remove all hands from the premises IMMEDIATELY and contact the Transylvanian authorities at 1-888-ARG-IT-ATE-MY-HAND!

Smee surveyed the crate in dismay. "Now where do you spose my smuggled crocodile went—oh look Cap'n, he likes yer other hand—my, what a jaw span he has!"

"MISSSSSSSSSSTERRRRRRRRRR SMEEEEEEEEEEEEEE!!"

He is Well-Tailored!

The "Transylvanian National Werewolf Forest, Park and Game Preserve" was rather like one might expect, dark, dense with trees and greenery, full of intimidating wildlife sounds from deep in the forest and the occasional wolf howl as if to assure them they'd reached the right place.

But, in case there was any lingering doubt, the vampires had erected a helpful sign for visitors:

Welcome to the **Transylvanian National Werewolf Forest, Park and Game Preserve**. *We hope you enjoy your visit with us today!*

You are presently **HERE** → *please refer to the guideposts throughout the forest to find the walking trails and public rest areas. Please don't stray from the marked trails into the forest or you may be mauled by a werewolf (lol!). Explore only at your own risk.*

Please remember the werewolves are an endangered species protected under the Transylvania Ecological Society Endangered Species Act (article 1037.b), therefore all weapons containing silver and flash photography containing silver emulsion are strictly prohibited. Outside food and drink is likewise prohibited outside of the camping and picnic area.

UNDER NO CIRCUMSTANCES SHOULD YOU OFFER FOOD TO A WEREWOLF!!
DO NOT FEED THE WERES!!

FEES: Park Admission: FREE
Vehicle Parking Fee: 3$ GTR
(Genuine Transylvanian Rubles)
Park Shuttle Ride: 15$ GTR
Werewolf Repellent (14 oz. can, non-toxic):
2$ GTR

Gifts and souvenirs may be purchased at the TNWF Gift Shoppe on your way out. **If any member of your party is mauled or eaten by a werewolf, please visit or alert (via the red phone on the guideposts) the "Safe Extraction of a Human Meal/Visitor Medical Center" immediately!**

Thanks for visiting the park today! Don't forget to "like" us on our Majick-Book page!
Follow us @ #i heart werewolf maulings lol!

As it turned out, they didn't have to stray very far into the forest to find a werewolf. *He* found *them*, actually.

Kent Clark (no relation) was nearly knocked over when he was unexpectedly and very energetically body-tackled by a hulking, wriggling, extremely-hairy figure. It was, upon examination, human.

Upon further examination, maybe half-human but mostly smelly dog tongue that was far longer than a person's could possibly be and very pink, laving its way past frighteningly large jaws and fangs, up and down Kent's bare face. His rear end hadn't stopped wagging back and forth since he laid eyes on Kent as if it expected to find a tail there. His ears were too pointed also, covered with small tufts of hair and they kept pricking up to the slightest sound.

"Oh, I've been WAITING and WAITING for you TO COME, Master," he said, all bright, cheerful and energetic, lovingly rubbing his head against Kent's hand as if wanting to be petted.

He was at least male, that much was clear, and young, easily in his late teens-to-early twenties, handsome and very tan. This was a creature that lived for the great outdoors and got plenty of natural exercise. He had more boundless, hyper energy than several toddlers put together.

The do—um, man lapped at Kent's face again, "My name is Tailor Wear of the UnderWear Werewolves Clan, and I HAVE JUST MET YOU but I LOVE YOU! OMG, you are the best master EVER, will you keep me, huh, huh, huh? My name is Tailor

Wear and I am a WEREWOLF and I love you, let us be BEST FRIENDS FOREVER—my name is—VAMPIRE!"

Suddenly his hairy ears pricked up again and his whole body went stiff, hair standing on end all over his head and even poking through his clothing as he sniffed at the air frantically, searching for the faint scent of vampire decay. Finally he relaxed, every coiled muscle that was ready to spring into immediate action slowly unwound and his fur—er, his hair settled.

"—I HATE VAMPIRES, I REALLY REALLY HATE VAMPIRES, they are so MEAN to us and don't like to PLAY BALL!"

"So, my name is Tailor Wear and I LOVE YOU, did I mention that?! I want to play with YOU and the BALL, the BALL, the BALL! Throw it, throw it, THROW THE BALL FOR MEEEE! I want to play, play, PLLLAAAYYY!" He shook his butt from side to side as hard as he could happily.

Obligingly, Kent Clark (no relation) tossed the ball and Tailor was off after it like a shot. It was hilarious watching him trying to lope on all fours when his arms weren't near as long as his legs. It was equally funny to see him try and catch the ball in his mouth.

He loped back with the ball proudly and dropped it at his Ma—um, at Kent's feet.

"Weren't you wearing a shirt just a minute ago?" Kent said, confused. Tailor nodded, tongue lolling out the side of his mouth.

"Yes Master. That happens a lot. I am always losing my human shirt master, because it is in my DNA—VAMPIRE!" While Tailor cocked his head up, sniffing out the possible vampire, everyone else just stared at his bare chest and chiseled abs, every muscle gleaming like it was freshly oiled.

"SRSLY, I think they got it wrong," Anne murmured, "I think it should be called woman's best friend, not man's." She smoothed back her shiny blond curls, adjusted her tiara and smiled becomingly. Tailor lolled his pink tongue out at her and scratched himself.

"Hey," Kent Clark (no relation) objected. "You, sit!" he ordered Tailor. Tailor sank obediently to his haunches.

"You should think this one over," he directed to Anne, "I mean, what's it going to do to your professional princess career if you're mommy to a litter of UnderWear cubs—" he paused, then tacked on "—SRSLY, IKR?"

"SRSLY? I hadn't thought of that. OMG, IDEK— it's like you speak my LANGUAGE," Anne gasped, staring at him in wonder. Then she removed her tiara and tapped his shoulder with it. "Ten points awarded to you from *Hubert Pfiffer! Boy Wizard!* for thinking of it!" she pronounced grandly.

"How magnanimous of *Hubert Pfiffer*," Kent Clark (no relation) grumbled. He was having some decidedly un-superheroic thoughts involving *Hubert Pfiffer* meeting a tragic end in a garbage disposal.

"*Boy Wizard*," Anne tacked on helpfully. Kent glared. A garbage disposal wasn't painful enough. There needed to be an angry rhinoceros involved somewhere.

Although that was given the fact that *Hubert Pfiffer! Boy Wizard!* would probably turn it into a magical unicorn that pooped colored candies and adopt it. Mmm, taste the rainbow.

"We still need to find the werewolf clan, wherever they are," Fu inserted then, looking at Kent. "We need to talk to them about helping us take on the vampires."

"Ooooohhhhhhh-memememeMEME-pickMEEEEEE," Tailor leapt up and begged by folding his hands in front of him like paws, wagging his butt frantically. "I can FIND the other werewolves for you, Master, because I can SMELL THEM OUT! I'm such a GOOD DOGGIE and a GREAT TRACKER! Did I mention that, huh, huh, huh?"

"Yes," Kent Clark smiled encouragingly, "What a good boy, Tailor." He patted Tailor on the head, which admittedly took some doing as the lanky werewolf was nearly as tall as he was.

Tailor beamed and sank back on his haunches, panting from the raw exertion of doing so much thinking and doting on his new master and behaving like a GOOD BOY all at the same time.

"Okay follow memememeMEME," he begged, paws—uh, hands folded in front of him. "Please Master come, come, COME, do not SIT DOWN unless you want to, Master but I am going to find WEREWOLVES now like a GOOD BOY! Come on, come on, COME ON!"

He loped off a few paces then loped back, circling around Kent's legs happily. "I LOVE YOU SO MUCH, Master," he insisted, "Can I lick your face again please, can I, can I, CAN I?"

"Yes, after you find the werewolves you can," Kent Clark (no relation) said kindly. Tailor beamed and wagged his butt harder.

"Oh I will, I will, I WILL do that, Master, I SO MUCH WILL FIND the WEREWOLVES because I am a GREAT TRACKER, and I CAN SMELL THEM, did I mention this? Follow me, Master, follow, follow, FOLLOW!"

He loped off again and the others tailed him deeper into the forest, with Tailor loping ahead as best he could on two arms and legs, then circling back around so he wouldn't lose the others.

Presently they came to big clearing where a large rock sat in the center. It appeared to be a gathering place for the werewolves. In fact, a few werewolves were lounging about in various forms of . . . perhaps the best word to use is, "natural undress". You'd never seen so much fur in one place in all your life.

They straightened up in a hurry though when Tailor led the others in, fur standing on end and as one, they emitted a low, predatory, rumbling growl.

"Strangers? At the Summit?" one werewolf barked loudly, the words sharp and staccato. "Strangers are not allowed HERE, Tailor of UnderWear."

"You shall be placed in the Territory Well-Marked in Yellow for this," another werewolf snapped its jaws at them.

Tailor immediately dropped to his haunches and begged. "NonononoNONO, I have only brought my new MASTER, who is GOOD and KIND! I LOVE HIM and you will love him too because he is GOOD and KIND! Do not put me in the Yellow Territory! I do NOT LIKE the Yellow Territory! It SMELLS greatly of YELLOW!"

"Indeed, my cub?" Another bark cut through the silence and it was the one all other werewolves listened to.

"Master, that is my father," Tailor said in a hushed voice. "My alpha wolf, Boxer Wear, the leader of the UnderWear Werewolf Clan." He begged solemnly and the older wolf just looked at him.

"Explain, cub. Why have you brought strangers here, who smell of Other Territory and—" the older werewolf sniffed the air disapprovingly, "—and VAMPIRES?"

Immediately the clan shot to their feet, and several werewolves shot to their hands as well, barking madly and excitedly. "Where? Where are VAMPIRES? Show us the VAMPIRES! We will rip them apart!"

Tailor barked along, excited. "Grrrrr, I HATE VAMPIRES! They are MEAN and do not PLAY BALL! Grrrrr!"

"QUIET!" Boxer the Alpha Wolf barked and every werewolf sank back down on his haunches, hushed. "We will let my young cub Tailor's new Master, who is GOOD and KIND, speak to us now!"

"Speak and tell us why you have come here, Master, and if you have brought along BISCUITS for GOOD DOGGIES?"

This met with an immediate howl of approval from the entire werewolf clan. If Kent Clark (no relation and also the new GOOD and KIND Master of Tailor) had brought along a box of doggie biscuits with him, he was indeed going to be very popular!

Just as the vampire who erected the warning about not feeding the werewolves would be very disassembled if, in fact, any of the werewolves could read what it said.

As it was, the guidepost signs erected throughout the werewolf forest were inspected and determined to smell of VAMPIRE but not FOOD nor BISCUITS and abandoned once they were Well-Marked in Territorial Yellow. Various werewolves had tried knocking them over but the wicked splinters in their tender paw-pads caused them to abandon that plan. The signposts were ignored by the werewolves after that, chalked up to the usual vampire mischief.

Vampires were always playing mean jokes on poor nice doggies that the werewolves themselves did not understand! That was why VAMPIRES were MEAN and BAD!

"Well," Kent shared a raised-eyebrows look with Fu while clearing his throat to speak up. It read something like: "This is my ball field. Now I know how this will work."

"The vampires are behaving like bad boys indeed! They need to be swatted with a rolled newspaper," Kent sounded solemn.

A menacing growl rose in several werewolf throats. YES! They agreed with Kent Clark (no relation), the Master of Tailor who was GOOD and KIND. VAMPIRES were very often BAD BOYS who Marked Territory In Places They Should Not! They needed Many Swattings and Noses Rubbed in the Bad Markings—Look, What You Have Done, Bad Boy!! This was very true!

"—they're working with the VERY BAD zombies and both want to harm many human masters, who are GOOD and KIND," Kent tacked on, thinking quickly, "And many fairies too, who are also GOOD and KIND."

The growl rose in intensity and vibration. Was this true? Were the bad VAMPIRES going to harm GOOD and KIND Masters? This was troubling news indeed!

"So, we'd like your help to fight the vampires on this," Kent Clark finished, and added in afterthought, "And I'm sure once the bad VAMPIRES are stopped, we can find you all some biscuits and play a game of catch together in the backyard."

The werewolves were very excited by this! Oh, what a GOOD and KIND Master this was, lucky Tailor! He could get them biscuits and he liked to PLAY BALL!

Almost immediately there was an outpouring of begging from many throats, Tailor was the loudest, "Oh pickmepickmepickmepickME, MASTER PICK MEmememeMEME! I will go fight the BAD VAMPIRES for you!"

There were also many loud, fervent declarations of instantaneous but eternal devotion for Kent Clark which, given the enormous size and shape of some of these werewolves, could only be looked at as alarming.

"QUIET!" Boxer ordered and again, the werewolves sank to their haunches in utter silence. "The Clan will all help the GOOD and KIND Master of Tailor our cub. We will Listen now with our Inside

Bark Voice while GOOD and KIND Master tells us what he wants us to do."

While Kent Clark (no relation) and Fu-Belle made arrangements for how the werewolves could assist in backing the war militia of the fairies while their party went on ahead to reason with King Armando (save for Tailor who refused to be torn from his new Master's side so they decided to allow him to accompany them).

Anne Genue wandered off by herself to explore, bored by the discussion of war. She hadn't gone but a few steps before spotting an oddly shaped tree and, being female, felt the need to impart this observation verbally, if only to herself.

"Hey look, Anne Genue! That tree looks more like a wardrobe growing in the forest, doesn't it?" she observed aloud, "There's even a door in it, see? I wonder if it will open."

She tugged on the door handle and then came face to face with . . .

"A lamp post? In the middle of a snowy forest— wha—?" She broke off as a faun ambled up on his hind legs, carrying parcels and wearing a scarf.

"Are you perchance a Daughter of Eve?" the faun gasped aloud, "A—*human*?"

"Am I—? Of course I'm human! Is there something wrong with you?"

The faun clapped his hands in joy. "You're from another world, aren't you? You must have come to save us from the witch."

"Just a lame witch? Not a dark lord whose name cannot be mentioned?" Anne frowned deeply.

"Yes, the witch, she who makes always winter and never—"

BAM! Anne slammed the door of the wardrobe shut as hard as she could on the mysterious faun and stomped indignantly away.

"Stupid portals to magical worlds," she grumbled. "They pop up everywhere! AYFKM? Why can't I find the one that leads to the invisible platform for wizard's school?! Hashtag-OMG-LOL!! Like that's asking too much?"

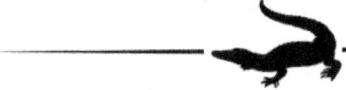

a page ran into the throne room of the Fairy King and bowed, "Unidentified flying gingerbread-house incoming, sir. It's hovering above the main city now, minutes from landing."

King Clarion beamed. "Ah, marvelous! Ding-Aling," he called to his wife, "Tinker-Belle has finally come home! Let us welcome her with open arms, my love."

He then nodded to the page, "Bring the gingerbread house in here when it lands and we'll open it."

It took four fairy guards to heft the gingerbread house into the castle for, though diminutive to a full-grown human, it was the perfect size for a fairy to climb inside. But how it was levitating above ground level helped them move it without harm, or use of a garden hose. They directed it to the middle of the throne room and it landed safely.

But, much to the fairies surprise when they opened it, they found inside not Tinker-Belle at all but the small, smuggled hand-eating crocodile who had slipped inside the gingerbread house while Hook and Smee weren't looking and sent the homing house flying back to Fairyland with the crocodile as its passenger. The small crocodile studied the fairies now with scaly, beady suspicious eyes, wondering how many hands it could get away from them before they caged it.

"Oh—My—*Manicure*!" Clarion gasped, horrified. "Ding-Aling, it's WORSE than we thought! Look, just LOOK at what that foreign dreadful land of Never did to our beloved Tinker-Belle. Look at her SKIN— and her lovely button nose, and her TEETH," he waved a hand over the scaly crocodile body and shuddered, "Darling, where do we even *begin* with this—*disaster*?!"

Ding-Aling likewise looked horrified. "Oh Clarion! I just cannot believe it! If only we'd known!"

"Her skin actually turned green with scales—do you suppose it's some kind of Neverland fungi staining? We'll need milk baths and—and the heaviest moisturizer we have, gobs and gobs of it. Bring the pumice stone, hurry!"

"I don't know if it'll be enough," Clarion murmured as the crocodile paced the room predatorily, "She's walking on all fours now, and that jaw—what do you suppose she has been eating over there to transform her jaw like that? She's become feral, living off the wilderness, my love! Our beautiful girl has even lost all of her lovely golden hair!"

"Evolutionary, survival of the fittest in those wilderness lands, I suppose," Ding-Aling winced. "Oh darling, do you suppose we can civilize her again, back into society? I just can't bear to send her back there, not after all this."

"I don't know, my dew-drop," Clarion shook his head solemnly, "I'm not even sure magic itself is strong enough to undo the horror of what has happened here—but we can most certainly try."

"Oh Clarion," Ding-Aling wept, "If only we'd never let her run off with that dreadful boy! But she seemed so happy with him and I never imagined—I never even dreamt—" she wept harder.

"There-there, my precious," Clarion soothed, "We'll fix this somehow. Anyway," he searched for a bright note, "Tinker-Belle always did favor wearing green. I think her new skin tone looks very handsome on her, personally."

"She even lost her wwwinnnngggs," Ding-Aling still sobbed, "Our poooorrrr beauuuuutifullll giiirrrlll!"

"But," King Clarion searched in vain for another ray of sunshine, "What a tail she's grown, huh? You couldn't ask for a more proud or magnificent tail than hers, I'm sure. Look at the size of it!"

Ding Aling only sobbed harder. The crocodile meanwhile sidled over to one of the fairy guards and dropped his jaw open wide.

"My goodness," Clarion murmured, "What a jaw-span she has—*oh dear!* I guess there isn't much food to be had in Neverland so she must be used to eating whatever is close by—but we can't have her doing THAT at dinner parties, now can we?"

His tone turned stern, "TINKER-BELLE: that is a no-no! You give that nice guard his hand back right now! Right this INSTANT! Don't make me tell you again, young lady!"

Surprise: Vampire Invasion!

TRANSMISSION TO THE GALACTIC COUNCIL
EXTREMELY URGENT
FROM: The Starship "Enter&YouCouldWinAPrize"
SPACE BLEEM DATE: 2001021002-sp.bl.star.yr.

BEGIN TRANSMISSION ...

WARNING!!! STRONG ADVISORY!!! Landing in Transylvania, PLANET EARTH, DO NOT!!!!! Planet EARTH, and Earth Solar System, Quarantined by Council from UFO Passage—IT MUST BE!!!!! ERHM!!!!!!

Our last mission, to scout/schedule possible future invasion on Planet Earth—*not good*, it went! Human Borders under Zombie Jurisdiction; therefore rerouted coordinates to Transylvania, we did! Vampire extraction from Transylvania successful!

But, once on board ship, BIG SURPRISE vampires were . . . *(static interference from deep space)* . . . US, they did, over and over and *OVER AND* . . . *(more static)* . . . tentacles flying against the walls, then vampire took the MK12 ProbeMaster-3000 . . . *(static)* . . . so sticky, poor Vyxblkzkal, erhm! Him, they grabbed and . . . *(static)* . . . heard him begging, "please, for the Love of God stop, no more" . . . *(static)* . . . wanted to touch it, NOBODY did . . . *(static)* . . . searched everywhere we have, but Ghulooongauhagh not found still, very worried we are, especially when those claw marks on ceiling we saw . . . *(static)* . . . talk about this in public, **WE WILL NOT!!!!**

MARK PLANET EARTH AS "NO INVASION ZONE" AND *TOUCH NOT VAMPIRES*, THE COUNCIL MUST!!!!! OR—"INVADED" YOUR BODY WILL BE!! ERHM!!!

... END TRANSMISSION

The Not-Related Family Reunion (of No Relations)

They were almost there, or at least, that's what Fu-Belle kept telling Mr. Oubliette each time he whined, "Are we there yet?" and Fu wouldn't let him slow-dance to a masquerade ballad about the "world falling down" to cheer him up. The hairy, strange little "Ettes" weren't around to distract Mr. Oubliette either. They'd been underfoot so much that Fu convinced Mr. Oubliette it was much safer for them to be sent home (wherever that might be) than eaten alive by vampires.

Certainly the mountain that housed Armando's castle looked close by, terribly huge, black, barren and imposing across the skyline, leaving our band of misfits worried less about reaching the mountain itself and more about how they were going to tackle the perilous and death-defying climb once they got there. Even a consommé mountain climber would take one look and declare it a deathtrap, pack up his gear and head home, after first stopping to barricade the entire structure with yellow crime scene tape.

First they reached the village at the foot of the mountain where, by reputation, the residents were supposed to be utterly terrified, locked and hiding in their ridiculously-cute and insanely fretworked little gingerbread houses.

To their surprise, the town was decked out in colorful lanterns and streamers, a brass band and a parade passing slowly through the town square as they arrived. The ginormous balloon of a vampire being led through as the grand finale was probably supposed to represent King Armando but at its size, it was anyone's guess. A little sign being carried in front of the balloon handlers announced the giant balloon was "sponsored in part by Majick-Book".

A bright banner hung between two adorable triple-decker fretworked houses announced it was: *"The 17th Annual (No Relations) Not-Related Family Reunion of People Who Are By No Means Related To Each Other Or Anyone Else"*.

"NW! How cool is that! Aren't you a (no relation) too?" Anne turned to Kent Clark (no relation) excitedly.

"Yeah, but I had *no idea* we had annual reunions for folks we aren't related to," Kent Clark said, shocked. "Boy, I can't wait to meet all my non-family members who aren't related to me or each other!

Wait 'til my non-related adoptive parents hear about this!"

"Oh, are you also a (no relation)?" a tall man wearing a sand-colored robe and utility belt stopped and looked at Kent Clark (no relation) inquiringly. Kent Clark (no relation for sure) nodded.

"Indeed I am! I'm as not related to you as it gets, man!"

"Steller!" the man clapped him on the back in warm, fraternal, non-brotherhood, "Glad to meet you! I'm WalkerSky Luke (no relation)! I'm also NOT a Knight-Jed-Eye (no relation). So which family are you not related to?"

"I'm Kent Clark (no relation)," Kent proclaimed proudly, "And I'm delighted to not be related to you, WalkerSky! These are my friends," He made introductions around the group and WalkerSky Luke (no relation) beamed and shook hands with them and showed off his fancy Sabre-Lite (no relation either).

"Come along then! You need to come down to the reunion and meet everyone," he invited so off they all went. Once they got there, they were greeted by a barrage of (no relations) and not related introductions.

"Hey, nice to meet you, I'm Man Spider (no relation) and I can climb up bare walls and hang upside down. It makes making out with a pretty girl interesting, I can tell you."

"Hi, I'm Wayne Bruce (no relation). I'm very rich and own a variety of personalized gadgets, like the Wayne Mobile (definitely no relation)."

"Hi all, I'm Ranger Texas Walker (no relation) and I like to carry a big gun."

"I'm Cruising Tom (no relation) and I'm told I'm handsome like a god (no relation)."

Even Velociraptor—er, Verethraghna the Persian god had to admit that was true. At times, basic biology and genetics favored mortals to ridiculous proportions, apparently operating under the assumption that gods had the power to favor themselves.

"But I don't believe in gods, simply science-theology (no relation to a religion, at all)."

Fu had to hold back the wrathful Verethraghna (deeply related to the entire Persian god pantheon) before he smote Cruising Tom (no relation) unceremoniously with a lightning bolt on the spot!

"Hold it, Veranda!"

"Verethraghna!"

"I said that."

"Plus, it's my unbirthday today and I'm proud to not-celebrate at a party that isn't for me with the people I'm not related to," Cruising Tom (no relation) continued brightly, undaunted. Someone else clapped him on the shoulder.

"Perfect. You know, it's actually my unbirthday too."

"No kidding? What a coincidence," Cruising Tom (no relation) said warmly. "Man, I wish I'd known. I'd have gotten you nothing at all."

"Nothing?" Mr. Oubliette brightened immediately, "NOTHING? NOTHING, TRA-LA—"

Biffy clapped a hand over Mr. Oubliette's mouth to shush him, then winced and wiped the lipstick off on his cheer skirt.

"This is a little not—I mean, IT IS confusing," Kent Clark (no relation) murmured.

Some other (no relation) leaned over to insist, "No, you haven't *seen* "confusing" yet! There was the year they held the (no relation) Non-Family Reunion on Opposite Day. Everyone was asking, "who was not-not related to whom" then reversing it. We were levied a huge fine by the Double-Negative Abuse Coalition."

"Well hello there, Not-Sarahs," a guy with big phoofy blonde hair, conspicuous eye-makeup, tights, black boots and a flowing, glittery cape joined them, "I'm the King Gobl—" he took one look at Mr. Oubliette, then backed off. "Oh—never mind, sorry."

Mr. Oubliette stared back thoughtfully as if there was something familiar he couldn't quite put his finger on.

A short, nerdy kid in large, round glasses tapped Kent Clark on the shoulder, "hi, I'm Pfiffer Hubert—" he announced proudly.

Kent Clark (no relation) fought back the involuntary and decidedly non-heroic urge to punch him dead in the mouth.

Anne's entire face lit up with pure ecstatic joy. She began hyperventilating, "OMG-OMG-OMG-OMG-OMG-OMG-ITS-HHHHIIIIMMMMM—" she frantically fanned both her cheeks, glowing bright red. Kent took a moment to reconsider the whole punching thing.

"—(no relation)," Pfiffer Hubert finished, a bit embarrassed. Anne gaped and shut her mouth with a huff, turning bright red.

"Oooohhhh, I HATE YOU SO MUCH RIGHT NOW!"

"Tut, that's no way for a princess to behave," Kent Clark (no relation) chided, taking great pleasure in it. "Minus 10 points from Pfiffer Hubert (no rela—"

"OH!! SHUT UP!" Anne marched away, indignant. Her tremendous hoop skirt saw that dramatic exit and threw in a flounce for good measure.

Kent darted a look around at his many non-relatives and thought what a perfect opportunity it was to launch his super alter ego. He looked around for a potted plant but was only able to find a conveniently placed phone booth.

Strangely the phone inside the booth didn't place calls or have a dial tone, but the booth itself was luxuriously-wide, with velvet changing curtains to pull around the windows and wrap-around bench seating, as well as several conveniently placed hooks and complementary clothes hangers. Many of the Not-Related-to-Superheroes crowd were invited to the event and the (no relation) Reunion Committee knew what their heroic target audience required in a pinch.

Soon Kent Clark (no relation) emerged from the Not-Related-To-A-Real-Phone-Booth with his hair slicked back and no glasses whatsoever to introduce his not-related super identity to all of his new not-related friends.

"Hello good citizens," he boomed, "I'm Super-Stupendous-Awesome-Man (no relation), I'm pleased to meet all of you."

"Uh wait—you're Kent Clark (no relation)," Wayne Bruce (no relation) said, lifting an eyebrow. "You just took your glasses off and slicked your hair back."

"What? That's utterly ridiculous," said Super-Stupendous-Awesome-Man (no relation), blushing. "I don't even know—that other guy, and besides, he wears glasses and I don't. As you can clearly see, I'm Super-Stupendous-Awesome-Man (no relation) as I said. I just happened to be, ya know, flying through the neighborhood looking for someone to rescue, and decided to drop in and introduce myself."

"No, I'm pretty sure you're Kent Clark (no relation). I saw you just a couple minutes ago, then you went into the phone booth and now you're pretending to be your superhero identity. Which is cool but seriously, you took off glasses? Glasses? That's the best you could come up with?"

"Look, I took my glasses off so you don't know who I am," Kent—(oops), Super-Stupendous-Awesome-Man (no relation) hissed back as quietly as he could. "I'm Super-Stupendous-Awesome-Man (no relation), okay? Get it? Just say "it's nice to meet you" that's it."

"Hey Kent Clark (no relation)," Man Spider (no relation) strolled over with a smile, "Why did you take your glasses off? And why are you wearing your underwear on the outside of your clothes? Changed in too big a hurry, did you?"

Kent Clark (no relation) had a moment of existential crisis but no one noticed.

"Don't worry bro. We've all been there too. We'll help you come up with something better for your alter ego," Man Spider clapped him on the back.

"You should've seen Zorro (no relation). He was off making the sign of an "O" before we pointed out a "Z" made more sense but he was a bit dyslexic."

"I like the glasses," Kent Clark (no relation) grumbled. "Anyway, that's not what I need help with. I'm 38 and my superpowers never developed. I can't fly or x-ray or use my heat vision. Nothing works. It's like I have an alien manufacturers defect."

"Don't you know anything?" Man-Spider (no relation) shook his head and pointed. "If you want to use your superpowers, you have to meet your dead, artificial-intelligence-preserved alien father in your Solitary Fortress so he can train you and give them to you. Duh! Basic stuff. Superheroing 101, even."

"Oh—well—no one told ME that," Kent Clark (no relation) said defensively. "It'd be nice if this alien superheroing business came with a manual. So where do I find this Solitary Fortress?"

"Best guess, high in the Transylvanian mountains," Man-Spider (no relation) replied. "It's got to be an isolated spot so no one can reach the Fortress but you. Climb to the highest peak, toss the glowing alien crystal packed along with you in your birth spaceship into the snow and the crystal should do the rest."

"Umm—" Kent shifted uncomfortably in his red cape. Man-Spider (no relation) lifted a brow.

"Don't tell me. You left the alien crystal at home, didn't you? DUDE—REALLY?"

"Well, how was I supposed to know?" Kent Clark (no relation) huffed. "It's not like I keep it in the extra pocket sewn in my cape just in case I need an alien crystal on-the-go or—oh look, here it is."

To his surprise, his fumbling fingers pulled the cold, narrow, alien crystal out of his cape's extra pocket with a little sticky note attached:

Kent dear (no relation),
Just in case you need your alien crystal on-the-go; I packed it in your cape for you. It might come in handy later.
Good luck saving the world, sweetheart!
There are sandwiches in the fridge when you get home!
Hugs & Kisses!
Love, Mom (no relation)

"My not-related adopted Earth mom is just the best," Kent Clark (no relation) said, beaming.

Man-Spider (no relation) nodded his agreement. "Sandwiches dude, you're lucky. That's an awesome not-related adopted Earth mom who found you in a ditch someplace and kidnapped you."

"So—high in the Transylvanian mountains, you said? Throw the crystal in the snow and it will do the rest?"

"It should," Man-Spider (no relation) said calmly. "I mean, you can order a "Do-It-Yourself Solitary Fortress" from the alien product catalog, but it's not recommended. The assembly instructions were written in hieroglyphics, and they can only pick up your dead-alien-father's transmission reliably about half the time. You'll be halfway through your superpowers download and suddenly experiencing "connectivity issues" which is a bitch when your heat vision melts your entire fortress to a puddle because the download corrupted."

"Really, you're much better off using your pre-packed alien birth crystal if it isn't stolen, damaged or defective from the crash landing at birth. If it is, you're probably screwed 'cause after 38 years on Earth, I don't think it's still covered under warranty."

"Guess I know where I'm headed then," Kent Clark (no relation) nodded politely. "Nice meeting all of you. See you guys at the next non-family reunion of us people who aren't related."

"It's gonna be awesome," Wayne Bruce (no relation) put in. "Word is Gelina-Bran (no relation) are coming and bringing the many, MANY kiddos. We can't wait!"

"Awesome! I may have to bring my wife, Twin Leia-who-isn't-the-Princess," Walker-Sky Luke (no relation) added, then seeing the looks directed his way, added quickly, "Oh no, we're not related. Er, to each other, or anyone else, we're just not related—to anyone! So it isn't like, *weird*, in case you were wondering that."

Kent left them discussing the upcoming reunion not-celebrity guest list as he headed out and told the party of new friends he was sorry to leave them but he had an urgent appointment to discover his heroic Destiny. Whether or not his companions believed this coming from a Kansas farm boy, they graciously wished him well and Kent fervently promised to check in with them later to see how it all turned out.

With that, he went Transylvanian mountain climbing—not for the faint of heart, mind you! Armando had done well with the whole craggy peaks and snowy desolation and packs of ravaging, fiercely hungry wolves.

But Kent persevered and got rid of most threats simply by stepping behind a tree and removing his glasses, slicking back his hair, then placing his hands on his hips in a very threatening manner. (But if you're looking for a spot to build your own frozen alien Solitary Fortress, it's perfect!)

After a two day climb and reaching the pinnacle of a suitably snowy and desolate mountain peak and crystal tossing, the Fortress erected itself from the crystal while Kent Clark (no relation) beat off some hungry wolves and vampire bats with a tree branch, then had to mend his cape with duct-tape on the fly until he could get it home for Marta Clark (no relation) to sew it back up. His dratted cape got tangled in some branches and near-choked Kent to death mid-battle, thanks to the wild, shrieking mountain wind. Despite how dashing it looked in flight, maybe all those no-cape safety advisories for superheroes did make a valid point.

Finally, the fortress was ready and Kent ventured nervously inside. It was all blue ice, cave-like and cold, glowing and spectacular. A voice spoke from the everywhere at once, echoing with the acoustics of all that empty space and startling Kent half the death.

"Hello, my son! I'm your father, A-Jar, and you are my beloved son, A-Skew, and the last surviving heir of the House of A-Komik and the hope of our people—

By the Kosmos, what ARE YOU wearing, my son? Is that how they dress you on this planet?" The ethereal voice broke off, puzzled. Kent shifted a bit in his handmade costume.

"Um, my mom made it—sir."

"Oh—yes. Marta Clark (no relation), good woman," the voice murmured nervously, "But you— look *older* than I expected. Are—are you still in high school, my son?"

"Yes," said Kent Clark, 38, admittedly 100% truthful. The voice coughed.

"Oh—well—I guess the yellow Earth sun causes accelerated aging in aliens. That, uh, wasn't in the brochure. Well, no matter—to your training my son, and quickly," the disembodied voice grumbled, "before you keel over from heart disease. Guess we'll skip over the alien heritage lessons for sake of time, and get straight to the good stuff."

He cleared his throat again. "You'll have to start bulking up with your Super!Pow Energy Drink. It comes in nine delicious flavors and your choice of heroic powers. Would you like to start with Rocket-

Cherry Heat Vision-Cola, Go-Go-Grape Super-Speed Gulp, or Cool-Limeade Susceptibility-to-Meteor-Rocks Surprise?"

As Kent Clark (also known as Super-Stupendous-Awesome-Man but never related) sipped his super-powered energy 44 oz. and learned how to manage his many deliciously-flavored new superpowers—

—Unbeknownst to him, Tailor Wear the werewolf sat on his haunches outside the Solitary Fortress and whined.

It took the werewolf cub almost a week to track down his new and beloved Master across the snowy mountains and the Fortress refused to allow the cold, tired little werewolf inside. It was an exclusive club: Aliens Only.

The exterior was smooth as glass, reflective as a mirror and no entrance presented itself although Tailor circled the fortress all the way around and sniffed it many times, marking his trail with a Territorial Yellow path in the snow, to hunt for one.

So poor lonely Tailor, cold and clinging to the torn remnant of a red cape stuck in the bushes (well, it smelled like GOOD and KIND Master Kent anyway) had no choice but to sit in the middle of the frozen mountaintop and await his beloved Master to come out.

17

Choose Your Own Adventure: Long-Lost Princess or Soulful-Eyed Vampiress!

O nce our heroes left the village behind, the steep climb to Armando's castle in the Transylvanian mountains wasn't as bad as initially anticipated.

Perhaps because they found a wide, well-lit and well-ventilated, air-conditioned staircase that Armando helpfully installed for any human girls who were worshippers of Howard—or Leonard? No, it was Stepford right, or maybe Robert . . . what was that vampire kid's name again?

The staircase was clearly marked "No Heroes Allowed" but, as Kent Clark (no relation) had departed to discover his heroic Destiny and there seemed to be no corresponding rules listed about war gods or fairy captains or cross-dressing cheerleaders (even Mr. Oubliette, whatever the hell he was), they figured it was okay to take the stairs and skip the horrifying death of falling off a mountain.

That felt like the smart plan until they discovered there was a certain prolonged torture in climbing a steep, seemingly-endless tier of stairs where the walls were lined with life-sized posters of a shiny, sullen teen vampire shot in various poses, presumably supposed to make him look *mysterious* and *angsty* but only succeeded in making him look extremely constipated.

Anne Genue took their minds off their suffering by regaling them with how *Hubert Pfiffer! Boy Wizard!* heroically stole fire from the gods for the good of all mankind. This came as news to Vegetarian—um, Verethraghna, the Persian god of war, who was pretty sure he'd heard it was Prometheus. He came to the same conclusion as had everyone else but Anne herself, he desperately wanted to punch Hubert Pfiffer right in the face!

(But everyone *loves* Mary S—oops. *Hubert Pfiffer*. Yes. We know.)

Apparently the remarkable *Hubert Pfiffer! Boy Wizard!* bored quite easily (geniuses, you know) so he invented Majick-Book and the Smart Phone while tinkering in his basement when he happened to have a Saturday free from helping mankind.

This news would come as much of a surprise to a former student at Harvard and a prominent software guru as it had to Verethraghna!

So Armando's slow-torture climb, though not intended as such, was very effective. To our heroes (again, all except Anne) it felt like the longest stairway climb in history!

However, they were surprised when they came to a colorful tile mural at the head of the stairs, the only part of the stairwell not slathered with sparkly vampire posters. The mural depicted a beautiful young girl who, strangely, didn't look unlike a younger version of Anne Genue. Everyone paused to stare at it—

Everyone, that is, except Miss Genue.

"C'mon, we're almost to the castle now," Anne urged them.

"But—that tiara in the mural, it looks identical to yours doesn't it?" Fu felt compelled to point this out. The others nodded their agreement.

Anne gave the mural a cursory glance. "Yeah, I guess so. Most tiaras kinda look alike, IDK. Diamonds, and WTV."

"Well—where did you get your tiara?"

"Found it hidden in a crevice in the wall of the remote, hidden, doorless tower in the forest where I was raised by a witch," Anne shrugged again,

"What's so weird about that? Maybe all remote, hidden, doorless forest towers have tiaras tucked away in the crevices? I'm no expert."

"Anyway, the tiara fit me, so . . . are we going?"

She just walked off while everyone else read the sign at the bottom of the mural:

> *The Lost Transylvanian Princess and Heir to the Transylvanian Throne. REWARD OFFERED FOR ANY INFORMATION! If found: please contact King Armando immediately.*

Exchanging a glance, the men all shrugged and tailed after Anne. If she wasn't going to make a federal case of the resemblance and staggering coincidences, well, why should they?

They exited the stairs to find themselves at the top of the mountain and just outside King Armando's vampire castle. The enormous black, spiked gates surrounding the imposing structure were solid iron, and to top that, securely padlocked.

If there was ever a moment for a secret key to materialize and perfectly fit the lock it was now. But Fate refused to play ball with them. Usually its timing was impeccable but it must have had the day off.

"Couldn't we just get inside the castle using the secret entrance?" Biffy asked.

Fu looked at him, "Do you know of one?"

"Personally, I favor that big sign with an arrow pointing to the hole in the stone wall that reads:

"Secret Entrance to the Castle", next to that very large hole in the iron fence."

"Oh! How kind of them to label it for us," Anne gasped. "They must know we're not from here."

"Sure. That isn't *at all suspicious*, a well-marked secret entrance," Fu mumbled. "Call me crazy but I think Armando likes encouraging visitors. Particularly those he can eat."

Once they got inside, the castle proved to be larger than a typical hotel resort complex, and equally confusing to navigate. It needed its own guideposts. Although our heroic party didn't *intend* to split up and search the castle, it happened more or less organically just from the sheer size of the place.

There were so many endlessly twisting, labyrinthian hallways that they kept turning corners and it felt like the bend they just came from was never the one they found while retracing their steps.

In a place like this, one might expect a magical king to pop up with a 13-hour clock and offer to show them their dreams—but today HE was dressed stylishly (and ironically given the setting) as a vampire with a red satin cape and black sequin fetish, wearing oversized white plastic fangs. He was also preoccupied searching for "false alarms" every time they turned a corner. Apparently "you got a lot of those in the Labyrinth" although Mr. Oubliette had the hardest time explaining what he meant by that random remark later. All they could give out of him after that was a huffy, "What's said is SAID!"

But all this confusion was probably why it took them a good 20 minutes to realize Anne Genue was kidnapped and not just lost in one of the endless castle hallways.

Actually it was because they didn't realize this at all that prompted Armando to get on the castle intercom and interrupt when he grew tired of hearing them bicker about which hallway they left her behind in.

Armando ended it finally by yelling across the PA system. "LOOK, she's KIDNAPPED, NOT LOST! *I kidnapped her* okay, your pretty little girlfriend! I've hidden her and you'll never find her now, you heroes!"

(This, given the size of the castle, was quite possibly true.)

"I've sent a contingent of guards to bring YOU HEROES to ME TO FACE YOUR ULTIMATE DOOM, mulhahaha—" Armando abruptly broke off, mid-evil chuckle. The intercom crackled with empty static.

"—of course, they do have to find you in my castle first. Which hallway did you say you were in again? Could one of you boys check for me, is that the NW or NE corner . . . damn, they all look so much alike! Wait, let me get the maps out—"

. . . *there was a sound of rustling paper across the PA system* . . .

"No, this is useless! I can never figure this out. I'll have to use the GPS app to locate you, okay don't move. Stay in the hallway where you are until I can get a fix—"

. . . *a few electronic beeps sound in the background* . . .

"Oh, this stupid GPS thing never works! "Locating coordinates" my ass! Yes, I'll accept the "Terms and Conditions" . . . okay, yes fine I'll pay any fees for services not covered under the apps free operations plan . . . YES, my current location is Transylvania . . . what? Why do I have to register my email address NOW, I just WANT you to WORK! NO, I DON'T KNOW my username and password, JUST GIVE ME A LOCATION—is that SO HARD???"

There was another burst of static across the PA system while Fu and the others just stared at each other. Armando's voice came through again. It seemed like he'd forgotten he was broadcasting this across the entire castle.

"Oh look at that, I can login through Majick-Book. That's cool. Ah here we are, "loading coordinates" . . . ah ha, I'll have your location in a minute, heroes so just hang loose and . . . WHAT??? What do you mean I'm OUT OF RANGE??? I'm OUT OF RANGE to a SATELLITE??? SERIOUSLY, ARE YOU BATSHITTING ME RIGHT NOW??? ARRRRGGGHHHH,

NO I WILL NOT "LIKE" YOUR APP ON MAJICK-
BOOK!!! DISLIKE! DISLIKE!! THUMBS-DOOOOWN!!!"

. . . *another burst of static and some very loud
feedback . . .*

"FINE THEN, we'll just find you WITHOUT THE
APP!! I really shouldn't have wallpapered all of these
hallways the same but—

ANYWAY, when my guards FIND YOU, AH-HA,
you will REGRET ever coming to Transylvania and
YOUR DOOM, you . . . HEROES, er," Armando
hesitated again.

"Well, my guards *will* find you eventually. In two
or three days maybe? So—feel free to make
yourselves at home while you wait. All the floors are
set up for basic cable and you can order room
service from any of the phones, it'll just be billed to
your room. See you in a couple days. This is King
Armando, over and out."

There was a period of surprised silence after the
intercom cut out, then another sudden burst of
static.

"Oh wait, I almost forgot: MULHAHAHAHAHH
AHHHAHHAAAA!!! Okay, over and out again, for
real this time."

The intercom/PA clicked off after a few seconds
but not before faintly heard in the background:
*"Dear Majick-Book, I would like to introduce this app
that's a real piece of batshi—"*

Again, dead silence. All of the men (yes, Mr. Oubliette too) were still just looking at each other.

This was a moment that clearly required a plan. A GOOD PLAN would be nice but they'd settle for any plan that came to mind.

"Let's split up and search these endless hallways for the girl" ranked marginally on the overall Plan Totem Pole a few notches below, "Let's split up and search for the masked, chainsaw wielding psychopath" and SEVERAL notches below, "Let's just order room service and watch cable TV until the castle guards find us".

But it was A PLAN and so, unable to top it, it was the plan they went with.

They each took a different direction and went to search their respective hallways, although both Mr. Oubliette and Verethraghna preferred the "point 'n click" method of teleportation to wandering through halls on foot. Yep, it's good to be a god—or whatever kind of magical entity Mr. Oubliette was.

Unfortunately due to the uncanny similarities in the hallways and bad sense of overall direction, Mr. Oubliette was, unbeknownst to himself, actually teleporting in and out of the exact same hallway for well over an hour. He didn't find the kidnapped Anne the first time . . . nor any of the other 1,536,292 times either.

In that same span of time, Fu-Belle had managed to zip down about half-a-corridor in flight in relation to his tiny fairy size. If there was any consolation, it's that the castle guards will find Waldo before they manage to find him.

B iffy the Cheerleader-Disguised Vampire Slayer turned just the right corner and discovered a lavishly-decorated boudoir in red silks and black velvet, which puts him ahead of the game if you're keeping score at home, since he's the only one who escaped the "identical hallway trap" so far.

Biffy grew very excited. This had to be where Armando hung up his wings for the—daytime? Surely! Whatever vampires called their daily slumber nowanights, or whatever? This was "Armando's kingly bedroom", and all Biffy had to do was wait here and he'd gank THE KING OF VAMPIRES HIMSELF!

Bonus, he'd get to like, totally rescue Anne from Armando's evil clutches too, which would put him WAY AHEAD of Kent Clark (no relation) who wasn't even HERE, in the department of totally winning her affections! Awesome! It was a two for two score!

He couldn't wait to login to Majick-Book to show-off for his poker buddies back home, "Hey dudes, while you were at the diner having coffee, I just TOTALLY GANKED Armando, KING of the VAMPIRES! *Biiiiitchin!* And I saved the pretty girl too—'cuz I'm just awesome like that!" He was already snapping pics of the boudoir and they were going viral as soon as he got a better Wifi signal.

His friends would be soooo jealous and he'd be, like, the most infamous vampire slayer ever—making the name "Biffy" synonymous with Slayerdom like, FOREVER!

Vampire slayers everywhere would be dressing as blonde cheerleaders and he'd become known as the "Chosen One"—there'd probably even be a TV show made about his adventures, though knowing Hollywood, they'd get some details wrong anyhow, like adding demons or ghosts to hunt and slay, junk like that.

But, to Biffy's surprise, it wasn't Armando he discovered unless "HE" was actually a "SHE" and if so, the descriptor "King of the Vampires" had far from done her justice!

Instead it was the most stunningly beautiful woman Biffy had ever laid eyes on! She was tall and slim, with beautifully long, flowing black hair and it certainly didn't hurt that she wore something straight out of the gothic-bodice-ripper dress catalog. It was all clingy red velvet and black lace with a flattering corset worked in and ridiculously tall stiletto heels no woman should wear unless she can defy gravity.

But what really captivated Biffy were her beautiful eyes—they were gigantic and incredibly soulful. If the eyes were the "windows to the soul" than hers were double-paned glass French doors! Biffy just couldn't help himself from staring transfixed into her velvety doe eyes.

Vampires traditionally were known for their mesmerizing gazes but she had Legosi and all the others beat. If Bambi's mother saw *these eyes*, she'd have shot this woman out of pure jealousy!

"Hello," the mysterious woman breathed the word more than spoke it. It was musical, elemental as water. "I'm Angellass, Mistress of the Night! And who are you, you handsome, dark, mysterious stranger?"

"Uh—I'm—Biffy," Biffy hesitated. "The Cheerleader" wasn't the way to go here. Of course, "The Vampire Slayer" left something to be desired too on this side of the Transylvanian Border.

"Uh, just—Biffy. And the cheerleader outfit, I can explain that."

"No need. Obviously, you're a vampire slayer trying not to look like one—everyone knows women can't be slayers, or slayeresses as it were! That's just silly," Angellass smiled. "Sort of like vampires, right?"

Her teeth were a little too pointed. "No such thing as vampiresses. Clearly, it's male-only gig on both sides of the coin."

She saw right through his disguise. Biffy was instantly in love—and strangely fascinated by the vampiress in question, but one thing still bothered him.

"You can't be—vampiresses don't have soulful eyes!" Biffy protested.

They shouldn't be stunningly gorgeous knockouts either, he wanted to add but couldn't think of a sophisticated way to say it.

"I know," Angellass agreed with a dramatic sigh. "I never wanted to be a monster. I never wanted to hurt anyone. I was a simple girl born to simple parents, but my simple life tragically was changed forever when Daddy slipped and fell in the shower. Then he forgot who he was and couldn't work and had to be spoon-fed like a child."

"Oh how awful," Biffy commiserated.

"Yes it was. Then about a year later, Mother slipped and fell in the same shower and lost her memory. She thought we were the neighbor's children and threw us out in the snow to starve, where one of my brothers immediately froze, a human popsicle, and he died."

"My goodness!"

"Then about a year later, Daddy slipped and fell in the shower again and the hair buildup clogged the drain so that the tub overflowed until he drowned and died."

"Golly!"

"Then my sister stepped out of the shower when there were no dry towels and she used a wet one, caught a cold which turned to pneumonia and she died."

"Wow!"

"Then my mother fell asleep reading in the bathtub and the book fell and crushed her windpipe so she died."

"Oh my!"

"Yes, then my other brother was reaching for the shampoo bottle when he got shampoo in his eyes, tripped over the side of the tub, fell and . . ."

"Died?"

"No, he was just bleeding from a gash to the temple."

"Well GOOD," Biffy brightened, looking relieved, "That's good then. Not that he was bleeding, I mean, but the not-dying bit."

Angellass nodded. "Indeed, why he didn't die for a whole 30 minutes until he bled out during the ambulance ride to the hospital and died of brain trauma."

"Oh—I'm sorry to hear that."

Angellass sighed, "So after my first and second husbands both died in the shower, leaving me an enormous fortune, and my vampire sire told me that there were zero shower-or-bath related causalities among the vampires . . . I don't know."

"All my family and lovers were dead and I was a young and rich widow and—at the time, immortality just seemed like a good precaution to take. Insurance against a death by shower, as it were, like the unfortunate fates of my loved ones."

"Yes well—" Biffy fumbled for a response. "I can see why it might."

"I was a bad vampire girl for awhile," Angellass sighed, "Drowning cute little puppy dogs and eating helpless kittens and fluffy white bunnies, just because I could. Oh those memories fill me with shame now."

"I guess eating that poor baby elephant at the circus was just spite, really. I thought the tumblers were terrible but that's no excuse. Alas, the circus folk grew angry with me and their gypsy fortune-teller placed a powerful curse over me as a penalty, that I should have "open eyes of the soul" and thus see all the suffering I've caused."

Angellass heaved another dramatic sigh and clasped both hands to her breasts becomingly. "And that is why I'm the only vampiress with soulful eyes! I can't eat anything now once the food starts screaming for help—I just weep like you wouldn't believe! Why, I haven't been able to snack on a little lost orphan in years."

"Oh. I'm sorry to hear that," Biffy wasn't, but he felt it was expected of him to say.

Angellass gave him a look that could only be termed as amused. "I suppose you must slay me now?"

"Oh no," Biffy rushed to assure her, "Slaying isn't *mandatory* per se. It's a case by case basis type of gig."

"And *obviously* you have soulful eyes so you're not hurting anyone—and—and I really think you set a good example as vampiresses go."

"It's very tragic," Angellass replied, dramatically pressing her hands to her chest again. Biffy tried not to stare.

"In another lifetime, perhaps we could have been together but now—NOW—well, it's FORBIDDEN! Alas! ALAS!"

Just the way she said "forbidden" made Biffy tingle all over, "Er, yes, forbidden. Obviously. Slayer, Vampiress, it would never work out. Yes. Er. Forbidden, I was just going to say myself—"

Out of the corner of his eye, Biffy noticed a stack of dog-eared romance novels by the bed. They all looked to be of the bodice-ripper variety and the book covers focused on a very bare-chested, rippling-with-muscles male vampire slayer, judging by the large cross and wooden stake he openly carried, coming to romance a very lonely shut-in vampiress dressed rather like Angellass was.

Oh. *That* sort of "forbidden". Right.

Suddenly Biffy appeared about two inches taller. He sucked in his stomach and drew himself up, flexing his biceps and trying as best he could to look like the bare-chested and hard-muscled "slayer" male models on the book cover.

"Yes," he deepened his voice an octave for effect, "But I ask, is it forbidden to love beauty, like a rose in spring and the morning dawn—" he caught her look and rapidly course-corrected his gallant hero speech, "er, I mean, like the starlit velvety night sky and—uh, magnificence of a bat in flight? If it's a crime to love these things, my dear Angellass—"

"Mistress of the Night," Angellass prompted. Vampires set a great store by proper titles.

"—Mistress of the Night," Biffy continued without missing a beat, "Then indeed I'm guilty for I cannot forbid this love in my own heart." He finished his speech proudly. No male-modeling book hero could've topped it.

Now dating vampires was traditionally listed in the slayer training handbook under, *"No! No! We said NO!"* but this was a rule Biffy had about ten minutes ago decided was old-fashioned and clearly outdated, with no concept of the *modern relationship dynamic* between vampiress and vampire slayer.

Though he admitted, this wasn't the rule he expected to take exception to. He'd expected to struggle more with "don't step out for a couple beers first before heading out to slay", a rule he'd already broken twice. The thought of dating the enemy hadn't once crossed his mind until now.

Now he could see plainly the old slayer handbook needed revision, some "If this, then that" clauses added, more in keeping with the *modern* slayer. This so wasn't a black 'n white situation; rather it was shades of gray!

Besides, Biffy mused to himself as he watched Angellass close in with the single-minded determination of a woman with centuries of reading and fantasizing, and a head fresh with erotic ideas she wanted to experiment with, *what's the fun of having a rule unless one broke it every now and again?*

The Sexiest Kidnapping on Majick-Book!

Armando was more than a little peeved. Not only had he not received his crackle ransom demand from King Clarion of the fairies, but he'd received word from Neverland.

Apparently the *real* Captain Hook up and rudely spoiled Armando's Brilliant Plan™ by telling Clarion he didn't kidnap Tinker-Belle after all (although there was some strange complication involving a tiny, hand-eating crocodile and a flying gingerbread house that no one could seem to explain).

Now Armando was forced by circumstances to invade Fairyland after all. In the middle of a war, he had to stop to plan an invasion. Really, it was such an *inconvenience!* One would think the fairies could see that, what with managing a war and all, Armando was far too BUSY to plan invasions at the moment!

Fortunately, Armando had developed yet another Brilliant Plan™! Even better than an invasion, it was a plan that worked for centuries, tried and tested by the handbook of villainy.

Naturally, Armando was referring to kidnapping the pretty girl and threatening her life. Plus, as a matter of convenience, pretty girls were a widely available resource. You could pick one up practically anywhere.

Yes, it was truly a brilliant plan! Even better than transforming the hero into a tiny flea then placing him in a box inside another box, mailing that box to oneself and smashing it with a hammer when it arrived. Although Armando rather liked that Brilliant Plan™ but the postage got expensive, true.

Armando had seen on his Super-Villainy Spy-Cams placed discreetly in corners of the "Howard—Leonard—or whatever that vampire's name was" Secret Staircase that a small band of heroes—well, possibly they were heroes, Armando was a little undecided on this point. He hadn't ruled out circus performers or renegade cross-dressing trolls.

Anyway, these heroes (probably) were sneaking up the back staircase and Armando noticed they had conveniently brought along a pretty girl with them for him to kidnap. That was mighty decent of them to do that so Armando didn't have to go out and find his own pretty girl, then do all the work of getting her emotionally bonded to the heroes, to then later kidnap her and threaten her life, blah-blah.

Instead these heroes had thoughtfully spared him the trouble so he could just jump right to the kidnapping bit. Clearly they had more consideration for what a busy vampire king he was than the fairies did!

And they brought a fairy along with them. Too bad it wasn't that annoying fairy captain that Armando hated so much for moving the fairy crackle caches around without the vampire king's permission. It was quite the coincidence that this fairy was wearing a Royal Fairyland uniform with captain stripes but it couldn't be the same guy— what was that infernal fairy captain's name again? Something with a "—belle" in it, right?

Anyway, too bad this fairy captain wasn't his nemesis but Armando was going to squish him anyway on basic principle, as a dire warning to all fairy captains.

This was just too easy! They'd entered the castle via the "secret passage" . . . and true, that was the more popular method. Armando had it installed after his visitors kept turning away from his huge black gates—well, sorry they were impenetrable but it was TRADITION to have those!

The secret passage conveniently had plenty of handy dark alcoves to hide in and snatch the pretty girl when they passed by. By which we mean the one who wasn't a cross-dresser.

The kidnapping bit went off without a hitch. Now that the girl was secure, Armando just needed to post his Brilliant Plan™ on Majick-Book and improve his rating!

Things weren't going too well on the MeIzSo Popular front. He'd been demoted two levels already from all the "un-friending" going on and was just a step above "dweeb". His score was rapidly tanking and he needed a significant victory in the popularity arena to keep from sinking lower. This kidnapping was brilliant (and *sexy!*) so that should do it!

Once he'd finished adding his new status, Armando noticed Alucard was showing online on his instant messenger.

That was even better! There was nothing Armando wanted more than to rub his rival's nose in his latest victory, except those Mr. Cool shades.

You received an instant message from KING ARMANDO SXEST NM ON MAJKB!

Sooo, I totally kidnapped the pretty girl today
from a band of heroes,
'Cuz I'm awesome like that!!!
What are u doin with your Saturday, Alucard?
Oh right, NOOOTHING!

You received an instant message from ALUCARD DNT SPL BKWRD!

Why don't you just bite me, Armando! Suck off!

You received an instant message from KING ARMANDO SXEST NM ON MAJKB!

Ehehhahahahhaahahaaaaa!
U will TOTALLY NEVER ever guess
where I've hidden her, Alucard!
PWNED FOR ETERNITY!

You received an instant message from ALUCARD DNT SPL BKWRD!

Right, sure.
You hid her inside your coffin
in the castle basement, didn't you?

Armando froze.

You received an instant message from KING ARMANDO SXEST NM ON MAJKB!

No.

She's not down there!
Don't go looking for her down there;
it's a waste of time, ALUCARD!
Cuz that's where she ISN'T!

Armando snapped his fingers and a vampire underling materialized on cue.

"Orders, your Highness?"

"Get the girl out of my coffin in the basement," Armando grumbled. "Then bring her to me."

A ding from his laptop interrupted and Armando turned back to find an IM waiting.

You received an instant message from ALUCARD DNT SPL BKWRD!

Oh she isn't huh?

You received an instant message from KING ARMANDO SXEST NM ON MAJKB!

NO!! SHUT UP, like u know ANYTHING, ALUCARD!!

You received an instant message from ALUCARD DNT SPL BKWRD!

I know she isn't in your basement!
You're too late, Armando! I've taken the girl, ha!
I told her to look deep, deeeeep into my eyes
and she replied that I lost 10 points from
some wizard bloke named Hubert Pfiffer.
Whoever that is? Friend of yours?

*Point is, now she's **mine!** You lost your captive,*
Armando!

Armando gritted his fangs. "Oh NO he didn't! It is ON now!"

"Your highness," a vampire rushed in to confirm. "The girl has escaped somehow. She's not in the coffin or the basement, Sire. We think she might have grown lost in one of your castle hallways, they are rather long—"

"I know where she is," Armando cut him off, "Alucard has taken her but he won't get away with it!" The vampire king fumed, "I'm going to RE-kidnap her back before he suspects anything, ha! The hell he's stealing MY Brilliant Plan™ which I STOLE FIRST so THAT!"

With a huff, Armando disappeared and after several long minutes, finally reappeared with Anne in tow.

"Was it that hard to find her, Sire?" the vampire guard asked, taking Anne's arm.

"No," Armando grumbled, "But she wouldn't invite me inside the room where Alucard was holding her until I could prove I knew who *Hubert Pfiffer! Boy Wizard!* was."

His laptop dinged again and Armando turned back to it to update his status.

You received an instant message from KING ARMANDO SXEST NM ON MAJKB!

Have girl back. Alucard, UR A LOSER!!!

You received an instant message from ALUCARD DNT SPL BKWRD!

No you don't!
I just found her in your bat cave,
and re-re-stole her back, ha!
You're so predictable, Armando.
It's the first place I checked, seriously.

You received an instant message from KING ARMANDO SXEST NM ON MAJKB!

Oh, and behind a MIRROR,
THAT was such a great hiding place—NOT!
Mortals throw back reflections in those, U know!

You received an instant message from ALUCARD DNT SPL BKWRD!

If you knew anything Armando,
you'd know that was a special
mirrored room that illusionists use,
as designed by the Great Houdini himself.
You should read an actual book once in awhile,
it'll expand your education . . .
Of course, you'd have to learn how to read first.

You received an instant message from KING ARMANDO SXEST NM ON MAJKB!

Fang U!

You received an instant message from ALUCARD DNT SPL BKWRD!

Real mature, Armando. Articulate too.
It's such a mystery why Stoker chose me
to star in his novel over you, isn't it?

Armando fumbled for a witty rejoinder that didn't start in "fang" and end in "you". While he mentally shuffled through options, his IM dinged again.

You received an instant message from ALUCARD DNT SPL BKWRD!

I'm returning the girl to you, Armando.
By what I witnessed in your castle,
I suspect you'll soon have much bigger problems
than me anyway.

You received an instant message from KING ARMANDO SXEST NM ON MAJKB!

What r u talking about?

If u mean the heroes, I have a plan to torture them!
See, I found this DIY torture chamber,
it has a scorpion pit and a lava bed
and a shark tank- o, never mind,

I'll just send u the link.

****You received an instant message from
ALUCARD DNT SPL BKWRD!****

Cool, love to see it.
But no, that wasn't what I meant.

Armando wasn't paying any attention, as he hunted through his internet bookmarks folder. He was trying to figure out why practically none of them had titles or anything to identify them besides a confusing URL that went something like: "www.hjsbdosafbkjxznbcjkdbvgkhsbghrjsnrbgfwjhbf. hash"

****You received an instant message from
KING ARMANDO SXEST NM ON MAJKB!****

Trying to send u link but I can't find it.
Have it bookmarked but iz such a mess!
Can't find batshit in here! Drives me batty!

****You received an instant message from
ALUCARD DNT SPL BKWRD!****

IKR? That's just how I feel.

You received an instant message from KING ARMANDO SXEST NM ON MAJKB!

U know, someone should make like a
better method of bookmarking!
Some way of filing it so u can find
what ur looking 4 @ a glance, right?

You received an instant message from ALUCARD DNT SPL BKWRD!

Totally! I'd be lost without my pin-boards,
it's how I keep organized.
All my notes and reminders and receipts ...
It's all pinned and sectioned so I can find
what I need when I need it!

You received an instant message from KING ARMANDO SXEST NM ON MAJKB!

Shut up! DUDE, I have a pin-board at the castle too!
It's fangtastic!
Like, y isn't there something like that online?!
An online pin-board?

Instead of just jumbling ur batstuff
in one spot, u could all "organize it"?

**You received an instant message from
ALUCARD DNT SPL BKWRD!**

OMG, YES! That WOULD BE fangtastic!
But with multiple boards that
you could subcategorize?
So you wouldn't have to clutter
all your topics on one board!

**You received an instant message from
KING ARMANDO SXEST NM ON MAJKB!**

YEAH, cuz u could personalize them,
like "Blood Cocktail Recipes" would be kept
separate from "101 Ways to Match
Your Opera Cloak To Your Bat Wings" . . .

Armando was growing really excited. He began jotting down ideas on a 3x5 index cards just as fast as they were hitting him, like lightning on the dead brain of a monster brought to life by a mad scientist! (Don't we all know what that feels like? *wink, nudge*)

**You received an instant message from
KING ARMANDO SXEST NM ON MAJKB!**

*U could pin wtev u wanted on ur boards—
links, pictures, articles, blogs!
& like u could tag them by topic for later,
& find everything under 1 tag!*

*Then, all the boards could be posted on like
1 BIG BOARD by TOPIC
so every-1 could see every-1 else's boards
and share with the whole community!*

*U could even cross-post ur boards to Majick-Book &
"like" them!*

**You received an instant message from
ALUCARD DNT SPL BKWRD!**

*YES, YES, YES! I PULMONARY-ARTERIES IT!!
Armando, that's an amazing idea!!!
See then, you could follow the topics you like
on other boards and repost your favorite
pinnings back to your own boards too!*

Alucard was clearly growing just as excited. Their frenzied IM chat didn't end for hours, and only after they had promised to meet up the very next evening at earliest twilight to discuss it further over a p.m. blood-latte and to bring along an expert in web development to consult with while they were at it.

In the process, they both seemed to forget they had hated each other for centuries.

Gods could sense one another passing through the aether, and they could even follow each other to the destination point if the timing was right.

So, it wasn't a complete surprise when Viagra—um, Verethraghna appeared in one of Armando's endless hallways and was followed there by his half-brother Mithras, contender for the grandiose title of "god of war". Getting two gods to share the same title in an ancient pantheon was like getting two toddlers to share the same popsicle. Someone was going to end up with the empty stick here but not without the motha of all kicking and screaming tantrums first.

While Verethraghna wasn't surprised by Mithras arrival, it was without any cool sound effects or dazzling lightning bolts and smoke. Instead, he just popped dully into existence as the Persians didn't have their special effects crew signed on yet.

Verethraghna glared at his competitor and half-brother. He'd been expecting him for awhile now.

"Mithras!" he roared.

"Verethraghna!" Mithras sneered back.

"That does it," Verethraghna huffed, "Let's step outside, pretty boy!"

"What "outside"? Has plague addled your senses, dear brother? Do you perchance mean "outside" on the precarious snow-capped mountainside where there's a massive blizzard affecting both aim and visibility? Where one ill-aimed energy bolt will bring down the entire mountain collapsing directly on our heads and we'll be buried for thousands of years? That "outside"?"

"Fine," Verethraghna grumbled, "We can stay INSIDE then to fight. There's ample battling room in the hallway, believe me!"

He folded his arms over his toga. "But once and for all we shall settle this matter between us, like gods!"

"I knew you'd come," Mithras hissed.

"Verily, pray foresooth? Well, I knew that you'd know I'd come," Verethraghna said, sounding triumphant, "That's why I cameth prepared! I brought along the BOW of the HUNTRESS GODDESS," he whipped out a bow and arrow from nowhere, looking extremely pleased with himself.

"It can turn you into any weak, mortal animal I wish you to be. Then I thoroughly shall destroy you *BROTHER*, ha-ha!"

"Verily indeed? Well I KNEW you'd bring the huntress bow SO I cameth prepared also, and brought the SANDALS of the MESSENGER of the GODS," Mithras crowed, looking equally smug.

From thin air, he produced a pair of golden winged-sandals and waved them victoriously in Verethraghna's face.

"They can outrun an arrow, faster than the wind itself! Also, I brought the three-headed guard dog of the Underworld who will tear you into tiny pieces *BROTHER*, ha-ha!"

"Verily, thou saith? Well I already *knew* you'd bring the 3-headed dog and the messenger shoes, so I brought the enchanted scroll of history so I can write him out of existence!"

Again from thin air, a lengthy scroll and quill pen was produced as Verethraghna continued haughtily, "Besides, I brought a centaur with me, so ha!"

A bewildered half-man/half-horse creature was summarily produced and added to the growing stockpile of godly weaponry.

"Well I also *knew* you'd bring an enchanted scroll and a centaur—so I brought a minotaur and the sea god's trident," Mithras huffed, tossing the half-bull monster on the pile and studying the trident a minute.

"Admittedly I'm not sure what power the trident would have outside of the sea—but I thought it might come in handy, you never know."

He tossed the trident on the pile as well, then folded his arms, "Oh and doth I forget it, HA!"

The two gods faced each other, nose-to-nose, gauntlet-to-gauntlet, eyes narrowed to slits as they continued to produce more weapons.

"I brought a sand shark!"

"Did you? I brought a harpy!"

"*Pathetic*, brother! I brought a time-traveling Christmas ornament!"

"Tis weak, *brother*! Because I brought enchanted love candy!"

"That's naught for I brought an invisibility helmet!"

"And I brought a king of thieves!"

Godly weapons were being produced from the aether like rainwater and added to piles summarily as the lists respectively grew and grew.

"Oh yeah! OH YEAH!" Verethraghna finally exploded. "Verily lo and behold, I brought a WARRIOR PRINCESS! Ha-HA! Beat THAT, BROTHER!"

"No fair," Mithras whined. "That's cheating! "Warrior princess" beats everything else in a god-to-god showdown, you know that's against the rules!"

"War god!" Verethraghna taunted and reached into the aether, then frowned.

"Sorry, false alarm. She's not a real warrior princess, I grabbed the psycho blonde wannabe. That's what I get for hurrying. My mistake," He shrugged and added the screeching, black-leather-bikinied blonde to his weapons pile. "Carry on then."

Mithras eyed the two piles with disdain, "Looks like we're pretty well matched THIS TIME . . . *brother!* But I'll be BACK! You can count on it!"

Verethraghna glared, "Looking forward to it . . . *brother!*" he hissed. "You're so on my list!"

Mithras paused. "Um . . . wait. Aren't we going to have some awesome fiery battle with smoke and lightning-energy bolts and some well-choreographed kickboxing sequence of martial artistry and advanced gymnastics not possible under the laws of physics?"

"We can't. We don't have the budget or special effects crew," Verethraghna reminded him.

"Verily brother, I hath told you already I'd CALL when I landed us a good movie deal for our pantheon. First, I must locate a mystic occult object known thus as an "agent" and perform such a holy ritual as "rights signing". Then, that Grecian pig Ares said some nonsense of regular baths," Verethraghna shuddered.

"A pox be upon him," the other ancient and aromatic-toga-wearing god agreed instantly. "Doesn't he know you can contract plague and other nasty diseases from over-bathing?"

"Alas, it seems to be the "thing" with mortals these days," Verethraghna sighed. "Mortals and their obsessions, ye gods—er, ye us!"

"Plus, Ares the Greek pig says we must start building a "web platform"—I know not of which he speaks but I can only assume it involves spiders. It's exhausting, trying to learn all of these complex modern ways."

"Yea verily, the mortals have grown very strange these past several centuries," Mithras commiserated. "They once had such simple needs: healthy crops, prosperous villages, fruitful loins and victory in battle. Now they require of us, their gods, to spin webs like spiders? But surely spiders are fair suited to this task and do it well enough?"

"Yea, 'tis a struggle, keeping up with modern thought," Verethraghna shook his shaggy head. "But soon, my dear brother, I shall win the approval of this "Hollywood" deity and then we shalt have worshippers aplenty as we once did and hold a foothold amongst the other modernized gods, such as the Greeks and the Romans and the Norsemen."

"Also," Verethraghna added, "We shall have many small statues crafted in our image, as represented by a comely mortal who bears our namesake and is very fair of face. They're known to these modern mortals as "action figures" and mortals prize these highly."

Mithras smiled. "Verily, this pleases me greatly. It is good for a victorious god to be known among his followers as a figure of action."

Verethraghna nodded. "Have patience but for a time, my half-brother, and all these things shall come to pass in their season. Then we will have many godly battles depicted in this age as have we in ages before until our names are once more cried in the heat of battle."

"Well—just don't go taking all the good lines or battle sequences all to yourself, dear brother," Mithras grumbled. Verethraghna shrugged that off.

"Soon there will be special effects, theme music and costuming enough for all! Go now; gather the other gods to make preparations! They may be in need of many baths to please these modern mortals."

Mithras recoiled at the hated word "bath". Whoever said cleanliness was next to godliness had clearly never stood next to a Persian war god and his toga.

"Then we must enroll in a good dental plan," Verethraghna stated grimly, "Mortals of this age are most insistent their teeth must be shining white at all times, not yellowed or brittle with age. They even replace the missing teeth with false teeth of gold or white pottery."

Mithras looked puzzled. "Oh, why?"

Verethraghna shrugged. "Verily brother, I do not know. Another mystery of this new age. I suspect it must be some symbol of one's chastity or purity before the gods."

"Ah. Verily, these modern mortals are very strange, brother."

"Indeed. Thou hast said it."

The ~~Fake~~ REAL Zombie Apocalypse!

"Y our highness! Your highness! The heroes are missing, Sire!" A frantic vampire rushed into Armando's throne room with the bad news.

"What?" Armando huffed. "I TOLD THEM not to leave the hall! Now they've wandered off somewhere in the castle and gotten lost, I suppose! Why can't heroes ever just do as they're told?! Fine time they picked to become a nuisance! They should've stayed put so we could capture them and torture them ruthlessly in a proper fashion!"

He rolled his eyes. "Well, don't stand there! Go—find them or—*whatever!*"

The vampire bowed. "Yes Sire, immediately Sire—but there is *urgent news* from the frontlines of the war that I must relay to you, Sire. The werewolves are assisting King Clarion of the fairies to turn back our troops from entering Fairyland—and the zombies, they are—"

"Hold the guano!" Armando held up a hand to stay him as his iBat phone loudly played a cheerful ringtone.

". . . *but since u been gooooone, I can't breathe for . . .*"

"YEEESS! Sweetness! My last BaTwing was re-BaTwingged 13 times already," Armando beamed happily with a triumphant fist-bump, then nodded to the other vampire. "You were saying?"

The vampire messenger stumbled to regain his train of thought. "The zombies, Sire! They've abandoned us outside the border of Fairyland! We're dreadfully outnumbered, Sire!"

Armando barely lifted his eyes from his iBat phone. "Is that so? Did you know that Tetris was so hard? Why do they keep on sending me those squares that I don't even need?" he huffed, his fingers going like crazy on the controls of his touch screen.

"Dat's right," a new voice cut in, one that wasn't either vampire. In fact, it belonged to the gray-skinned, green-teethed zombie leader, now framed in the doorway and grinning at the messenger and Armando.

"Tho it ain't right 'xctly. See, dis is mo of an "ambush" than abandonin yo vampires." The zombie walked in and grinned even more, "Oh yeah. Surprise."

Armando huffed, "What? What is the meaning of this? Aren't you supposed to be overseeing the troops you zombie—leader—" he fumbled hopelessly for identification and came up blank (not that this was uncommon), "—fellow?"

"Yo vampires, yo all tink yo soooo smart," the zombie sneered. "Yo dun tink we zombies has no brains, no brains a'all."

"Umm—" Armando eyed the gaping hole in the zombie's rotting cranium where there did, in fact, seem to be a significant lack of brain matter left. The zombie cut him off.

"Yah, yah—well, we zombies dun outsmarted yo vampires, so how bout dem app—dem—app—dem red tings wot are fruits, huh?"

Armando paused, feeling like there was an important connection he missed somewhere in the conversation.

In the prolonged gap of silence, his iBat sounded off proudly, ". . . *been goooooone . . .*"

"I'm—sorry?" Armando finally came back with, "I really don't follow you—?"

'Yo ain't da king no mo! I AM!!" the zombie shouted. "Yo vampires are fo away in Fairyland and—and zombies, us, we here in Tra—in T—in HERE!"

"And we takin it, wot, Tra—Tr—we takin it ALL, see? Fo us, see? Zombies," he hesitated and scratched his mostly empty head, "which is wot we is," he finished, in case Armando needed clarification.

Armando looked highly offended. *"WHAT?!* You mean you're betraying ME? ARMANDO? KING of the VAMPIRES?" His tone indicated the very notion was unthinkable. The zombie tried snapping his dry, corroded fingers, and this wasn't the best move as one fell off in the attempt.

"Right, deres da ting! *Betray*, yah, dats wot we do. We take dis place here and yo vampires be our sla—our sla—" the zombie frowned.

"Slaves," Armando supplied, a razor edge on his tone. The zombie snapped again and lost another finger for it.

"Dats it, wot? I—I keep yo fo yo know lots of words, tings, wot?"

"And *you know* I can just rip you to pieces right now?" Armando huffed, absolutely furious, "Not that there's far to go, you're practically ripping yourself to pieces as it is! VAMPIRES have TREMENDOUS STRENGTH, you traitorous, detestable, smelly MORON!"

The zombie lifted a hand and there, clenched tight in one almost-complete-minus-a-couple-digits-fist, was a sight (and a smell!) worse than the rotting, reanimated corpse himself.

"GARLIC!" Armando hissed, drawing back in terror from the hideous alum. He lifted his opera cloak to shield his eyes, his sensitive nose. "NOOOO! Put it away, PUT IT AAAAWAY!"

The zombie sneered. "We all zombies, we dun have some, and some o' dem crosses and—and—water wot dun bin blest, so—so now how bout dem app—dem red fruits? Now yo vampires do wot WE SAY! Or we puts garlic in all yo beds and puts yo out in da blazin hot sunshine."

Armando glowered in hot, defeated silence, shielded protectively behind his cloak.

"...*movin' ooooonnn, YEAH YEAH, thanks*..."

"Yup. So. I da king now," the zombie preened. "So da first ting is, where da kitchen at? I gots mad 'brain cravings' now, from all dis tinking."

"The castle kitchens are on the FIRST FLOOR," Armando huffed again, arms crossed. "Have fun trying to find them. Start with any hallway and work your way downward."

"Or," his lips curled sardonically up in the corners, "I have a GPS app you could use."

*a*rmando's castle was currently full of the undead. Granted, his castle was *usually* full of the undead, but right now they were the wrong species of undead.

Zombies were everywhere; stinky, smelly, mostly rotted and corroded zombies around every corner, every bend, every damn endless corridor in the whole castle and they'd already overpowered what few vampire guards Armando had left. Between that and the garlic bulbs they were toting on them, they were pretty much filling the place with the horrific smell of disintegrating human flesh.

If this was the *Zombie Apocalypse,* perhaps the worst part of the whole experience was that it didn't come packaged with a stronger brand of deodorant.

("Zombie Fresh" 24-Hour Super Protection, with extra strength formaldehyde . . .)

Fu-Belle was still flying up the original hall where he started from (remember he's only a 1/4 of an inch tall and Armando's hallways are impossibly long) when he ran into, or rather he FLEW into, an unexpected and better-smelling surprise!

Actually, it was Kent Clark (no relation) who had shown up just in the nick of time to rejoin his traveling companions and do some damsel rescuing, both "Newly Trained" and "Super-Powered" not to mention super-pumped.

"Hey Kent," Fu greeted him. "I thought you were off to the mountains to discover your Destiny . . . or whatever you Kansas boys do in the Transylvanian mountains."

"Oh I did discover Destiny," Kent replied. "It tasted like grape mostly. But I figured you guys might still need my help."

"Oh-kay, cool," Fu wasn't sure about the grape flavored and sure as hell wasn't going to ask. He collected his thoughts.

"So Armando took our girl Anne Genue and we all split up to search the castle for her. Then these zombies showed up, hell if I know why. That's pretty much the recap, save for the longest stairway ever with the sparkly angsty-teen vampire posters and believe me when I say you got off easy."

"Anne's been kidnapped," Kent gasped. "Then there's not a moment to lose! We must save her!"

Forgetting himself and his audience of one, Kent whipped free his nerdy horn-rimmed disguise, slicked back his curly black hair with his palm, then gasped when he realized he'd just done this right in front of Fu-Belle!

Shame Mr. Oubliette and his portable changing Chinese screen weren't around (portable changing phone booth still in production).

"Oh—wait! I didn't mean to change in front of—look, this isn't what it looks like, I swear! I'm really NOT Super-Stupendous-Awesome-Man (no relation)! I know what you must be thinking—"

Fu groaned, rolling his eyes. "Kid, look—just *go and save the girl!* I didn't see ANYTHING, okay! I was looking the other direction this whole time and, "oh my god, where did you come from, Super-Whatever-Man and where did my friend Kent go, blah-blah-blah." Feel better now?"

He gave Kent Clark, uh, the "Super Whatever" (not related) a tiny shove to get him started.

Convinced, the Super-Whatever went off on his heroic rescue mission and, with his new superpowers, he was able to make the rounds of the castle halls faster than the others.

Eventually he stumbled on the room where they were holding Anne. As he dashed in with his impressive super-speed (that tasted mostly of grape), he called to Anne.

"Never fear good citizen, I'm here to save the daaaaayyyy—AURGHHH!" His fluttering cape caught in the doorjamb and choked him, cutting off the rest of his sentence.

Anne looked disappointed. "Oh hello Super-Stupendous-Awesome-Man (no relation). Thank you for coming. Guess *Hubert Pfiffer* couldn't make it, huh?" She sighed. "He was too busy with the greater good deeds for humanity, I suppose."

Kent Clark folded his arms. "You know that stupid boy wizard isn't even REAL don't you," he grumbled, tone decidedly lacking of super-heroic tact or sensitivity. "You could give some REAL GUY a shot here. Like my—um, friend, Kent Clark (no relation) who is really a nice guy and he'd be here to save you himself heroically if he could but he—"

Super-Stupendous-Awesome-Man (no relation) had to think fast on the spot, not an easy feat for 38-year-old alien superheroes, "—he, uh, needed to use the toilet again, unfortunately. Too much grape superpower—um, s-s-s-soda, I meant, too much grape soda, which he found in this place in the mountains and met his, um, long-lost dad who wasn't an alien or anything—it's *complicated.* Actually, I happened to be flying by so—um, that's how I know all this but he should tell you the story himself later."

Super-Stupendous-Awesome-Man (no relation) took a deep breath, ignored the way Anne was staring at him like he lost his mind and got back on track with the rescue,

"So—let her go, YOU FIEND!" This remark was directed to the vampire minion who was guarding Anne so she wouldn't escape, not Anne herself.

The vampire backed away from Kent (or "Super-Whatever" if you prefer). "Wait, hold on. I haven't fought with a superhero before, so time out, okay?"

He crossed his hands in a large "T" signal, whipped his iBat out of his opera cloak and quickly typed into the search feature: "How to defeat an alien superhero?"

Since Kent Clark (no relation) was raised to be polite, he waited patiently while his current vampire nemesis skimmed the highlights on the "Super Villains Wiki" and crossed to a cupboard in the room neatly labeled: "Hero Defeating Toolbox" and thumbed through the shelves.

"Bribe money, don't need that . . . supernatural weapon, no. World domination device, nope . . . ah yes, here's the one, brightly-glowing green meteor rock."

He cross-checked it against the detailed image shown on his iBat for confirmation, then, smirking, he tossed the rock at Kent Clark. "Here Wonder Boy, catch!"

"Are you serious?" Anne gaped, "You're facing down a SUPERHERO and he's the size of a freakin' LINEBACKER! He's gonna CRUSH YOU and you toss a sliver of rock to—*REALLY?!*"

This last word was snapped at Kent Clark (no relation) as he fell to his knees choking and gasping, body writhing in instant agony.

"A ROCK? *AYFKM?!* Do I really have to do EVERYTHING around here including MY OWN RESCUING, for *MYSELF*?" Anne huffed. She threw up both hands, totally exasperated.

"Some superhero you are!" She stomped over, picked up the meteor rock without blinking an eye and tossed it out the window.

"There! OMG, that was soooo HARD! Can't imagine how I managed to defeat A ROCK all by myself!" she rolled her eyes. Still wheezing, Kent Clark (no relation) managed to find his feet, thoroughly embarrassed.

"Can we just go now?" Anne Genue spun sharply about, facing the exit door.

"Hey," the vampire guard protested loudly, "You can't do that! It's against the rules! The superhero is supposed to save himself with his powers or die miserably while the super villain commences with their evil plan. That's the way it's done! You can't just rescue him and spoil it all!"

"We haven't got time for that!" Anne snapped. "Our "hero" was just taken down by A ROCK, if that says anything about his probability of survival. I'm not betting the farm here, so I need to get this whole rescuing show on the road."

"Did you know there are Transylvanian children who've never heard of *Hubert Pfiffer, Boy Wizard?!*" she thumped down the newspaper she'd been flipping through during her captivity and poked the offending headline with an accusing finger.

"Right here! I was reading all about it in the Transylvania Times while I was held captive. There are *actual schools in Transylvania* that have banned the book series entirely! Some political crap about "the separation of vampirical tradition and pop culture dissimilation" . . . it's an OUTRAGE!"

The vampire looked like he was trying to interrupt but Anne left no room for disagreement. "There's so much to do! I have a letter-writing campaign to launch, a protest rally to organize and picket signs to make—sorry, but I can't stay put for this kidnapping *nonsense* any longer! Thank you for all your hospitality but if you try to stop me, I *will* hurt you! I have a frying pan and I *will* use it!"

In fact, she'd snuck the cast-iron kitchen implement out of the weapons cabinet while the vampire guard wasn't looking and was now hefting it high with a fanatical gleam in her eye.

The vampire guard weighed his available options. "Oh. Well, um, in that case, thank you for being my captive and good luck with your escape, ma'am. The corridor to the left will take you to the elevators; from there you can catch a ride down to the first floor and exit the castle through the main lobby."

"How very kind, thank you." Anne marched out, head and frying pan held high, with the caped superhero she rescued trailing rather sheepishly behind her.

Yo castle bin overtaken," the zombie leader proclaimed, tone proud. "Today, da castle! Tomo, da whole wor—er, Trans—uh, da place where we iz at."

"Fine, take Transylvania," Armando waved it off, light and airy. "I'll hand you the keys. We vampires were evacuating anyway. We just hadn't made the formal announcement."

"Wot?" the zombie leader looked puzzled. He wasn't expecting such easy acquiescence to his hostile takeover.

Armando smirked. "That's right, my friend. Not so smart now, are we? Good luck running the place! Enjoy the tremendous expense and the constant upkeep, how it snows 364 days a year, the treacherous mountain terrain and thick impassable forests. Not to mention your always ravenous, filthy and illiterate neighbors, the werewolves. You might want to stay inside when a full moon hits, just sayin."

Armando wiggled his fingers in a dismissive gesture. "Anyway. bye now! We'll send you a postcard later, bitchez!"

". . . *thanks to u, now I get what I waaaant . . .*"

"Where yo goin den?" the zombie asked, brow furrowed. Armando yawned, patting his fangs.

"Who, us? Not far. Just to the moon. So go on, keep this planet. It isn't like we even need it now. It's very—" Armando hunted for the word, "—oh, *nice*, I guess, if you like that sort of thing. Could be a decent vacation spot to visit, I suppose."

"Wot? Da moon?"

Armando rolled his eyes. "Seriously, don't you follow me on BaTwingger? You should really do your homework if you're going to betray us and conquer the whole country and all. I mean, I've only been

BaTwingging about it for, like, WEEKS now. We're leaving Transylvania and instituting a new vampire colony up on the moon! *Duh!"*

He began to pace, ignoring the zombie's incredulous stare. "The environment is so *perfect* for vampires! We sent up test shuttles months ago, just to try out the new digs, and I have to say I really like it! It's so quiet; all cool, dry air. None of that blazing Earth sunshine guano, and it's guaranteed to be 100% garlic and holy water free!"

He turned back to face the zombie leader, spreading both hands apart. "So, we're evacuating Transylvania to permanently relocate to the moon. It's exactly the right spot for a vampire to hang his wings up and relax! Up there, the cool, endless night lasts forever and ever!"

The zombie looked shocked. Clearly it hadn't occurred to him that there were worlds to conquer beyond the boundaries of his own home planet. Being undead had opened up new frontiers of human—well, *zombie* exploration!

"You can keep Transylvania," Armando yawned, politely patting his protruding fangs.

"To be honest, I was a bit worried about the resale value. I don't think I'll be able to recap the purchase price. It's grown overpopulated, overrated, overcrowded—and oh Pulmonary Arteries, don't get me started on the pollution and global warming on this planet Earth! Please take this trash heap off our hands, I beg you."

"Yo will take us zombies to the moon, slave!" the zombie leader ordered.

Armando huffed. "What? Zombies in space? I think *not!* Seriously, we already let you have your little *Zombie Apocalypse* and double-crossing scheme. Must we do everything for you?"

"Besides, if I let you zombies come along, I'd have to let everyone else come and colonize with us too! Where would it all end, I ask you? We'd have the same problems as we did here on Earth: overpopulation, interracial warfare, gross pollution and global warming destroying the moon colony . . . no, sorry. I won't have it."

"YO WILL TAKE US WITH YO, SLAVE!" the zombie leader was growing hot now. Armando yawned again.

"Oh no, my friend! YOU wanted Transylvania remember? That's what we agreed on and the deal is final. Sorry, but the moon colony is off-limits to zombies. Vampires only!"

There was no telling what the angry zombie leader might have done next if Armando didn't break his poker face then. First with a wide grin, then going for broke, he threw his head back and laughed loudly.

"Holy guano! You just like, TOTALLY BOUGHT THAT! Bwahahahahahah! Seriously, no I mean, *seriously?!* I just EPICALLY batshitted you there! You, my devious zombie friend, were BATSHITTED, HA! I SO have to BaTwingg this one!! OMG, my friends list will DIE! Moon Colony, bwahahahahaha! *Vampires! On the MOON!* That's SO my new Majick-Book status!"

"*. . . guess u never felt that way, but since . . .*"

"SHUT UP!" the zombie leader finally snapped at him. Eons of traditionally empowered human captors bullying their helpless prisoners came rushing to his aid. That was the way it was supposed to go. The prisoner wasn't allowed to mouth off or get the better of you. Some instincts are ingrained deeply in the human spirit, undead or no.

Armando ignored the angry zombie leader. He was much too busy adding the fifth "hee" to his status update.

"*. . . YEEEEEEAH, I GEEEETTTT WHAAAAT I WAAAANNNTTT . . .*"

His iBat sounded off like crazy with all the shares across various social networks. The "Vampire Moon Colony" had already gone viral and would be popular on his friend feeds for awhile, he could tell. (Alucard already commented "LOL for immortality!" and "good one!")

Armando beamed with pride and a sense of accomplishment. His MeIzSoPopular social status could only benefit from this. He was back on the rise again.

Did it even matter if his country was just taken over by zombies? Hmm, maybe that would actually get him more shares on Majick-Book? He'd have to think of a catchy status about that. The point was, he was sure now he'd be at the "Mr. Cool" level now by the end of the week!

Later, reports stated this was how the *second* "Zombie Apocalypse" came about. Technically it only involved one zombie, albeit a very angry and vengeful one, and the length of lead pipe.

Poor Armando, had he been conscious, would be much more traumatized by what happened next to his beloved iBat! It was just as well he was smashed first before the phone so he didn't have to witness the violence, though the constant social activity feed and unfortunate timing of notification ringtone was hardly the fault of the technology.

With that, the zombie leader hefted the still-unconscious Armando on his rapidly disintegrating shoulders and marched, armed and dangerous, to find some brain to eat. He also went to locate his zombie troops who needed to witness the defeat of the mighty vampire king at the hand of their leader.

Yes Virginia, There *is* a *Hubert Pfiffer!* Boy Wizard!

O ur tableau of heroes met up not a moment too soon. Though as Fate would have it, they were aided in their efforts as each was caught and brought together with the others by the zombie forces, leading to torture, mutilation, death threats and the eventual slow, painful demise these sorts of situations generally entailed.

Kent Clark (no relation) had changed back to his farm boy alter ego and was sulky over his epic failure to rescue and impress the girl, and that she now held suspicions over the weakness of his bladder. Was she hopelessly infatuated with his caped crusader side, no!

Instead, all she'd talk about was how wrong it was that Transylvanian citizens were legally prohibited from reading about the many highly-improbable adventures of *Hubert Pfiffer! Imaginary-Yet-Still-Manages-To-Be-A-Total-Pain-In-My-Ass-Wizard!*

Seriously, you killed yourself to unearth and develop your stupid alien birth powers and what was it all worth in the end? You got super-powered and it still didn't change a damn thing! You were treated like a big Uber-Nerd from Kansas (with a weak bladder) by your dream girl, while Hubert Pfiffer (who was a REAL NERD, and NOT A REAL PERSON AT ALL even at that) still got the girl and the glory!

While Anne was busy organizing her protest rally against the book censorship, Kent Clark (no relation) resolved he was going to be preoccupied with organizing a HP!BW! book burning!

Biffy (the Vampire Slayer until about an hour ago) didn't appear too bothered by the fact that Kent Clark (no relation) was the rescuer of pretty Anne. Nor did he seem too surprised to find out that Anne was the one who did the actual rescuing.

He had ditched the cheerleader outfit and was now shirtless and dipped in what one could only hope was cooking oil, bearing his pizza and beer love-handles left and right to do any bodice-ripper cover photo proud.

He also seemed distracted, absent-minded even, sort of like he'd been making out with a pretty girl for the suspicious length of time he'd been missing in action and not, as the others were, lost in the labyrinth of castle hallways.

He was fascinated with a slip of paper held in his hand. It had a heart drawn around a European phone number, one of those with about 35 digits and a + sign (not that he had any idea how to dial that, but Biffy wasn't accustomed to having to ask for step-by-step instructions after a pretty girl just said, "call me").

Anyone piecing these clues together might also take note that Biffy had, just in the past hour, changed his Majick-Book relationship status to: "It's so complicated you'd need a decoder ring".

Mr. Oubliette was likewise distracted. He'd grown bored with the search and rescue, so he settled down with Armando's HD 1080p cable television until the zombies finally unearthed him in one of the rooms and separated him from the boob tube. It wasn't as long as you might think; he only had time for 3 wardrobe changes but it was long enough for Mr. O to catch the film, *"Hubert Pfiffer! Boy Wizard! and the Philosopher's Sequined Slippers"* on local cable.

Mr. Oubliette found that he rather liked it and was already determined to attend wizard school himself and play a magical flight sport in mid-air! He was sure he'd be amazing once he manufactured a hairspray strong enough to withstand "wind-hair".

Predictably one of his costume changes had been the philosopher's sequined slippers, but Mr. O had also role-played the head wizard of a magic school and a royal, headless ghost in the past hour-and-half of the movie. He was considering reading the book series as well, if only for a better description of the wardrobe.

Tailor Wear had faithfully followed his master's scent all the way back from the snowy fortress. He was the only one grateful to the zombies for being taken into captivity since it had reunited him with his GOOD and KIND Master Kent Clark (n.r.). He was so grateful in fact that he tried lapping the decaying faces of the zombies who captured him, but only once.

Viagra (the Persian god, not the little pink pill) returned feeling the full support of his ancient pantheon behind him (a rare treat among gods) in this Hollywood venture he'd embarked upon.

So far the response to his first draft of an exciting action-packed script containing gods, vampires, zombies and werewolves interlocked in an intense species war for survival was favorable—but those "Hollywood agency" high priests and priestesses were *very demanding*! They wanted an ending to the project before they offered it as a burnt sacrifice to the Land of Movies highest deity: His Almightyness, the Hollywood Producer!

Why the script to be finished, Verethraghna wasn't sure, as it underwent many, many, many revisions after that, invoking many sacred Hollywood incantations such as "marketability", "demographic" and "social campaign platform". It was therefore a mortal sin in Hollywood to approve a first draft of anything, and was punishable by low budgets and automatic B-movie effects.

Nevertheless, the Persian god had returned to the Zombie Apocalypse simply to spread his name around and to see how it all ended. This was apparently a special ritual known as, "social networking".

He was very busy post-capture grilling every zombie he could with: *"what was their character(s) motivation?"* The zombies responded that they liked to eat brains and wanted to live somewhere that by federal law had no rifles. Apparently they had attempted conquering the State of Texas before Transylvania but that had led to a nasty surprise.

And, *"if this were a film script, do you think this might be a good spot for an extreme martial-arts action sequence involving, say, a war god who was Persian, all-powerful, intelligent and yet also extremely handsome?"* The zombies felt it could be the right spot, depending on which action hero was cast in the role.

It should be noted that Verethraghna was the only one captured who wasn't complaining about the zombie's rotting flesh stink, though they likewise seemed to have no complaints on the state of his ancient, unwashed, matted animal skin toga.

Fu-Belle in the meantime remained worried about the safety of his new friends. Well, the human ones at least, considering they were the ones on the zombies main menu. For them to be reunited after all their adventures, only to be beset by a greater danger—gee, one would almost think it was scripted.

True, they had a superhero with them, such as he was in his hand-sewn cape and footie pajamas. They even had a god among them, older than time but it worked for immortals, and—*and they had Mr. Oubliette too*—Fu didn't dare speculate what advantage that might prove.

But the crush of the zombie hordes was overwhelming. Was there some outbreak of genetic warfare that caused an overall zombie plague in the human realm? Fu hadn't heard about anything like that but this appeared to be multiple generations of undead legions here!

Sure, the term "zombie apocalypse" indicated more than one or two stragglers but . . . but . . . *all this?* The empty ballroom that the zombies had shuffled their captives into was spacious (it took up nearly the entire second floor of Armando's gigantic Transylvanian castle) but they were still pressed for space by thousands upon thousands of decaying, undead and reanimated human corpses everywhere!

Who knows what might have happened to our heroes next—but everyone was startled, distracted from the dire situation by a loud clatter, followed by flashes of green light and smoke filling the room. No one knew what the ruckus was. But whatever was causing it, it was emanating from the huge fireplace.

A figure emerged from the smoke arguing or, given that he appeared to be all alone, perhaps loudly grumbling to himself though his tone was decidedly argumentative.

"You STUPID Flue! I SAID I wanted transportation! Not TRANSYLVANIA! T-R-A-N-S-P-O-R-T-A-T-I-O-N! Don't you ever LISTEN right?"

Though the boy in the chimney gave no identification, nor even acknowledged there were others in the room to witness him, he was immediately recognized by all of them. His distinctive likeness was stamped on every book cover across many countries, and apparently even across *many worlds and universes* as well.

"*Oh my God! That's Hubert Pfiffer! Boy Wizard!*" someone said, in a tone of awe.

Everyone in the room stared at him, in shock and growing excitement. It *was* THE Hubert Pfiffer, that legendary boy wizard, far superior of a deity than a god! Surely he was, for after all, the god's greatest claim to fame was merely the creation of mankind. Did *the gods* invent both Majick-Book and the Smart Phone in the space of a solo Saturday afternoon? Hardly.

Hubert did in fact look to be a boy wizard, as the name would suggest. He was short, wearing the formal uniform of a British children's preparatory boarding school, and he also wore thick round glasses.

Anne, for reasons inexplicable, was instantly in love—perhaps proving that love is indeed blind or yes, possibly invented by Hubert Pfiffer.

"HUBERTTTTT PFFFFIFFFFFER!" she shrieked at an excited, canine decibel loud enough to awaken the dead.

"OMGOMGOMGOMGOMG! THIS IS REALLY HAPPENING! I'm your BIGGEST FAN . . . can I have your babies—er, autograph?"

"Oh stupid, STUPID Anne Genue," she began scolding herself before Hubert could even reply, "Of course he doesn't have time for autographs! He's HUBERT PFIFFER! BOY WIZARD!"

She didn't allow him any quarter to get a word in before continuing all in a rush, "OMG, OMG, OMG!! ILU so much, like you just don't even know, and I've read ALL THE BOOKS and I've earned my first year wand already and I hope this year will be my year to earn the *Pfiffer Cup*! It's my dream! Maybe even by the end of the semester."

She turned then and glared full force at all the guys, "SEE?! HE IS REAL, I TOLD YOU SO! NOW YOU SEE I WAS RIGHT! HA!"

In a general manner of speaking, it was never a good day to be a man finding himself next to a woman who'd turned out to be right where he was wrong (though mind you, it was far from an uncommon situation).

But it'd prove to be *far worse day* to be *the real Hubert Pfiffer! Boy Wizard! within arms-reach of other men who'd been hearing about him the entire trip here!*

The zombies suddenly became incidental as Hubert Pfiffer was surrounded by a wall of very angry testosterone. Anne didn't bother to notice though poor Hubert couldn't help but to notice. Even Fu-Belle was almost as tall as he was, and that was only the start of his problems!

"I'm so glad you're here! I just knew you'd save us," Anne gushed, her pupils practically transformed into hearts. "Can't you do something to get rid of these zombies for us? I'm dying to see a real Hubert Pfiffer spell done live and in person!"

"Um, you mean work a spell, right?" Hubert Pfiffer asked nervously. "Well—the thing is . . . the thing is, see—spells are complicated, um. There's special magic words you have to say, and you have to get them just right or things go terribly wrong and that's *really bad.* Um."

"So, how is that a problem for the prodigious boy wizard who invented cheese doodles," Fu asked nastily, glaring at the kid, "and sign language?"

"And stole fire from the gods, who'd like that back by the way," Verethraghna growled. A lightning bolt with which to smite him was already forming on the tips of the Persian god's fingers.

"And invented the Smart Phone and Majick-Book," Biffy hissed, cracking his knuckles.

"Not to mention, inventing TRUE LOVE itself," Kent Clark (no relation) added, balling his super-fists so hard that the oxygen in the air around them was already sporting bruises.

There was a slight hesitation on his part, because of Hubert's size and thick glasses and Kent's new superpowers, that this behavior might be construed as "bullying" (a big no-no in the Superheroes handbook, tantamount to "using your powers for evil" or "not rescuing little kitties from tall trees"). But Kent was prepared to risk it.

It was looking less and less like a good day to be the famous, young, amazing *Hubert Pfiffer! Boy Wizard!* Right about now, a fancy new fast-getaway broomstick or invisibility cloak gifted out of a clear blue sky to Hubert mysteriously with no explanation by an equally mysterious but oddly generous benefactor with limitless resources would come in mighty handy for the young and soon-to-be-deceased legendary wizard! It was very strange that it didn't happen in real life when it never failed to occur right on cue whenever Hubert Pfiffer was in grave peril in one of his books.

"Um—well, stories of my accomplishments might have been slightly exaggerated. For narrative effect," Hubert Pfiffer said nervously.

"Slightly? *Slightly?*"

"Exaggerated? You don't say?"

"Narrative effect, huh?"

Nobody sounded much impressed. Hubert nodded convincingly.

"Well—blimey, I mean, *it is supposed to be fiction*. You understand that means it's not real? Anyway, what did you expect? The books *were* authored by my mum."

The men (and gods, and fairies, and—well you get the picture) all exchanged glances and scrambled to find a copy of the novel to check. This wasn't difficult as Armando had the boxed hardcover, 7-book, leather-bound "Spell-Binders" special edition copy, because even vampire kings on remote mountains in Transylvania had read the *Hubert Pfiffer! Boy Wizard!* books. As if there was any doubt.

Sure enough, the author's name was clearly embossed in gold on the spine of the book: *Mildred Pfiffer*.

Ah, yes. Funny how no one had ever noticed it before. Suddenly, it began to click into place for the very disgruntled body of men.

"You mean you didn't actually *invent* chocolate?"

"Or find the lost city of Atlantis while excavating your bathtub?"

"Or travel back in time to the Garden of Eden and beat that lying snake Satan into the ground with a stick?"

"Or invent TRUE LOVE?" Kent Clark (no relation) added again, sounding extremely sarcastic. Hubert Pfiffer shifted, a little uncomfortable under the intensity of their glares.

"Oh, is all that in there?" he asked. "I never read the books myself, but Mum said they were based loosely on some of the letters I used to write her from school. She said they were very good."

The luckless Mr. Pfiffer had just proceeded to sign his own death warrant. It would've gone down very badly for him indeed had it not been for Anne, whose disapproving glare was the ultimate impediment against male physical violence.

"Oh, I'd be happy to tell you all about your marvelous exploits. I've got them all memorized," she gushed, in the throes of utter fangirl joy.

"But, couldn't you do something about those pesky zombie armies in the meantime so we can talk? Turn them, I dunno, into ants or something?"

"Um, I—could—try," Hubert Pfiffer said, again sounding very nervous.

"No doubt he could invent a cage for them out of a pack of chewing gum and tweezers, then capture and imprison them all single-handedly," Fu grumbled.

"Or no doubt he could take them and reform them into workers for Santa Claus to make cute little toys for orphaned, one-legged children so the elves could take the year off and go on vacation," Biffy snarled.

"Or he could go back in time and keep them from ever dying in the first place and convince them to turn to a life of charity and goodness," Verethraghna sniffed.

"Or he could invent a whole new human emotion for them, something far bigger and grander than TRUE LOVE," Kent Clark (no relation) balled his fists up again. That infamous claim of Hubert's seemed to be a personal effrontery to him.

Tailor also growled at Hubert loyally, not sure what the problem was but could tell something was bothering GOOD and KIND Master Kent.

"I'm sure whatever Hubert Pfiffer chooses to do with those dreadful zombies, it will be utterly brilliant, more than we could think of and solely for the betterment of mankind."

Only Anne sounded perfectly sincere when she said this and she beamed at Hubert Pfiffer encouragingly, who in turn looked (to be blunt) scared spitless.

As a collective, the men in the room folded their arms across their chests and coldly stared. Was anyone here volunteering to play a round of wizard's chess on a giant chessboard as a timely distraction so *Hubert Pfiffer! Boy Wizard!* could slip past his enemies and go on to victory and glory?

From the looks of the faces, that was a unanimous "oh *HELL* no!"

Hubert turned to face the hordes of thousands upon thousands of hungry zombies, all eyeing him like his brain looked mighty tasty.

"You have to say the magic words, darling," Anne beamed lovingly at him. "*Incantus Corporous Ant-hillus*. Then wave your wand like so," she made a complicated gesture with her left hand.

"It's a very simple spell. Any first year wizard could do it. But I know you're just feeling out the wand's *intensity* first."

"Of COURSE," Hubert jumped on that like a mad dog on a scrap of raw meat, "I'm feeling out the wand's intensity, that's what I'm doing. All wizards, er, have to do that before casting a spell cuz, um, you can get into real trouble if you don't feel out your wand's intensity."

He cleared his throat, very nervously. "Right, so . . . ummm?"

"*Incantus—*" Anne prompted.

"*Innncaaantus—*"

"*Corporous—*"

"*Corp-orrr-ousss—*" Hubert seemed to be stuttering over his pronunciation.

"*Ant-hillus.* Then wave in a figure 2-8."

"Ant-hill-us," Hubert mumbled, then fumbled nervously with the wand. Anne clucked her tongue.

"Oh no, I said a 2-8 . . . no, that's not it, Hubert darling. Look, here, like this," she placed her hand over his with a warm, adoring smile and in a slow, careful motion she demonstrated how he was to maneuver the wand.

"That's perfect," she praised him. "No doubt you just forgot that spell; it's such a simple one. Obviously you're much more advanced."

"Obviously," Hubert Pfiffer mumbled, pushing up the brim of his round glasses. Unfortunately the spell had no effect whatsoever. None of the zombies transformed into tiny ants.

This may have been because, unbeknownst to Mr. Pfiffer, his wand had the magic valve switched off and was set on "training mode". But it still caused a stir among the zombie hordes.

"Hey, dat dere is . . . uh, Hooberrt Pfiffer, I tink," said a zombie, proving that you could be missing half-a-brain and dead for the better part of a century and still recognize *Hubert Pfiffer! Boy Wizard!* on sight.

"Ooohhh, I need him to sign his name fo my kid," another zombie exclaimed. "My kid, he dun shoot me in da head with a long-range rifle if I meeted da real Hoobert Pfiff-fiff-fiff-fiff—er and dun git him to sign somethin."

The zombie didn't seem to grasp where to punctuate the "fiffs" with the "er" and Anne zeroed in like a laser beam ready to educate him on how to address a boy wonder.

Within minutes, *Hubert Pfiffer! Boy Wizard!* was surrounded by an adoring, undead public, begging for autographs and offering bribes of brain or flesh (whichever was his preference), wanting to hear all about how he defeated Dark Lord Whatshisface.

Anne was practically beating them off him with a stick. Even her hoopskirt was fighting for space enough to swish.

"He's MINE, I saw him FIRST," she huffed, glaring at the zombies. She waved her frying pan menacingly in the air as a warning to any insolent, "touchy feely" types. "I WILL KILL YOU! You may *look*—but DON'T TOUCH THE PFIFFER!"

The men looked on in wonder. Astonishingly and right before their very eyes it had, most unexpectedly, turned into a very *GOOD day indeed* to be *Hubert Pfiffer! Boy Wizard!* Any moment now, mysterious benefactors would be rushing in with unique, powerful and equally mysterious gifts for the boy wizard! It was their cue!

But after all, what could you expect? As they say, STBYANHPBW! (Sucks to be you and not *Hubert Pfiffer! Boy Wizard!*)

Shortly the room was organized into two queues of patiently waiting zombie fans, plus a few vampire guards who'd simply wandered in at the right time and two bewildered teen girls who were searching the castle for the attractively-sparkling Leonard and had decided that *Hubert Pfiffer! Boy Wizard!* was an acceptable celebrity substitute.

One queue was arranged for those who wanted autographs and photos and the other queue merely wanted to shake the hand of the real *Hubert Pfiffer! Boy Wizard!*

Meanwhile Hubert was quickly rigged to Armando's castle PA system and he nervously, punctuated with many "um's" from a long time fear of public speaking, was broadcasting over the castle intercom the valiant story of how he defeated Big Bad Dark Lord What-The-Flaggnog-Ever, with coaching from Anne on the sidelines.

She helpfully interjected every time he got stuck on parts of the story (such as, THE STORY which he starred in, but had never read) therefore Anne was the one doing most of the talking. The zombies ooohhh-ed and ahhh-ed appreciatively at every suspenseful moment while our heroes watched this in stunned silence.

Fu-Belle couldn't believe the magic spell that had come over everyone. It was mesmerizing, stronger than magic, the luck this kid had! Kid couldn't even work his own wand—but somehow he'd still come out on top, just like in the books.

Kent Clark (no relation) was envious-green and utterly convinced that *Hubert Pfiffer! Boy Wizard!* had never even kissed a real live girl before! *Invented "true love", pah!* The mere fact that Kent hadn't kissed a girl either (at age 38) didn't overly concern him at the moment.

Biffy, the shirtless, Not-Currently-A-Vampire-Slayer, was standing eagerly in the autograph line and streaming live web feed to Majick-Book from his smart-phone.

Holy crap, the REAL *Hubert Pfiffer! Boy Wizard!* and Biffy was meeting him in person! Sam and Dean would be sooooo jealous, nothing like this ever happened to them on a vampire raid. Seriously though, Biffy resolved he was coming back to vacation in Transylvania every year!

Mr. Oubliette was deciding, in matters of costuming, what it would take to be *Hubert Pfiffer! Older By Several Hundred Years Wizard!* tomorrow. However, his version of the traditional wizard's cloak and wand involved more glitter and sequins than usually allowed by most British preparatory schools, even under fantasy novel standards.

And Verethraghna, the Persian war god, was currently musing over how this kid apparently had seven, not ONE, but SEVEN! big-budget, money-grossing, fully approved and merchandised, Hollywood blockbusters named after him, AND APPARENTLY, also STARRING HIM!! WOW! Just the *merchandising rights* to that franchise *alone*—oh, the very *thought* made Verethraghna feel little dizzy! *How had he done something like this?*

Why, that was more box-office blockbuster films made for ONE KID, a mortal kid no less, than all the movies based around ancient god pantheons put together? Here lies the history of hundreds of early, primal civilizations packaged in better CGI special effects, glorious 3-D color and THX sound enhancement and spectacular battle sequences than the ancient pantheons dared to dream of—but what modern audiences inexplicably WANTED to see on the big screen was a short, stumpy, nerdy kid in round glasses at school?

Verethraghna wasn't modernized enough of a god yet for "seriously" but that summed up his perspective in one word.

As Hubert Pfiffer descended the podium, gulping down water from a plastic bottle that mysteriously bore his image scanned on the label (Yes, it was a *Hubert Pfiffer! Bottled Wizarding Water!* normally 10$ GTR retail but this now being a celebrity venue, the price had skyrocketed to 25$ GTR), he was offered a disgusting bowl of chili-cheez nachos that only the truly starving or truly color blind would consume. Nothing came organically in that shade of neon orange, let alone cheese. However, this didn't prevent the concessionaires from hocking nachos to several of the zombies at 15$ GTR a pop.

To his surprise, the Boy Wizard found his face was branded on everything he saw around him, despite him only having been in Armando's castle for maybe 20 minutes, tops.

Ah yes! The franchisee merchandising salespeople had arrived, and already there were booths lined up along the ballroom walls with a plethora of *HP!BW!*-branded-everything-you-could-possibly-want-or-imagine, from "I Heart HP!BW!" T-shirts to coffee mugs, wall posters to 8x10 signed glossies; iBat or iWolf phone covers (iZombie still in production) and reusable tote bags ("Save the Ecosystem with HP!BW! Live Wizarding-School Green!").

Collectable hardcover editions of each of the books were available, signed in "magical golden disappearing ink" by the Boy Wizard himself ("Say an Incantation to Make HP!BW! Signature Magically Appear on the Page! Impress Your Friends!") Even a stack of "New Zombie Translation" editions of the 7 novels were available just for this venue ("Don't be left out of the fun! So you can't read *Hubert Pfiffer! Boy Wizard's!* marvelous adventures just because your brain is half-missing? Here, buy the easier-to-read copy with included *Wizard-to-Zombie* terminology lexicon!").

The zombies couldn't even make it past the marketing blurb, but they were snatching up the books in droves anyway. The cover photo was clear enough.

No one, possibly not even *Hubert Pfiffer! Inventor of True Love!* himself, could bend the physics of space and time quite like a major marketing franchise when faced with a massive celebrity venue chockfull of fans to which they can sell licensed products!

Christmas had come unexpectedly early for HP!BW! franchisee holders and every precious second that ticked by while Hubert was on the podium and they didn't have booths in place *was a second where someone wasn't buying an ordinary bottled water with HPBW's face stamped on it at FIVE TIMES THE NORMAL PRICE!*

It's unclear how franchisee owners find this stuff out but they're certainly quick about it! It's rumored they were there at "Washington Crossing the Delaware" in 1776 with a booth featuring tiny American flag wall pennants (with 13 stars) and "Team Betsy Ross" T-shirts.

It's widely assumed that black holes, impossibly complicated physics and lightspeed are all involved in this mystery somehow, possibly with a technological device centuries ahead of its time. (Somebody please tell the Doctor to start locking his time-space bending vehicle up at night).

Yes, modern technology will catch up at some point but by then, the franchises will have figured out how to telepathically market to you utilizing your own natural brainwaves and will charge you FIFTEEN TIMES THE NORMAL PRICE FOR BOTTLED WATER, and make you think it was your own brilliant idea! This is what your average franchisee marketing rep dreams about every night and asks Santa Claus for in his Christmas letters, which he then mails to the North Pole as "postage collect from recipient".

As Hubert Pfiffer stared at his distinctive likeness, slathered on every sellable item as far as the eye could see, Anne sidled over to him, wearing a large "I Heart HP!BW!" T-shirt draped over her pink princess dress and munching on a "Very-Berry Wizard's Cone of Magically-Delicious Cotton Candy", and happily plunked down a thick, heavy sheaf of paper into his arms.

Hubert Pfiffer looked down at it, puzzled. "Um . . . what is this?"

Anne openly beamed, proud as a mother with her new infant. "Well, I was just thinking—see, I kinda wrote this story about—well, it's about YOU, darling, sort of—although I wouldn't call it a *fanfic* per se, because fanfic really sucks, IKR?"

"But this is like, NOT A FANFIC but, a REALLY, REALLY GOOD STORY about this girl whose so not a Mary Sue character AT ALL that goes to your school! See, her name is Princess Anne, um, no relation to me of course," Anne blushed, trudging her toe in the ground.

Hubert Pfiffer, with something of a "deer in the headlights" expression, blushed too. "Um . . ."

"—and Princess Anne is just like, WAAAAAY pretty! I mean, TRUST ME, she's like, SO MUCH PRETTIER than any know-it-all, big-haired wizard-girl in the books, as if!"

"Anyway, so she goes to wizard's school and some, like, adventure stuff happens to her and she all like, finds out she has like these amazing wizard's powers see—"

"Um . . ."

"—and she like meets Hubert Pfiffer there and he totally falls in love with her at first sight, and they get married and she has his baby, which is so gorgeous BTW—"

Now Hubert Pfiffer was looking highly uncomfortable, cornered and not a little panicked. "Uh, um, well—" his eyes darted this way and that for rescue. Where were his "Defense Against The Dark Spells" professors right now? This situation was starting to look worse than being eaten alive by zombies.

"—but their baby has like, you know, these AMAZING wizarding powers cuz like, it's both their powers combined, and so it's all like, this BIG DEALIO, like will little Huberta Pfiffer follow in her parent's footsteps to become a truly great wizardess or will like, she go all dark side with her powers and ally with the forces of the Dark Lord—"

Hubert Pfiffer stared at the 400+ pages in his hand with something akin to horror. It was alarming that Anne Genue had gone to the extent of having her amateur story professionally leather-bound.

"—so I thought you might pass that on to your Mom for me," Anne beamed even more, experiencing that hopeful, optimistic glow all fanfiction writers encounter when they think they've finally cracked the secret cipher code on how to be as beloved as the real deal and go legit, from hobbyist to paying gig.

She wasn't due to receive the soul-crushing disappointment until months later, when the polite rejection form letter would come from one of Ms. Pfiffer's army of personal assistants. It would gently explain that while Ms. Pfiffer was always delighted to hear from her fans and was thrilled her story made such an impression and would definitely take their suggestions under advisement.

However, it would deliberately leave out the bit where Anne's carefully-bound fanfic was dropped in the incinerator unread past the first paragraph, a lengthy description of Princess Anne's pink ballgown, who clearly was (no relation) to Anne Genue, and who was also the future Mrs. Pfiffer and soon-to-be-legendary Wizardess and mother of little *Huberta Pfiffer! Indeterminate Wizard!* which she then wore to her very own "Wizard School Acceptance Grand Ball" at her wealthy family's 500,000 acre palatial estate.

But she *wasn't* a Mary Sue character, let's get that straight. Despite how everyone *loves* those characters at first sight, especially if they are the very famous hero of the book!

"Okay," Hubert mumbled his agreement, probably because he didn't want to be beaten into a smudge on the floor with a frying pan by an offended, slightly rabid fangirl.

"I'll show your story to Mum. Can you, um, help me get out of here now?"

Anne gasped. "Of course! How insensitive of me! Mankind *needs you* and you have so much still to do for the greater good, and here I am selfishly hogging you all to myself."

"Yeah, and I'm all out of flue powder," Hubert mumbled again, pushing the brim of his glasses.

"I think I can help," Mr. Oubliette said, stepping forward and fumbling in his Man!Purse. Anne eyed him closely.

"Wait. Are you actually *wearing* the Philosopher's Sequined Slippers?"

"The what—?" Hubert looked lost. Anne waved him off.

"Oh, they are these magical ruby shoes that can transport you to different worlds, and the Dark Lord tries to steal them to use as a weapon against good wizards and you—oh never mind. I'll tell you what you did to stop him later." She turned back to Mr. Oubliette suspiciously.

"Fine, but this better be a good plan or I'll hit you over the head with my frying pan! Don't test me!"

"Duck behind the screen, quickly," Mr. Oubliette ordered Hubert who did so, slipping behind the enormous fold-out Chinese screen. There were a few flashes, tosses of glitter in the air and again that mysterious sound of hair dryer running, then another strange sound that went something like, "TWWWWAAANNG!"

When Mr. O folded up the screen again, there stood Hubert . . . well, *probably* Hubert. He was the right size and shape but there the resemblance ended.

Instead of wizarding school robes and a wand, he was garbed in strange attire; a black and blue rhinestone-studded corset-waistcoat, black cape, a pair of thigh-high glossy black boots, and skin-tight black breeches. His round glasses were also missing and his dark hair was inexplicably longer and looked something like a mullet crossed with a severe electrical shock, feathering on down to his shoulders.

In one black-gloved fist he held a crystal orb. No one knew why. In the other hand, mysteriously, a small, leather riding crop. (Again, we have to point out ... why?)

"Oh!EM!Gee!" Anne shrieked. "HUBERT! WHAT THE HELL HAVE YOU DONE TO HIM?! WHAT IS HE?!"

"I don't know," Mr. Oubliette studied him, thoughtful yet pleased. "He looks good though, doesn't he? I outdid myself."

Anne looked ready to pop a blood vessel. "I'm getting the frying pan," she hissed but noticed the zombies were letting Hubert pass, probably because they didn't know what he was either.

The last thing any of them remember seeing was Hubert tapping the glass of the crystal orb he held, murmuring, "Hey, is this thing on?"

Witnesses say he vanished in a puff of glitter before the sentence was even finished.

Everyone was distracted from the magical disappearance of *Hubert Pfiffer!* when the leader of the zombies strode in, still clutching his length of lead pipe with the unconscious form of Armando strung triumphantly across his shoulders like a limp lion skin.

(Oh, did you forget that cliffhanger already? No, don't flip back a couple chapters—we'll catch you up. The leader of the zombies not only tricked and betrayed King Armando, but he kicked off the Second *Zombie Apocalypse* by knocking Armando unconscious with a lead pipe).

He climbed up to the podium, dropping Armando in the process, took the cordless microphone still rigged to Armando's castle PA system and the intercom clicked on.

"Greetins, yo! We zombies iz vic—we victor—we dun won Trans—where we iz at!" There were some scattered applause from the crowd.

"Da king o vamps iz put down!" This drew a cheer from the watching hordes. The zombie leader lifted the smashed iBat in the air where all could see it.

"And his annoyin' little CELL PHONE too!" This drew another cheer.

"Yah well dey can take away our lives," the zombie leader yelled, revved up with excitement, "But dey can no never take OUR UN-LIIIIIVES!" Now the crowd was a roar.

"Unless dey dun shoot us in da head with long range rifles," one zombie piped up from the crowd helpfully. The zombie leader glared and fumbled for recovery.

"Fine yah, dat, but dey can't no never take—" he scratched his mostly missing cranium, "OUR—FREEEEDOMMM!"

"Unless dey dun lock us in jail cells and—"

The zombie leader shook his weapon threateningly at the mouthy zombie in the audience.

"Look! If yo dun wan no big hole in yo head like Armando, shut yo brain-hole NOW!"

Wisely, the other zombie backed off.

Fu-Belle had a sudden flash of inspiration. Zombies were once human, right? Well, humans and fairies shared a very special and complicated relationship.

The thing was, Humanity (for reasons inexplicable to either race) were born with a consistent flaw in their genetic make-up. They *wanted to believe* that fairies were sweet, kind and generous little magical beings, just because they were tiny and cute or whatever . . .

Yes, this could work if he did it right. He whipped out his very best, "I'm a good fairy, yes you can trust the shit out of me," expression and flew over to the zombie leader, fumbling in his crackle pouch for his collapsible wand. No wand was strictly necessary, but it added to the theatrics of the occasion. Humans did have certain expectations and fairies had to give a good show.

He stopped when he reached the podium, trying to look the helpful type, "I'm the sort of fairy who gives away crocks of gold coins for free".

"Why HELLO THERE," he said brightly to the zombie leader, wishing he'd brought along his make-up kit. Unlike most fairy males, Fu-Belle didn't wear make-up just for fun, but there were times when it helped to sell the bit. You had to look good, downright magical even. Much as Fu hated to admit it, the sparklies helped.

"I'm your fairy god—er," Fu paused. Fairy *godmother*, though traditional, was definitely off the docket. Although he was a loyal patriot of Fairyland, there were some things even he refused to do for his homeland.

"—I'm your fairy god *law-enforcement officer* and you're such a good human and law-abiding citizen that I've come to help you—no, bless you! Yes I've come to bless you, that's what I've come to do."

"I gots a fairy god law-enforcement officer?" the zombie leader said, puzzled. Like any other human, he'd grown up a steady diet of "altruistic fairies helping good humans make their dreams come true" bedtime stories, such as slaying dragons with glass slippers or however it went.

But that didn't sound entirely right.

"Of course you do! Every good and law-abiding human has one," Fu nodded reassuringly. "Why haven't you ever heard how Cinderella got to the ball? With the valuable assistance of her kindly fairy god law-enforcement officer. Seriously, it's a classic fairytale. Look it up."

"Um—" the zombie leader hesitated. Again, something felt off but missing most of his brain he couldn't put his finger on the detail that bothered him.

Besides, his human DNA and misleading animated film classics watched all through his childhood, the heavily sugar-coated ones with an idealistic view of reality, were practically screaming at him to trust this fairy! After all, it was just so SMALL and SHINY and ADORABLE it must be kind, noble and good as well! Only *bad* witches were *ugly*!

And fairies were GOOD creatures, everyone knew that. Clearly this pocket-sized, adorable fairy, albeit armed to the teeth with all the weaponry it could carry but that was probably *traditional* with fairy god law-enforcement officers, was so impressed that he'd led the entire zombie army to victory without breaking any human laws.

That's why his fairy god law enforcement officer was going to help him out, absolutely free of charge. Made perfect sense, right?

(Think about it with the idealistic logic of a sugar-coated animated children's film . . . ah, there you go).

"Um, I—"

"PERFECT!" Fu full-wattaged him with a blindingly-white and shiny smile.

"Now today my friend, you could have one whole wish granted absolutely *FREE OF COST* as part of our Fairy/Zombie Neighborhood Goodwill

Program—OR—" he let the bait dangle provocatively. The zombie leader was wide-eyed.

"Yah? YAH?? OR WOT??"

"OR—" Fu rolled the word enticingly, "—You can SPIN the BIG WHEEL O' WISHING to WIN MORE wishes, cash and prizes up to 100,000$ GTR, if THE PRIZE IS RIGHT!!!"

The zombie leader paused while the zombies all shouted excitedly at him.

"Take da free wish, take da free wish!"

"Wot, yo rotted in da head? Go for da big spin! Go for da big spin!"

"Wish fo mo wishes den!"

"Ah-ah," Fu lifted a restraining finger at the zombie who said it, "Sorry friend, that's against our terms and conditions, which you must *sign first* before we can grant your wishes today."

He smiled brightly again and held out his glittering iFairy device. "It's SO easy! Just touch the "I Agree" button on the screen there to consent to our Terms and Conditions page and CLAIM YOUR FREE WISH! No purchase necessary."

The zombie leader looked at the staggering and very lengthy paragraphs of fine print which scrolled on down the page for miles. "Do I have to read all dat letterin first before signing?"

Fu kept his shiny smile fixedly in place. "No-no, of course not, it's so simple. Just press "I Agree" right there on the touch screen, and we can get started . . ."

". . . I'm a real Nigerian prince and if you'll help me move 15,000,000GTR$ out of the country . . ."

Fu-Belle coughed. "Oh no, my friend, that's—uh. another program we're doing." He quickly scrolled down his iFairy.

"You're looking for this button here, where it says "I Agree". See it? Just click that, there's a good boy."

The zombie leader tried to think it through and gave up. It was a good fairy he was dealing with here so why not? He clicked the Agree button and Fu tried not to break his poker face.

"Now, we are obligated under Fairyland Law to inform you beforehand that any winnings received today may be considered as income by the Human World's IRS system, and held for tax liability as required by your human laws. The wish recipient is responsible for paying any and all taxes from their earnings today, due in the Human World, and the fairy granting the wish is not liable for the taxable portion of the wish or prizes awarded. This advisory is applicable in all states where required by law, including Utah."

"Also," Fu added, "Fairyland Law currently prohibits resurrections of the dead as granted wishes, due to complaints about the smell and condition in which dead loved ones arrived, although," he glanced over the throngs of watching zombies and finished brightly, "seems like you already have that part covered."

He took a quick breath and refreshed his game show smile. "So, my zombie friend, where are you from? I hear that you like conquering new countries, eating flesh and brain tissue; you dislike headshots from a sniper rifle and in your spare time, you slowly disintegrate."

"Well, I—"

"That's SO NICE, WELCOME to our SHOW! We're so glad to have you with us today!"

"Now, you can cash in your wish right now for immediate granting . . . or trade it in for 3 BIG SPINS on the WISHING WHEEL! Which are YOU going to CHOOSE?"

The zombie leader glanced at the audience again, who were energetically screaming one or the other at him, "I'll—I'll—trade in da wish and spin da big wheel," he said finally.

Fu smiled still, though his cheeks were starting to ache. "Final answer, my friend?"

"Do it—Do it—Do it—" chanted the eager zombie audience. The zombie leader agreed and with a wave of Fu-Belle's wand (pure showmanship, obviously) a giant wheel appeared suspended in the air. Amidst the encouraging cheers of his zombie friends, the leader gave the wheel a big spin.

"Crock o' gold, crock o' gold!"

"Ooo, dat vacation home in the Caribbean! Looks good, wot?"

"New car!"

"No-limits Express Card!"

The wheel slowed and the audience gasped, then cheered loudly as it stopped on, "Vacation for Two Zombies to Maui" square.

"Two more spins," Fu-Belle said warmly and the zombies went wild again. What a great fairy god-law-enforcement officer! Everyone oughta have one!

The second spin brought the "Crock of Gold" square and even more cheers.

But in the zombie leader's final spin, catastrophe struck! At first, the ticker appeared to land on "Bonus Free Spin" but at the very last second, it tipped back to the previous square, "Bankrupt, All Is Lost."

The zombies all groaned loudly together. *Tragedy struck*—and their leader was doing so well!

"Aw, that's too bad," Fu-Belle commiserated shaking his head. "Such a shame. Better luck next time, my friend, but thank you for playing."

"Oh well," the zombie leader sighed, "I dun git no wishes granted den, huh?"

"I'm afraid it's a little worse than that," Fu broke the news gently. "See the Bankruptcy Square, as covered under our Terms and Conditions which you agreed to prior to playing, means you literally *ARE* bankrupt!"

"Everything you own reverts to Fairyland, including any land rights you may own such as, oh for example, the recently-conquered country of Transylvania—and including, as is traditional in fairy/human contracts, your first-born child. Technically, every zombie present here with you counts as your first-born child as the undead cannot bear children (also covered under the Terms and Conditions, Lawful Seizure In Lieu of First-Born subsection) so you and all of the zombies present are now slaves to Fairyland under the dominion of his Majesty, King Clarion."

With a little twirl of his fairy wand, every zombie was manacled together in chains, foot and wrist. The zombie leader sputtered, struggling against the bonds.

"Hey! No fair! You didn't tell me dat in da rules ting!"

"Actually, we're not legally bound under Fairyland Law to verbally disclaim the end result in the event of game bankruptcy, so long as it's clearly covered in the Terms and Conditions which you didn't read. Fairyland and all fairy game hosts are not held liable if you didn't read or clearly understand the Terms and Conditions before signing them and playing."

"But—but—" the zombie leader stared helplessly out over the sea of his shackled undead troops, slowly coming to the realization there might be a hint of false advertising to the general belief and tales told about "good" fairies.

Fu patted his shoulder comfortingly. "Life lesson, my zombie friend: always read the Terms and Conditions before signing them."

Armando, now back on his feet again with no sign of head trauma (vampires heal *very fast*) beamed at Fu-Belle in a way that showed he hadn't found out just yet about the fate of his iBat.

"That was very clever, you young—uh, what was your name?"

"F.U.-Belle, Sire," Fu introduced himself.

Armando looked thoughtful, "Such a coincidence. I had an enemy fairy once, I believe— his name was also Belle."

"Well, "-Belle" is very common among fairies, Sire. Practically all of us have it." Fu said politely.

Armando nodded. "Yes, well, obviously you can't be him. He was a dreadful sort of fellow, moving things about without proper clearance and all that. I can see you're a fine young specimen of— of fairy, er, fairyhood. So about Transylvania—"

"—now a magical colony under Fairyland Jurisdiction and therefore ruled over by King Clarion," Fu finished warmly. Armando looked uncomfortable and fidgeted.

"Um—yes. Um, I don't suppose your King Clarion would—come to a compromise about that?"

"Technically I hold the contract for now." Fu said calmly, "The agreement rests with me until I turn it over to His Majesty back in Fairyland. So I'm fully authorized to say you can have Transylvania back, Armando—"

"Ah! Good lad!"

"—IF you declare a truce with King Clarion and promise to never again attack or pursue a state of warfare with Fairyland!"

"What?" Armando sputtered. "You mean there are "terms and conditions" involved?"

"There are *ALWAYS* "Terms and Conditions" involved in fairy contracts, Sire. That's the point where humans go oh-so-desperately wrong in their theology because it's not free magic—but it is ultimately *their choice*, just like it's now your choice. You can choose to abide by our conditions, or you can give up Transylvania forever."

"Also, there will be no more vampires stealing fairy crackle from Fairyland to rub and make themselves sparkly. That's our magic, not yours! It's *not* for vampire use!"

"WHAT?! But how are we supposed to trap the humans without sparkly fairy crack?" Armando groused. Fu shrugged.

"Fairy "crackle" actually, and figure it out for yourself, Armando. You did it before without us. Invite a few strangers up to your castle for a wild party, pay someone to help your vampires market themselves better, or put some pop-ads on Majick-Book: "Hey, wanna be bitten?" You're pretty creative, Sire. Eventually you'll find something else that works for you."

Armando merely pouted.

"Well? I need an answer here," Fu crossed his arms. "Cause I can hitch a ride back to Fairyland and tell King Clarion that Transylvania is all his now. We'll send some fairies help you vampires pack and clear your stuff out."

"Fine," Armando grumbled. "Draw up the contract and I'll seal it or sign it in blood and call my vampires off and you know, whatever else I need to do. "Like" it on Majick-Book?"

"It's all eMajick these days," Fu murmured, "So just press the "I Agree" button on the terms and conditions. The eMajick technology does the rest."

He held out his iFairy and Armando did as instructed, starting to check for his iBat, mysteriously ringtone-less for over 20 minutes now, but was first distracted by Fu's touch screen.

"What? WHAT? ARE YOU BATSHITTING ME, WHY DO I HAVE TO ENTER MY EMAIL ADDRESS NOW?? I SWEAR I'M GONNA FIND THE MAKER OF THESE MAGIC APPS AND EAT THEM!"

"No, no," Fu said hastily. "That's just if you want to be added to our Fairyland mailing list for valuable fashion tips and wish coupons. Here, you can just xout of that screen prompt, see?" He closed up his device and slipped it in his fairy pouch.

"That agreement binds you for immortality, you know. Neither you, nor any of your future generations of Armando can break it, er, Armando. The Laws of Magic will hold you to it."

Armando, currently still the 23rd incarnation, sighed. "Yes of course."

Meanwhile, Anne Genue drifted away from the zombie drama to admire a wall mural in Armando's ballroom, which in fact was the same wall mural as the one in the secret passage.

"Well, isn't she pretty," Anne murmured, "The lost princess? I love her hair . . . hey!" Like the magic of *Hubert Pfiffer! Boy Wizard!* a light switch suddenly clicked on in her brain.

"WAM," Anne insisted, throwing up a hand. "OMG! I'm totally the "lost princess" aren't I? That's why I have her tiara and she kinda looks like me," she gasped, as more light switches fired, "That mural in the tunnel. It's me, isn't it?" She spun back around and marched over to Armando, waving the frying pan at him. "Hey, are you my real dad?"

"Aw, my darling lost daughter," King Armando beamed. "I've been waiting for you to find your way back to me for years. When your mother and I split up, she took you with her."

"But, you're a vampire," Anne frowned, "And I'm human. Shouldn't I be a vampire like you if I'm your biological daughter?"

"You did always take after your mother; same blonde hair, same humanity. I can't say as it's a good look for you but I wasn't consulted on the matter. Your mother was human too," Armando observed with a sigh, "What can I say? Dating humans was all the rage at the time and I thought it was cute. Young love."

"Oh. Well—I see. I guess that clears it up," Anne murmured. Armando gazed at her fondly. It seemed he'd forgotten he kidnapped her only about an hour ago.

"My dear, I knew one day you'd find your way back here. I used to release a swarm of vampire bats every year on your birthday in hopes you'd see them and find your way back home."

Anne frowned, "Vampire bats? Don't they only come out at night?"

"Why yes of course, my dear."

"You used to release black bats—at night? Every year?"

Armando beamed, "Yes darling, did you see them?"

He looked so delighted Anne forced a smile, "Of course I did, Father. Every year on my birthday, yes. I came home because—of the birthday bats. I must've known they were for me."

"Um," she thought hard, "So I really am a princess, huh?"

"Yes, a princess of Transylvania," Armando nodded, "We haven't too much to offer in the way of culture but there's the Transylvanian National Forest and Game Preserve, and the highest peak on Mount Armando and naturally, the 3rd largest wizard's school located in our capital city, Zxyzagorria—"

"Excuse me? Did you say Transylvania has a wizard's school?" Anne's eyes suddenly gleamed bright.

"Yes, my dear daughter, it's a fine venerable institution of higher learning. Not for much longer though, I'm afraid. Your proud birth home of Transylvania will be a ghost town with all the vampires starving to undeath shortly." He shot Fu-Belle a pouty, accusatory look.

Fu smiled, "Now-now, you can't steal the crackle from us fairies, Sire—but I'll drop the hint with King Clarion, and he might enclose a few crates in your Christmas basket. He's a pretty generous gift-giver around the holidays."

"And Sire," Fu knew where Armando's heart lay and the first trick fairies learned as how to play to their audience, "King Clarion also voted your name the Sexiest Vampire Name on Majick-Book. I wasn't sure you knew?"

Armando beamed. "He did? Really?"

"Oh yes Sire," Fu insisted, knowing Clarion had never even heard of Majick-Book but anything to smooth troubled waters.

"Why he logged on faithfully every day to vote and put out an announcement to the rest of the fairies to vote for you. We were so pleased to hear about your win, Sire! Clearly it was destined to be!"

Armando preened. "Well I'm not surprised," he stated, still beaming, "Armando clearly WAS the sexiest name and I shall have to return the favor and vote for Clarion as well. I mean as fairy names go— it—well, it—it doesn't seem to have "Belle" in it, for one thing."

Fu-"Belle" winced. "Yeah, it's nice to be king," he mumbled out of earshot, then glanced back at the chained and subdued zombie legions.

"Hmm, now those I'm not so sure what to do with. I don't think Clarion will be pleased with me if I drag thousands and thousands of dirty, putrid rotting zombies home to Fairyland. Even with the extreme makeover possibilities."

Armando tapped his chin. "Right, about that . . . I have an idea, actually."

The uber-efficient Neverland Post delivered several large crates to the Crocodile one fine morning, covered with many Transylvanian Royal Air-Mail stamps and marked "DO NOT OPEN: Contents are Extremely Volatile" which naturally the Crocodile ignored.

There was a letter on top, written on fine stationary with, "From the Desk of KING ARMANDO" and it read:

TO: His Honore, The Crocodile of Neverland,

Arrrrrrr! Me hopes this finds yer in good health!

This is Cap'n James Hook and I'm sendin' yer a wee peace offerin, Mr. Croc-O-Dile. I ken yer been tryin' tae eat me fer yrs, but no haaaaarrrrrrd feelings, eh matey? Let's both bury the treasure once and for all, aye?

Inside the wee crate arrrrrre some DELICIOUS, crunchy zombies fer ye! They may be a mite past their freshness date, aye, but methinks yer soon adjust tae the taste o' them.

They been giving me good vampire matey King ARMANDO a wee bit o'trouble down in Transylvania but I think they'll make ye a *nice hearrrrty breakfast and yer can keep them all fer yerself! Arrrrrrr!*

Yrs Regards, Cap'n James Hook, pirate.

XOXOXOXOXOXO

Naturally the Crocodile couldn't read a word of Armando's letter but, once he worked the crate open with his teeth, he did adjust quickly and happily to the taste of zombie meat.

So Captain Hook, as well as the mermaids, indians and other pirates which had the misfortune of falling victim to the crocodile's enormous appetite, reaped the benefits of the zombie diet. The Crocodile had no need to pursue his dinner across the island now when he had several crates of long-lasting food at his disposal.

Just like that, the greatly anticipated and much feared "Zombie Apocalypse" (yes. the first one) was well and truly over.

No one in the Human World even missed it.

The Last Gay Unicorn

One of the little known facts about the Transylvanian portals is that there's a portal designed to tempt goblins across the border from the land of Underground.

It doesn't take much effort. Goblins can be bribed with a few live chickens and a handful of cheap plastic jewelry. What's most little known about the portal however, is who constructed it in the first place.

The Transylvanian vampires, who weren't responsible for this portal since no vampire would ever be desperate or hungry enough to drink the blood of a goblin, thought it was a practical joke by the werewolves. They left it alone as they were impressed the weres developed such a sophisticated sense of humor.

The werewolves assumed the mad scientists were behind it to provide them with an unlimited supply of scientific test subjects that no one would miss.

And the mad scientists blamed the vampires but then, as heretofore stated, they were utterly barking mad so who knows why they thought so?

In truth, that particular interdimensional portal was built, stocked and consequently monitored for activity by the Goblin-Reversal Purification Society, an organization that catches stray goblins who range across the border.

By means of 100% natural, organic, raw magic (not the cheap, over-processed and refined using artificial dyes and sweeteners sort of magic you get nowadays) they reverse-engineer the goblin-transformation process, turning them into human children and releasing the children back into their natural habitat in the Human World.

It was a touch 'n go process. Catching the stray goblins was the easy bit (frankly an armless guy in a wheelchair could catch a stray goblin) but not many of the creatures were bright enough to make it all the way to the portal from castle at the center of the labyrinth, not to mention how some fraggin aardvarks living under the pathway rocks kept changing around the GRPS road-signs.

But the GRPS persevered on in their good works as best as they could, and had organic, whole-leaf tea imported only from countries using fair trade import/export routes with the 'Allo Worm every third Wednesday of the month.

The word of the Tea-Drinking Worm this month was that the Goblin King had gone strangely missing and no one had seen him in two weeks. This would be declared a national holiday, except without their King no one had any clue how to hang decorations.

Any hope of the goblins banding together for a rousing group rendition of *"Ding-Dong, King J Is MIA!"* complete with solo from the Lollypop Guild, was fruitless as the goblins couldn't even remember how to do the 'voodoo rhyme' right, despite how many times over they'd heard it. It started out like, "yo re'mine me of da thing wots like dat odder thing, uh wot was dat thing . . .?" and didn't get much better.

Regardless, it felt like the tide was beginning to turn in their favor. No new goblins were created and in the meantime, more and more curious goblins were venturing out of the Goblin City in search of "new tings wot they couldn't remember were called". Some eventually stumbled over the portal and crossed through, discovering intelligence and how to eat using a fork again.

The GRPS encouraged walk-ins for volunteers were hard to come by. Most of their volunteers were individuals who'd been rocketed out of their comfort zone when a loved one or family member was abducted by a supernatural entity such as the Goblin King, although there were a few volunteers whose motives were altruistic. Mainly however, this was the type of charitable cause that inspired more personal vendetta than altruism.

Little did the GRPS know that the missing sovereign of the Underground would walk right into their offices that very afternoon! Mr. Oubliette had been up late watching Armando's cable again (channel reception was better in Transylvania than the Underground) and he was brought to tears by the soulful animated feature: "The Last Gay Unicorn" in which the young, titular gay unicorn Rocco embarks on a quest to find out why his species is extinct and he's the last of his kind.

After a number of adventures, assisted by a friendly sorcerer who helps him take on mortal form, culminating in the unicorn falling for a mortal prince (and an eye-opening discussion on the dynamics of reproduction) Rocco decides to return to his former life as a gay unicorn, sacrificing his personal happiness for the greater good and survival of his species, made richer by the experience of knowing love.

After sobbing his way through six boxes of Kleenex, and surrounded by used room service trays and soggy, blackened tissues that almost budged his many layers of waterproof mascara and eyeliner, Mr. Oubliette decided that today he'd continue Rocco's quest to be a gay unicorn and find the other members of his endangered species.

When he wandered in through the double doors of the GRPS, he was dressed as a gay unicorn of the rainbow, half-Pegasus, 80's retro fashion variety. His rock icon hair was frosted pink and blue, he wore a small silver horn on a headband and for reasons unknown, he'd pinned a very small pair of fat, iridescent wings to his back which, in another lifetime, probably were innocent throw pillows before they were forced to suffer this indignity (as if being iridescent and wing-shaped wasn't cruelty enough). They flapped back and forth hopelessly.

His spandex leotard and costume was dusted with shiny spangles and would probably be considered the best thing ever if you were a girl between the ages of 5-9 in the mid-1980's. There was a large amount of rainbow-striped tulle involved.

In fact, everything was rainbow-striped. Even the animated gay unicorn hadn't been able to work in so many pride rainbows.

"Oh Hello!!" the perky receptionist greeted him with a "We're One Big Team" attitude that would've made any corporate training coordinator weep with joy. Some sense of pressing and growing curiosity forced her to add, "And, who are you?"

"I'm a gay unicorn," Mr. Oubliette explained.

"Oh—" the perky receptionist fumbled for words, "well, that's lovely! We don't get . . . many of those in here. In fact I don't think I've ever met a gay unicorn."

"We're very rare. Our species is dying out," Mr. Oubliette clarified, then added sadly, "In fact, I may be the very last one. We've been declared an endangered species under Transylvanian law and we're covered under the newest National Protection Act, but—I fear it may already be too late! We face extinction!"

"Oh, I'm very sorry to hear that."

"Yes," Mr. Oubliette agreed, very solemn, "It's such a pity. Gay unicorns are extremely rare and beautiful creatures. They bring tremendous luck to mortals when they're wished upon."

"I'd imagine so," the perky receptionist agreed. Mr. Oubliette beamed.

"I've undertaken a quest to see if any others of my species still remain and to find us a safe habitat where we can live in peace with the rest of our gentle kindred."

"Oh, that's SO wonderful! I do hope you find some other gay unicorns."

Mr. Oubliette nodded, "Yes. As I travel on my great quest, I'm doing good and generous works of charity for those in need. Gay unicorns naturally wish to help wherever they can."

"Of course I understand," the perky receptionist smiled warmly. Mr. Oubliette tilted his head, nearly dislodging his silver foil horn headband.

"I've never heard of your charity. What is it you represent here at the GRPS?"

"Oh I'd be happy to explain! We're the Goblin-Reversal Purification Society! We take innocent little children transformed into goblins by the terrible, monstrous Goblin King . . ."

"He sounds dreadful indeed," Mr. Oubliette agreed.

". . . and we transform those goblins by use of fairy reversal magic back into sweet little children so they can return to their natural homes in the Human World."

"What a worthy cause. Can I perhaps be of assistance?"

"Oh yes, if it isn't too much trouble," the perky secretary beamed. "We *always* welcome new volunteers but we wouldn't want to keep you from your very important quest. Surely the world needs more gay unicorns and we understand if you need to move ahead with that."

"It's no trouble. My unicorn brethren would want me to help and I must make them proud when I find them," Mr. Oubliette insisted.

"A gay unicorn is always selfless, trustworthy, loyal, helpful, friendly, courteous, kind, obedient, cheerful, thrifty, brave, clean and reverent."

The perky receptionist clapped her hands in joy. "Marvelous! Why, you'll be a tremendous asset to the team, I'm sure. We're so happy to have you!"

Just then, a newly captured goblin was led through the lobby. Upon spying Mr. Oubliette, he immediately dropped to one knee, sputtering, "Oh, yer Highness!"

The perky receptionist turned surprised eyes on Mr. Oubliette.

"Are you a prince," she asked, her tone awed and full of wonder.

"Why yes, of course," Mr. Oubliette intoned, though he too was surprised but figured it made perfect sense so he went with it.

"All gay unicorns are born of royal blood and nobility. We are all princes and princesses in the unicorn bloodline."

"I didn't know that," the perky receptionist said in wonder. Mr. Oubliette held out a gloved hand and to everyone's surprise, a crystal orb formed on his fingertips.

"Wow! *Unicorn magic!* Amazing!" the receptionist gasped.

"Yes," Mr. Oubliette beamed. "We gay unicorns have many amazing powers. Watch!"

He tossed the crystal at the small, fugly goblin and in a theatrical burst of glitter, the goblin vanished and in its place was a small, adorable, rosy-cheeked child. All the other GRPS volunteers, now watching in rapt attention along with the perky receptionist, burst into a spontaneous round of applause.

"Gay unicorn magic can turn goblins back into children! How wonderful!" the receptionist gushed.

"Why it must be the purity of your unicorn souls interacting with the innocence of the child. How utterly extraordinary!"

"Yes, it must be that," Mr. Oubliette murmured. In truth, he was just as surprised as everyone else by his power to transform a goblin back into a human child. He didn't remember this part from the movie.

Just then, our innocent and pure of soul (today) Gay Unicorn physically collided with someone he knew very well.

No, it wasn't Pinocchio's Blue Fairy, although she was present and just leaving for her lunch break. She was usually the one the GRPS depended on to reverse the goblin process through use of her fairy magic. She knew Fu-Belle because they had a brief fling before she left Fairyland to run off with a wooden puppet boy and his cricket conscience.

That was considered pretty weird, even by Fairyland standards.

"Well, hello SARAH," Mr. Oubliette drawled for about the millionth time upon meeting a strange girl and so he was again surprised when this girl pulled back and shrieked at the top of her lungs.

"YOU!!!"

A tall, grown-up and very lovely Sarah Williams backed away from Mr. Oubliette in rising horror.

"How did you come here? How did you get in? Oh God's mercy, SAVE THE CHILDREN! SAAAAVE THE CHILDREN!"

She might have been all grown-up but one thing was clear: Sarah hadn't lost her penchant for dramatic scenes.

The others looked on in bewilderment as Sarah suddenly changed directions mid-emotional wave from fear to fury, turning to beat her fists against Mr. Oubliette's rainbow-covered chest while she shouted, "YOU GO AWAY! YOU HAVE NO POWER OVER ME!! YOU HAVE NO POWER OVER MEEEMMMEEEMEMMEMEE OR ANYONE ELSE, OR THE ENTIRE WORLD, SO GO! GO AWAY NOW!"

"Sarah, what are you doing?" the perky receptionist tried to intervene, having never seen the slender brunette break into hysterics like this before. Hysterics yes, Sarah had those about twice a week but not like THIS!

"He's such a nice gay unicorn, and he's on a mission to find his family. He came here to help us today. Now I'm sure we can settle this matter calmly, rationally and most of all, professionally," the receptionist's voice held a note of disapproval.

"*HE STOLE MY BABY BROTHER!*" Sarah shrieked, seemingly in favor of keeping hysterics firmly on the docket. She was very good at them.

"HE IS THE GOBLIN KING AND YOU JUST LET HIM WALK IN? WHAT ARE YOU KIDDING ME?!

Look," even her pointing indicated mute hysteria, "See his picture *RIGHT THERE* on our "Most Nefarious" wall?"

Everyone scrutinized the photo of the Goblin King on the wall in silence. True, there did seem to be a loose resemblance between the regal figure pictured there and the rainbow-colored unicorn currently in their lobby . . . but weren't gay unicorns related to royalty? Perhaps it was just a family resemblance then?

"I'm telling you he's the Goblin King," Sarah stressed, dramatically stomping a foot. "Don't let him fool you, he's evil! EEEEEVVVIIILLLL—" she seemed to enjoy rolling the word on her tongue like a piece of hard candy.

"He stole my baby brother when we were only children and though I'm not sure why he's here or why he's dressed as a gay unicorn—" Sarah faltered with the sheer improbability of the Goblin King dressing like a gay unicorn and desperately rallied, "—but it's clearly a vile deception as part of some— uh, nefarious scheme that can only lead to a bad end, I'm sure of it!" Her tone was triumphant she'd finished out strong though she'd lost steam in the middle.

Mr. Oubliette, royal designation currently unconfirmed, stared at Sarah. Although the way every goblin in the room was now lying subserviently prostrate on their faces before him might have been a tiny clue to his real identity.

Then again the argument can be made that these *were goblins*—it was entirely possible they were lying prostrate and subservient to the potted plant beside Mr. Oubliette, or perhaps they were simply terrified of gay unicorns.

"Peach?" Mr. Oubliette suddenly and generously offered, extracting said tainted fruit from his rainbow-striped Man!Purse and holding it out to Sarah with a smile.

Sarah's glare could melt sheet rock.

"I WILL *SHOVE* THAT PEACH RIGHT UP YOUR TWISTED—"

"*Miss Williams!*" the perky receptionist cut her off with a disapproving cluck. "Let's use our inside voices please and kindly remember that we have goblin-children present."

Sarah glared at them, both defiant and wholly unrepentant.

"Don't be a hater," Mr. Oubliette urged sadly. "We gay unicorns are naturally kind and gentle souls. We always forgive others for their hate. It's because our souls are pure, you know."

If Sarah's glare was smoldering before, that was nothing compared to the flames now.

"WHY YOU SICK BA—"

"I'm sure we can settle this without yelling or name calling, Sarah."

"BUT HE—HE—it's NOT FAAAAIRRRR!"

As Mr. Oubliette stared down into the fiery eyes of the human and vaguely familiar girl defying him, he felt something stir faintly in his memory banks. He'd been here, the exact situation somewhere, someplace before . . . some other lifetime perhaps?

Possibly HIS other lifetime—

Wait! Yes! That was it! Now he had it all!

"I wonder what your basis for comparison is, little girl," he hissed, and folded his arms. Like a sudden clap of thunder, it was all back. His kingly outfit, the regal manner, the eldritch appearance, the arrogance . . . but now so was *HE!*

HE was BACK; for it was clear the Goblin King now *remembered* exactly who he was. Or rather, who he IS now that he remembers everything. Yes, that was it.

Sarah gasped. "You! You ARE the Goblin King!"

"Well, I'm certainly no gay unicorn," he sneered back, voice smooth and lyrical like elemental water. He then blew another crystal ball off the tip of his fingers and it lit the room with a flash. All the goblins in the room vanished just as quick.

"Those are my subjects," he added, cruel just as he could be. "They were wished away to me and therefore mine. I warn you not to try me. "

"You won't get away with this," Sarah huffed. "We'll keep fighting you forever to return those children home."

"It's only forever, it's not long at all," The King (formally known as Mr. Oubliette) mocked her. He began to tick off his gloved fingers.

"Under Magical Law, subclause 35.a, section 2, paragraph 8, *'once invited on the premises, a supernatural entity can immediately reclaim any confiscated property lawfully taken by means of contractual human/fairy interaction such as trickery, bribery, wishing, or magical means as allowed under the universal clause of humorous misdirection.'"*

He smiled thinly. "You should've read up on your laws of magic before messing about with me, Sarah."

"Actually, that particular subclause is under scrutiny by the Magical Court," the GRPS legal aide piped up. "There's a good chance it'll be overturned by the Higher Courts because there's a general consensus that the legal definition of "trickery" used is too broad. It's merely a blanket subclause that supernatural entities use to duck behind for illegal abuse of supernatural powers against the natural order of the universe."

The Goblin King glared at the aide, for in fact that *was* his favorite magical law to duck behind whenever his activities were called into question by the magical authorities.

"Until overturned by the High Courts, it's still actionable," he snapped, "and you have to comply under the laws of magic and turn any goblins back over to me."

"But we can have an injunction filed against you," the legal aide came back like the lash of a whip, really earning his commission today.

Plus, he had a long-time score to settle with the Goblin King over the loss of his favorite pet turtle when he was a boy of three and was just wishing things away to see what would happen. He'd never forgiven the underground king for what happened next.

"By doing so you're violating Magical Law subsection d, paragraph 6, in which reverse-trickery "finders keepers" clause applies and the goblins are currently in our possession as well as the use of reverse-trickery to bring them to us, which overrides your original claim on them and renders all property recovery claims null and void."

The Goblin King glared harder. There definitely would be a refresher course on the current laws and statutes governing magic for this Supernatural Ruler as soon as he got back to the Underground, well as some long talks with the Supernatural Entities Appeals Supervisory Board.

Seriously though? If you couldn't abuse your power once in awhile, what was the fun of being a supernatural entity?

"Fine, you win for now . . . but I'll be back. Farewell Sarah until next time," he leered at her before vanishing in a flurry cloud of magical silver glitter.

It was possible this was just a side effect of his magic and wasn't intended as malicious, though the tiny flecks spread everywhere like little slivers of suffering, particularly down in pant waistbands where they itched like hell and were a pain to fish out later.

But really, what were the odds?

Now that all the excitement was officially over, everyone went home. Unlike the trip to Transylvania, the trip back wasn't as exciting or filled with a plethora of new and friendly faces.

Most of our band of heroes took the S.S.S. home, now back in commission, with only a minor black hole scare along the trip ("The S.S.S. Maintenance Team Has Been Notified And We Will Look Into The Issue. Thank You For Choosing The Supernatural Subterranean Subway As Your Preferred Method Of Interdimensional Travel!").

Save for Kent Clark (no relation) who crossed back to his hometown of Tinyville through the Transylvanian portal, and Biffy Winters who mysteriously decided to extend his stay in Transylvania (he was last seen web-searching, *"How to Dial a Transylvanian Telephone Number for Human Dummies"*). It was the perfect spot for a slayer to keep his skills sharp.

Anne Genue also stayed in Transylvania, both to pursue her lifelong dream of inheriting a throne as a full-time princess and bossing as many vampires around as she liked. One must assume she was pretty happy in both vocations.

She also engaged in a lot of HP!BW! cosplay, though she wasn't a popular character after she insisted everyone refer to her now and in the future as "Mrs. Pfiffer".

Kent Clark (no relation) arrived home safe and with Tailor Wear in tow, who loyally refused to be separated from his GOOD and KIND Master Kent.

Kent's parents (no relation) were thrilled to see him alive and fully super-powered but were considerably less thrilled that he brought home a wild, full-blooded Transylvanian werewolf which ate voraciously. Humans were considered "on the werewolf menu" though in truth a full-blooded werewolf was powerful enough to take down a raging bull.

Kent's parents (still no relation) felt this might be "too much responsibility" for Kent to handle all at once, between the extensive training from his alien father and the new superpowers to learn without throwing in a werewolf that could gobble up the citizens of Tinyville on top of that.

It was a lot to handle even for a mild-mannered middle-aged man still enrolled in high school—although his graduation oversight could well prove to be accidental. Tinyville High still held massively record-breaking annual enrollments when one considered the logical elements of the town's overall population, the overall percentage of which would actually be high school student age, and vast meteor-rock exposure turning everyone in town into raving psychopaths!

Even though Kent Clark (no relation) protested he could make his own decisions being 38 and all, his parents told him he couldn't keep the werewolf as a domesticated pet. Tinyville had enough supernatural problems as it was and no one wanted to consider the consequences of green meteor rocks turning a werewolf psycho.

So the Clarks set about finding a nice ranch in the country for young Tailor to live on, preferably one with a large wild game population that needed to be downsized in a hurry and kept under control (like darkest Africa). They also began training Tailor to develop a taste for doggy kibble.

Verethraghna was on the S.S.S. as well. Although Persia didn't exist as a world empire now (lost in the "sands of time") but that was no problem. The S.S.S. made frequent stops along the non-existent aether for homeless gods to rejoin their now-extinct pantheons before heading over to the Jurassic period to pick up and drop off visiting dinosaurs.

However, Verethraghna disembarked at the wrong stop first for Mt. Olympus and had a brief fist-fight with Ares (the god of war, not the god of love) while waiting on the next train. Since the fist-fight was concluded without godly effects—sadly, Ares special effects crew had been let go during the recession and Verethraghna's effects crew had not yet signed on, it was visually unimpressive and nobody got an Oscar for it. Verethraghna didn't add it to his war god resume and Ares delegated his part in the godly skirmish down to Strife.

Mr. Oubliette promptly returned to the Underground where, after celebrating his grand return by nostalgically drop-kicking a few goblins (ah it was just like he never left), he immediately enrolled for refresher master courses at the Underground Community College on the current Magical Laws and Statutes.

However, as it was a class taught by goblins, he passed the bar exam on his very first day just by spelling the Goblin King's name correctly—his OWN name, it should be noted! Few goblins knew what their famous monarch's name was, and fewer still (including the instructor of the class) could spell it.

Shortly after, Mr. Oubliette re-enrolled in a *non-goblin taught* institution of higher learning.

Fu-Belle returned to Fairyland a conquering hero, fresh from his victory over the vampires and zombie forces, as well as the newly enacted peace treaty between Fairyland and Transylvania, and the alliance with the werewolves. All this proved a far greater accomplishment than he even set out to do.

He didn't receive much acclaim for it from King Clarion who, upon hearing the tale, merely remarked, "Oh, that war affair? Was that still going on? I'd forgotten about that. I thought it ended last season." He glanced over at his wife.

"Yes dear," Ding-Aling agreed, "Warfare is out of fashion this season. It's all about saving the environment and living green for fall."

"I thought so," Clarion nodded his satisfaction, then waved Fu-Belle off, "There, you see? Do try to keep up, Captain."

However, the notoriety of Fu's success made the friends feeds of Majick-Book and Fu-Belle ended up getting 5 free makeover offers from his fellow fairies. By Fairyland standards, it was the equivalent of a homecoming parade with floats, balloons, fireworks and a marching band, plus a gold medal for his heroism.

More personally rewarding for Fu, Clarion agreed to let the acclaimed fairy captain train a special contingent of werewolves to serve as an elite protectorate squad to guard over Fairyland. Between werewolves as Fairyland's newest and strongest allies and the help of Tinker-Belle the tiny, hand-eating crocodile, Fairyland was well-protected now against any future squabbles with their magical kinfolk.

Clarion was happy with the arrangement because as law enforcement, the werewolves came cheap. All they wanted for reimbursement was a good home and a doggy biscuit (fairies demanded at least a new summer wardrobe before they would even consider the job).

Armando was equally happy with the arrangement because he received a bi-monthly stipend of fairy crackle from Clarion for use of the werewolves services (not including the crate tucked in his Christmas basket) and Boxer, the Alpha Werewolf, received a stipend of doggy biscuits.

Unfortunately for King Armando, it was already being speculated on Majick-Book that the human's craze over "shiny vampires" was dying off and, (are you ready for this?), "sexy, brain-eating zombies" were *the New Black!*

Word about "The Zombie Apocalypse" had gotten out somehow (#1, not #2) and it was so totally HOT and NOW, *THE NEXT BIG THING!!*

It was all over BaTwingger and Majick-Book, with Apocalypse Survival Guides and Top Ten Lists, and even a blockbuster movie starring *Hubie Pfiffer!*

Lord of the Undead Wizards! The merchandising franchises were excitedly gearing up, trying to figure out what they could stamp a decaying corpse on and hike up the price for twelve times over.

What?! Nnnnnooooooo!!!

Armando was outraged! *Really?* He'd just given all his zombies AWAY, dammit—he had crates and crates of the damn things before he shipped them off to Neverland . . . *WHY DIDN'T ANYONE TELL HIM zombies would be trending NEXT in the Human World, HUH?*

No more shiny vampires?? What was he going to do then with all the extra glittery, glow-in-the-dark fairy, uh—fairy magic kegger stuff?

It's not like he COULD USE IT IN SOME OTHER FASHION could he, ya know, e.g. to mark the walls of his dark, endlessly-twisting, identical castle hallways with glow-in-the-dark directions like a mall directory sign so that people didn't get lost in them all the time—

HEEEY, wait! Now, *that* was an idea!

Armando beamed. He was just *sooo brilliant!*

Just wait until he posted on Majick-Book that the zombies tried to conquer Transylvania *first* before the Human Realm! The *Zombie Apocalypse* had actually kicked off and *started* in Transylvania! Why it practically starred the vampires through the whole thing!

Armando could put in plenty of tourist areas and gift shops all around Transylvania, with a trendy zombie theme for the humans, and retrace their steps! Why, he'd be back on top in a flash!

Transylvania would absolutely become the *Sexiest Destination* on Majick-Book! *Vote for it!*

And They All Lived ~~Something~~ Ever After!

S o that draws our story to its close. "And they all lived happ"—oh, now you want to know what happened to all of them? What, "and they all lived happily ever after" just isn't good enough for you now?

But it's a long-held storytelling ending tradition—but—but it was first ending ever told by learned monks high in the Appalachian Mountains—but it's a *sacred* ending, like *true love*—but it's the only ending that holds the key to eternal youth—

No? None of this doing anything for you?

Alright, fine.

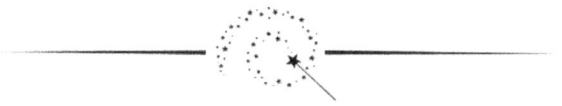

KENT CLARK (no relation) and **ANNE GENUE** dated awesomely for about a year or so until Kent Clark (no relation) collided with the bossy, emancipated reporter-gal of his dreams struck with the same affliction of never recognizing him sans glasses while Anne Genue was predictably swept off her feet by a prince who got misplaced from his fairytale (after the fifth restraining order was filed against her by Hubert Pfiffer). Some love stories are just written in the stars really.

Still, rumor has it they keep in touch on Majick-Book and Kent Clark (no relation) drops out of the sky to see Anne whenever he's rescuing someone from Transylvania. Mind you, she still hasn't figured out who he is when his glasses are on and they stick to places with restrooms close by for his weak bladder.

BIFFY WINTERS the Vampire Slayer carried on his *torrid* and *forbidden* love affair with **ANGELESS: Mistress of the Night** (the soulful-eyed vampiress) and romantically gave up slaying for her as a token of his love. Right up until she went soulless-evil and killed a great many puppies again so tragically he had to slay HER! The loud weeping you hear is the breaking heart of many emo-fans sounding off all over the internet. After that, there didn't seem much point in swearing off the slaying gig.

However, he did swear very LOUDLY when he got his phone bill, with 1,509,623.22$ GTR (Genuine Transylvanian Rubles) in roaming charges due for all the calls, texts and Majick-Book mobile updates he did from Transylvania. Oh yeah, the "Includes Everything Plan" with unlimited long distance, friends and family talk, data & text plan—that *only covers the Human World* in the "includes" section, didn't ya know? Those roaming off-network charges, *that's where they get ya!* Eventually Biffy had to get himself turned into an immortal just to budget out a reasonable payment plan with his mobile carrier.

Mr. OUBLIETTE went back to stealing children and turning them into goblins, much to the considerable annoyance of the GRPS who grumbled about him over their fair trade, organic tea cups.

He also became a spokesperson on behalf of the endangered species of Gay Unicorns and did a PSA for their preservation society where he rambled on about his day spent living as one of them and what a life-altering, eye-opening experience it was. "The Last Gay Unicorn" was shown in schools all across the Underground and free tissues were provided.

It's also said that Mr. Oubliette ordered the 7-book Spell-Binders boxed collector's edition, personally signed by Mildred Pfiffer herself, of the *Hubert Pfiffer! Boy Wizard!* books and became such a big fan he attended the midnight opening of *"Hubert Pfiffer! Boy Wizard! and the Deadly Riddle"* in full costume including, of course, the philosopher's sequined slippers.

Word is, he shipped Ms. Pfiffer a fanfic about an extremely handsome and charming Goblin King who goes to wizard's school and, besides finding out he has natural and fantastic wizarding powers, he revamps the school's entire spring wardrobe, crossing swords with the school's EVIL and far worse, BADLY-STYLED Professor Snope! We haven't heard back on whether that fic was tossed in the incinerator unread or not.

King **ARMANDO WINGSFIELD PENTAGRAM** and **Count ALUCARD** later became the founders of Majick-Pinning-Board, the hugely successful online pin-board community that pretty much skyrocketed their Majick-Book street cred beyond their wildest expectations and made them the darlings of every female and gay unicorn who'd ever been born! The Fairyland Chronicle did a special 12-page spread on just the fashion boards *alone*, with pictures! The two vampire overlords were swimming in "Likes" and "Friends Requests" more than they could hope to handle in a lifetime, even immortal ones.

They also became BFF's versus Frenemies and hold a standing date for blood-lattes every Wednesday where they happily discuss how Majick-Pinning-Board is doing and their respective weekly successes on Majick-Book. They grew so close in fact that they developed one of those cute, super-couple nicknames, and were referred to as "Armacard" on Majick-Book thereafter (though Alucard often misspelled it as "Dracamra").

You'll be happy to know that Armando far surpassed the level of "Mr. Cool" on MeIzSoPopular and shot to the highest level of advancement in the game, "Mr. Awesome!", where his little cartoon-y guy got to drive around a black '67 Chevy Impala, kill monsters, sleep with every pretty girl he came across and wear a super-cool leather jacket left to him by his father, as well as tiny black shades.

Finally, King Armando also had his long-lost, beloved human daughter back, and was never so happy in all his 23 generations as now.

VERETHRAGHNA, (aka/ Velociraptor) the Persian War God, landed a terrific movie deal from a top Hollywood producer to star in the summer blockbuster hit: "*ALIENS VRS. VAMPIRES VRS. ZOMBIES VRS. WEREWOLVES VRS. GODS: ULTIMATE-MEGA-ARMEGEDDON THE MOVIE WITH CGI EFFECTS, SHOWN IN MEGA-OMNIVIEW 4D*" so long as he signed over the rights to his life story, bathed regularly, shaved and ditched the smelly toga.

He was able to work out guest appearances for the rest of his Persian pantheon, but when he made the savvy business decision to keep the merchandising rights for the entire "Velociraptor-Chic" clothing line (even Hollywood couldn't pronounce Verethraghna) well, that's where he really cleaned up! He ended up wealthier than the Greek god Hades who operated under the arrangement that, *"Sure, the dead can take it all with them but someone terrified of ending up in Hell will pay the god judging his life whatever price he asks".*

Now the Greek, Roman, Egyptian and Norse pantheons are totally jealous of the Persians, and reputedly are busy with merchandising negotiations for the next film to incorporate their immortal pantheons. Money talks in a recession, even to gods and goddesses!

TAILOR WEAR of the UnderWear Werewolf Clan was adopted by a very nice, normal family with kids who owned several balls and loved to play and give doggy biscuits to their little endangered species werewolf. But it's been rumored that he ran away from home; he was, after all, a full-blooded Transylvanian werewolf, not a domesticated wolf.

Along with Prince Phillip, the gay unicorn, who stopped returning Armando's calls ages ago, to help him find and reunite the near-extinct species of gay unicorns. It's said they got along so well because both Tailor and the gay unicorns were pure of soul.

HUBERT PFIFFER! BOY WIZARD! never returned to Transylvania, possibly because he knew Anne Genue would be eagerly lying in wait for him.

Not much is known about what happened to the famous and heroic boy wizard. We can only hope he is out there in the world somewhere, committing many brave and selfless acts for the good of humanity! Maybe he's even discovering that one next big miracle to bring to mankind that will even surpass *true love* itself, or fathering little *Huberta Pfiffer* to follow in his footsteps!

If he does, we're quite sure Mildred Pfiffer will be there to take it all the details down for our delectation, with a ready pen and a light, humorous prose. We look very forward to it!

THE SMALL HAND-EATING CROCODILE went to Fairyland Finishing School to become reintegrated with Fairyland Society where he later stayed on as an instructor, because his delightful behavior and etiquette after graduation was the talk of Fairyland and his exceptional table manners were used to impress foreign dignitaries.

All of Fairyland's best cosmetologists and dermatologists tried their best, but they never were able to remove the green, scaly staining from his skin or get his wings and golden hair to grow back.

But the crocodile still advanced to the level of "Chief Designer" the highest honor ever bestowed to a fairy. His fashion taste was universally declared throughout Fairyland as "Fabulous, Darling!" despite his considerable handicap of being butt-ugly.

He also broke his bad habit of eating hands, although this also impressed visiting dignitaries and kept them well in line. All Clarion had to do was let the rumor intentionally slip out about, "Tink's old hand-eating habit, which we put a stop to but she regresses sometimes when people aren't being cooperative" and any incidents caused on Fairyland soil were thought long and hard about first.

It never dawned on Clarion or Ding-Aling that the Crocodile wasn't their Tinker-Belle, and was conspicuously male and reptilian, but perhaps it was just as well as Tinker-Belle never did leave Peter Pan or Neverland to come back to Fairyland. So in that respect, Clarion and Ding-Aling got to have her back and be proud of her achievements and the crocodile got to have a home in Fairyland, and it really worked out best for everyone.

F.U.-BELLE the PIXIE did well for himself back in Fairyland. Thanks to his brilliant military mind and adept handling of the werewolf troops, Fu was eventually promoted to General of Fairyland and left to handle all matters of military and border defense, untroubled so long as he kept his werewolves in fashionable dog collars for the season.

That way the rulers of Fairyland could handle the bigger, pressing matters of the day, such as why can't anyone invent a nail top coat that lasts the week, or a lip gloss that lasts the whole day? Top fairy cosmetologists are working on the problem as we speak. However cosmetic testing on werewolves was strictly banned across Fairyland after that first round of trials. No one wants a repeat of *that* situation!

Finally, there's a rumor circulating in the gossip column of the Fairyland Chronicle that the Blue Fairy left the wooden puppet boy and she and Fu-Belle were caught flirting shyly back and forth on BaTwingger. Our source says that only time will tell if something more serious develops—but it looks very promising!

There! Are you happy now? *slams book closed*

Obviously we already know the story ends with: "And they all lived *happily—well—*

. . .

—well *fine*, they *did* live happily. For *awhile*. Until the ice age hit, that is.

Anne Genue's ChatSpk Codex

Having trouble with Anne Genue's many ambiguous acronyms?
*(Too bad. You have to guess them all—**J/K** = just kidding!)*
This cheat sheet is for those of you not fluent in "chatspk".

- **IRL** = In Real Life (p.95)
- **B/C** = Because (p.95)
- **NP** = No Problem (p.96)
- **NMB** = Not My Business (p.96)
- **IMHO** = In My Humble Opinion (p.96)
- **RTM** = Read The Manual (p.96)
- **YSDWAL** = You So Don't Win At Life (p.103)
- **NYD** = No You Didn't (p.101)
- **BCNU** = Be Seeing You (p.119)
- **FWIW** = For What It's Worth (p.95)
- **OIC** = Oh, I See (p.99)
- **GR8** = Great (p.99)
- **ID(E)K** = I Don't (Even) Know (p.98; 115)
- **STH** = Stuff Totally Happens (p.115)
- **ROTFLMAO** = Rolling On The Floor Laughing My Ass Off (p.115)
- **SRSLY or SRS** = Seriously/Serious (p.97; 130)
- **RLY** = Really (p.101)
- **WAM** = Wait A Minute (p.115; 273)
- **IRK** = I Know, Right? (p.149; 253)
- **RBTL** = Read Between the Lines (p.130)
- **AYFKM** = Are You Freakin' Kidding Me? (p.157)
- **LYLAS** = Love You Like A Sister (p.103)
- **VBEG** = Very Big Evil Grin (p.99)
- **SRY** = Sorry (p.202)
- **NW** = No Way (p.164)
- **WTV** = Whatever (p.179)
- **ILU** = I Love You (p.241)
- **BTW** = By The Way (p.256)

And of course we can't forget Anne's favorite: **STBYANHPBW** = Sucks to be you and not *Hubert Pfiffer! Boy Wizard!* ☺

Anne Genue's Fangirlisms

Maybe you aren't familiar with certain phrases commonly used by fans? Let us educate you on how to "speak fannish".

FANDOM

The storyline, plot, characters, and setting of a particular show, movie, book, or other thing. This is also used as a term for the fictional world in which a show, movie, or book takes place.

FAN CONVENTION

A huge gathering of fans centered around their fandom, often with special opportunities like meeting the celebrities, buying specialized merchandise or meeting other fans from all over.

FANFICTION (OR FANFIC)

The term for unauthorized stories written by fans and set within the fandom they enjoy.

MARY SUE (OR GARY STU) CHARACTER

A character which is either too perfect, too extreme, or otherwise badly written. Generally speaking, he (or she) is written as the hero (or the love interest respectively) and has no real conflict or opposition, often a manifestation of the author's own fantasies or desires.

LARP (LIVE ACTION ROLE PLAYING)

A term for when a fan play-acts a character from their book, movie or TV show fandom, usually along with other fans of the same fandom.

NEWBIE (OR NOOB)

A term used for a newcomer to a fandom.

SPOILER

Any info which gives away parts of episodes or movies.

Cast of Characters

Meet the quirky and fun characters you may encounter within the pages of Majickal. Here's a quick introduction to get you started!

F.U. (Fu)-Belle, Captain of the Fairy Peace Corps

Pragmatic and sensible (perhaps because he's half-human) he is the unsung hero of our story. He is only a quarter of an inch tall, and has unresolved anger issues over the mandatory "-belle" attached to his name. He alone recognizes the absurdity of the world around him but there's not much he can do about it.

Kent Clark (No Relation) . . . and We Mean It!

We know who you're thinking about but he's not related to *that guy*. In fact, his planet blew up a whole different galaxy as that alien you're thinking of so, *their alien planets aren't even related!* Kent Clark (no relation) just wants to be an ordinary alien superhero like the guy he's not related to but he's so mild-mannered he's still in high school at age 38. His mom sews all his costumes for him. He really believes when he removes his glasses that no one can recognize him.

King Armando Wingsfield Pentegram, the 23rd

The other 22 Armandos were him too, reinvented. The shallow and self-absorbed king of the vampires, addicted to social media and has a castle so large people starve to death just trying to find the nearest bathroom. Ongoing rivalry with famous vampire Alucard and occasionally LARP's as a pirate.

Mr. Oubliette

A mysterious and enigmatic supernatural being suffering from an identity crisis that prevents him from recognizing who he really is. Tendency to change identities often, complete with outlandish outfits, makeup and 80's rock ballad numbers. (Isn't it such a pity?)

ANNE GENUE, PRINCESS-IN-TRAINING

A pretty girl wants to be a professional princess (you didn't know they had a community college program? Princessing 1.01: "Elegant Handwaving") Talks perpetually in chatspk. Major-fangirlism over *Hubert Pfiffer! Boy Wizard!*, her favorite fictional character (but then, aren't we all?) Beware: she carries a cast iron skillet and knows how to use it!

BIFFY WINTERS, VAMPIRE SLAYER

A normal guy dressing as a cheerleader. No it's not because he likes wearing mascara . . . (fine. He does a little). But it's a clever disguise to hide the fact that he's a vampire slayer 'cuz everyone knows girls can't slay vampires right? (Aren't they supposed to be the "weaker sex" or something? *stifles evil laughter* Sorry.) Ultimately destined to fall in love with a beautiful vampiress 'cuz that's just how the story goes.

VERETHRAGHNA, PERSIAN GOD (AKA VICODIN, VIAGRA, VELOCIRAPTOR . . .)

An ancient Persian god annoyed because the other pantheons like the Romans, Greeks, Egyptian, Norse gods all have big Hollywood blockbusters, but the Persians are being snubbed. Dresses *old school*: big bushy beard, toga, staff, no baths. Might also help if he had a name anyone could actually pronounce.

TAILOR WEAR, THE WEREWOLF

An enthusiastic and very attractive young werewolf who loves the great outdoors and becomes loyally devoted to his new master, Kent Clark (no relation). Really hates all vampires, considering how they act superior and don't like to play ball.

KING CLARION AND QUEEN DING-ALING OF THE FAIRIES

The goodhearted, albeit shallow rulers of Fairyland. They hold stronger opinions over whether the dress is Blue/Black or White/Gold than the total annihilation of their race.

C. J. Connelly Books

THE STORY DOESN'T END WITH MAJICKAL . . .

Today marks a full millennia since the Great Land of the North was held fast in the grips of a terrible curse, an everlasting ice age that made it Always Winter but Never Christmas! 100 years that curse persisted till it was finally broken by four legendary kings and queens who took back the land and a majestic lion who killed the ice witch who cast the spell. Exciting though the story was, its luster faded as a thousand years went by and the Northlanders all but forgot the magic and bravery that brought them such peace and prosperity today.

. . . but even though the witch was dead, the curse wasn't. Little did anyone realize how devious the Ice Witch was . . .

CRACKLE DUST BOOK 2:
ICE, ICE AGE!

COMING TO BOOKSTORES NEAR YOU:
WINTER 2017

(Psst, prepare for a long winter this year! Just sayin'!)

About the Author

Want to know more about the woman behind the curtain?
Get a sneak peek of her profile on Majick-Book!

Majick Book

C. J. Connelly

Species: Human Female **Age:** Mortal
From: Human Realm aka/ Zombie Territory
Profession: Author of Majickal; Other Series
Special Powers: Writer. Artist. Pro Sarcasm.
Wishlist Power: Book-writing while I nap
Relationship Status: Taking Applications
(Click here to view C.J.'s criteria now)
Arch-Nemesis: Nominate on SuperMatch
Profile Status: Locked to Top Secret Mage
Visit Me at: http://www.cjconnellybooks.com

Photos

Stalk Elsewhere?
BaTwingger: @CJConnellyBooks
Majick Pinning Board:
CJConnellyBooks

Majickians you stalk

Mildred Pfiffer
9,662,491,388
mutual
majickians

King Armando
2, 285, 465, 112
mutual
majickians

**Rocco
the Last Gay
Unicorn**

Stalk this Majickian (add to Stalk list)

C.J. Connelly
So I guess now isn't the best time to tell you
I have a sequel planned.

about an hour ago

C.J. Connelly
I just published #Majickal & I'm so excited!!
You're all in it!! How do you feel about that?
Sound off in the comments below, okay?

13 hours ago

F.U.-Belle, Kent Clark (N.R.), Biffy Winters,
and 63 others gave this post **the finger**

King Armando just nominated you for the
Sexiest Novel on Majick-Book (Vote now)

Mr. Oubliette hearts this post so hard he
changed his relationship status over it (View now)

You can find more about C.J. on her website.
Check it out at: www.cjconnellybooks.com
Or follow her on Twitter: @CJConnellyBooks.
And don't forget to ~~stalk~~ "like" her on ~~Majick~~ Facebook! ☺